THE *Artist's* REDEMPTION

A SWEET REGENCY ROMANCE

K. LYN SMITH

ISBN: 978-1-7376579-3-4

The truth is rarely pure
and never simple.

- Oscar Wilde,
The Importance of Being Earnest

PROLOGUE

1818
BRIARLY, SOUTHWEST OF LONDON

L ADY REGINA TOWNSEND SPENT HER reputation on a rogue. A poet with a French accent as false as his promises, who'd quickly fled at the first hint of scandal. Now, six years later, she marveled at how the ripples from that singular choice continued to shape her life.

"I'm with child," she said, and three pairs of eyes narrowed on her.

A month ago, her announcement would have been cause for celebration because a month ago, she'd been married to Anthony, the ninth Earl of Foxwald. Admittedly, her marriage had been dull and uninspiring, but another child—especially an heir— would have been welcomed.

Now, however, she was newly widowed, and the

disclosure of her condition was not well received. She pressed shaking hands against her still-flat abdomen and resisted the urge to pick at a thread on her skirts.

Roger Chesterton—the tenth Earl of Foxwald, she reminded herself—straightened from his relaxed stance at the mantle. He was a tall man, broad of shoulder, with dark hair combed back from a high forehead. The scent of tobacco was strong on him, turning Regina's sensitive stomach. Some may have counted him attractive, but in Regina's experience, attractive men were not to be trusted.

His lady sat on the edge of a gold velvet settee, her ivory skirts carefully arranged to drape about her in a soft fall. Fair-haired and smooth-skinned, the new Lady Foxwald presented an elegant, if icy, picture. At Regina's words, her hand stilled on the Foxwald rubies at her throat, and her jaw tightened.

And Mr. Arnold, the family's new solicitor, stood behind the settee with one hand on the smooth velvet. Regina thought he must have had an advantageous view into the shadow of Lady Foxwald's bodice, until Regina's words pulled his gaze from the lady's charms.

The doors opened, and Peterson stepped in. "Dinner is served, my lord."

"Not now, Peterson," Foxwald snapped. The elderly butler bowed and retreated, closing the doors behind him.

Lady Foxwald sputtered then regained her voice. "That can't be right. How—when?" She narrowed her eyes on Regina. "Who's the father?"

"My husband," Regina assured her, narrowing her own eyes at the insult. "In the normal fashion."

"Arnold?" Foxwald asked, snapping questioning eyes to the solicitor.

"Send for the midwife," Arnold advised. "We'll need to validate her claim."

"Even if she is *enceinte*, there's no way to know who the father is," Lady Foxwald insisted. "A midwife is pointless. There was the incident with the poet, if you'll recall," Lady Foxwald reminded everyone, then turned back to Regina. "Your reputation hardly lends credence to your assertion."

Regina felt her customary poise falling away as her frustration rose. "For heaven's sake, I assure you, this child is Anthony's."

Although she and the poet had been discovered *fully clothed*, Regina felt certain she would suffer for her poor choices indefinitely. Like a pebble dropped in a still pond, her ill-advised actions had sent ripples across the waters of her life, beginning with the loss of her reputation on the poet's swift defection.

Following Albert Durand's departure, Regina had dried her tears and vowed not to waste another. It had never been her way to bemoan that which she could not change. She strove instead for flawless comportment that could not be gainsaid. If her demeanor was a little stiff, at least it was irreproachable.

The next ripple had come in the form of an unexpected marriage. When the poet struck out for parts unknown, Regina's father struck a deal with the eighth Earl of Foxwald. Townsend's ruined daughter for the earl's ailing heir. It was a bargain of last resort for both fathers.

The elderly Foxwald had despaired of his only son's poor health and childless state and had long lamented that a distant cousin would inherit the earldom. A wife for his languishing son had been a glowing ember of hope too tempting to ignore, the wife's scandalous past notwithstanding. And so, Regina had found herself married with embarrassing haste to Anthony, ailing son of the Earl of Foxwald.

Dry-eyed, she determined to make the best of her ill-fated marriage. She and Anthony settled into a dull existence at Briarly, where Regina bore him a daughter but, to her father-in-law's distress, not the desired heir.

In time, the old earl died, Regina's own father passed, and Anthony's health grew worse. Regina remained by her husband's side until he gave up and left her too. She should have mourned. Tears were expected, but they wouldn't come.

The next ripple occurred shortly after Anthony was lowered into the ground, when Mr. Arnold shocked Regina with the news that her husband had made no provision for his countess and young daughter. Even the dower house, which should have settled on her as Anthony's countess, had been let, the income returning to fill the coffers of the new earl.

She missed Anthony's previous solicitor, Mr. Underwood. A grandfatherly sort with graying hair and kind eyes, he would have delivered the shocking news of her reduced circumstances with considerably more empathy than Arnold had.

But she'd always been good with sums and quickly realized she had nothing. No. Thing. At four and twenty, she had no income, no assets, no husband and no future with which to provide for her small family.

Stunned, she could only watch as the new earl arrived at Briarly with his countess and reorganized the household. Long-time retainers were dismissed, and new staff were installed. Only Peterson, the aged butler, remained. Regina suspected that was because he alone knew where all the silver was kept.

The new earl had taken up residence in the study, smoking cheroots and reviewing the estate's ledgers. His lady ordered decorators to begin work on the family wing, and Regina was removed to a guest chamber.

Plans were drawn for renovations to the grand ballroom. The draper presented fabrics for the drawing room while footmen stripped paintings from walls and hung Chesterton's extensive collection.

The speed with which the new Lord and Lady Foxwald had transformed Briarly was staggering. Suspiciously swift, as if they'd anticipated and planned for months. Years, even.

Shortly after removing to the guest wing, Regina found a maid pulling dresses from her wardrobe. A footman was placing her vanity things into a small crate, and both of them averted their gazes when she entered.

"What are you doing?" she asked.

"I'm sorry, my lady," the maid replied. "The new countess thought you'd be more comfortable near the nursery."

Regina's eyebrows lifted. She was being further removed, then, to the third floor. She supposed she ought to consider herself fortunate that the earl allowed them to stay, for she had nowhere else to go.

But as weeks passed, yet another surprise rippled across the surface of her life. She was with child.

She'd felt peevish for some time but had passed it off as anxiety about her changed circumstances. But with the added signs of fatigue and tenderness in places that hadn't been tender before, she could no longer deny her condition.

She had anticipated her announcement would not be well received. At best, it was sure to put a halt to the earl's plans for Briarly. At worst . . . well. She didn't think Lord and Lady Foxwald would appreciate a return to their pre-noble status if she carried a son, so their current skepticism was expected, if not welcome.

And so, on Arnold's advice, the midwife was summoned to confirm her claim. Yes, the midwife confirmed, Regina would bear a child in six months' time.

"Where does this leave us, Arnold?" Foxwald asked gruffly.

Arnold explained that since an heir couldn't take possession of the land *en ventre sa mère*—

"In English, Arnold," Foxwald growled.

"Since an heir can't take possession *in the mother's womb*," Arnold said, "the earldom does indeed pass to you as the presumptive heir. However, the succession won't be finalized until the countess—the dowager countess, that is—is delivered of her child."

Foxwald snarled at the solicitor's words and glared at Regina.

Over the next days, he grew more and more short-tempered, and Lady Foxwald's insinuations became bolder and more outlandish.

Regina overheard from a maid that Peterson had been questioned regarding any frequent male visitors to Briarly. It was absurd, but the Chestertons were intent on retaining their new nobility.

When Regina suggested that further work on Briarly be postponed until the birth, Foxwald snapped out a hand and gripped her wrist hard. She forced her spine straight, although she couldn't hide a wince. He squeezed, his blue eyes flat as he smiled at her grimace.

"Do you think a son will change anything?" he asked. "If"—he stressed the word—"you bear the next earl, he'll require a guardian until he's of age. Arnold has already seen to the paperwork."

She felt the blood leave her face. His words caused her to recoil in a way his hand could not. If he couldn't have the earldom, it seemed Chesterton was content to manage it. As guardian to an infant earl, he would have full access to the estate—full authority over her child—for the next two decades. Full authority while she would have none.

She began to pray for another daughter. A child that would be of no interest to Foxwald. If she bore a daughter, she was certain he would cast them out. Where they would go, how she would support them, she had no notion, but anything would be preferable to living with Chesterton as guardian to her son. Or worse, being cast out of Briarly while her son remained.

———

Two days later as Regina descended the stairs for yet another uncomfortable supper with the earl and his lady, she lost her balance. Crying out, she reached for the banister—twisting, turning and grasping—to no avail. She thumped to the bottom of the marble staircase and lay there, waiting for her breath to come. An eternity passed before air whooshed into her lungs.

"My lady!" A footman rushed to her aid, helping her to her feet. A physician was summoned and declared all was well with the babe, though Regina had bruises and lumps aplenty. No tears, she reminded herself, although the backs of her eyes burned. Tears would serve no purpose.

She requested a cot for Penny, her daughter's nurse, and asked her to bring four-year-old Tilda. She didn't relish Tilda's knees and elbows in her back, but she wished to be near her daughter. She wanted to assure herself Tilda was safe, because she'd felt the slight but distinct pressure of a palm between her shoulders in the moment before she fell. Detected the faint scent of tobacco.

She couldn't dispel the cold that frosted through her. It spread into every corner like ice crusting a pond despite the warm June night.

"My lady," Penny whispered in the dark.

"Go to sleep, Penny," Regina said.

"Sorry, my lady, but I can't. It's that worried I am for you."

"The doctor said I'm fine. The babe's fine," Regina whispered. Tilda curled against her in her sleep, and the dim moonlight caught her features. Regina's heart clenched at the sight of her small nose and puckered lips, fine dark curls painted to her forehead with her little-girl sweat.

"Yes, but for *how long*?" Penny emphasized the words for dramatic effect. She had an imagination fit for a gothic novel, but Regina couldn't dispute the shivers that continued to chase her spine. "You can't stay here," Penny said on a harsh whisper.

"What can I do?" Regina asked. "Foxwald will find me no matter where I go." She thought of her acquaintances in London. Many had cut her after the Poet Scandal of 1812, only to renew their acquaintance upon her marriage. (A countess was a valuable card to have in one's deck, after all.) She couldn't rely on them for assistance, and Foxwald would find her if she went to any of them anyway.

"I've been giving that some thought, my lady."

Regina waited for Penny to continue. When she was silent, Regina finally asked, "And?"

"My mum went to live with my sister last year. You remember Agnes?"

"Agnes? She married and lives in Ipswich now?"

"Yes. Well, mum received a pensioner's cottage on the coast, but she's gettin' on and couldn't keep up the place, so she went to live with Agnes. No one lives there now, and there's not many wot know of it. We can be there in a lick."

If she recalled correctly, Penny's mother had served four decades as housekeeper for a viscount near Brighton. Regina turned onto her back and chewed her lip. Penny's suggestion was tempting, but . . . "Thank you, Penny, but I only have a little pin money. It's certainly not enough to live on."

Penny shuffled on her cot. "You'll have to take it from the earl," she said. "It's the least you're entitled to after wot the old earl left you but nothing."

"I can't steal from the earl," Regina shout-whispered. Tilda stirred and settled again. Regina lowered her voice. "I can't steal."

"What if you're carrying a son? He won't give up the earldom, even for a proper heir. You'll never be safe."

Regina feared Penny was right, but she didn't know what to do. She had very little money of her own, even if she took the few gifts Anthony had given her. She might have enough for a few months, possibly longer if she economized, but no more.

And then she thought of the financial papers she read every morning. She followed the reports and enjoyed predicting which investments would yield the best return, but investing required funds. She curled around Tilda and tried to settle her thoughts, but it was a long time before she fell asleep.

Two days later, Regina became wretchedly ill after supper. At first, she assumed her nausea was related to the babe, but then her stomach seized with violent cramps and a chill sweat broke out on her skin.

She told Penny the poached fish must have been off, even while Penny assured her no one else had sickened.

Had that been the only incident, she might have convinced herself it was but an unfortunate event. But combined with her fall down the stairs, she couldn't ignore the danger that threatened.

The doctor returned and pronounced both she and the babe were well but weakened. He advised a sturdy bone broth. Penny advised she flee. And soon. Regina couldn't disagree.

She curled around Tilda again and began plotting. In the next days, she and Penny gathered clothing which they passed to Penny's brother to hide. He'd drive them to Beddington where they could catch a stage for the rest of the journey. They planned a circuitous—and distressingly expensive—route that would hopefully distract any would-be pursuers from their destination.

Regina gathered the few small trinkets Anthony had given her over the years and secreted them in a small cloth bag. She shook her head at the small cache and pressed a hand to her mouth. It wouldn't be enough.

She watched Foxwald pull bank notes from his desk, and she marked the drawer, stomach turning.

She still didn't think she could *steal* from him. What if she were caught? But what alternative did she have?

———

THE NIGHT THEY WERE TO leave was clear and dry. Regina left a vague note on her vanity—enough to suggest she'd gone to visit friends, but no more. She'd taken to eating her meals in her room, spending little time with Foxwald and his countess. With luck, it would be some time before they realized she'd gone.

Penny carried a sleeping Tilda down the servants' stairs to the garden while Regina steeled herself and walked on light toes to the earl's study. Faint light shone beyond the edge of the door. She peered around the heavy wood, careful not to make a noise.

A brace of sconces cast flickering shadows along the wall. The French doors leading to the gardens reflected the candlelight, blind to the night beyond. The chair behind his desk was empty. She looked toward the leather sofas and the chairs in front of the cold hearth. Also empty. She glanced behind her, listening. The hallway was silent and dark. If she was going to do this, it had to be now. She couldn't believe her life had been reduced to this. Not for the first time, she cursed Anthony, her father and poets everywhere.

She hurried to the desk, crouched and waited, listening. The old manor house popped and she jumped. She clearly did not have the constitution of a criminal. She forced her heart to slow then reached for the drawer's brass pull and gave a slow tug. Nothing. She pulled harder. It was locked.

Well. She hadn't counted on that.

She surveyed the desk in the dim light. Was he stupid enough to leave the key? Possibly . . . but no, there was no key. All she saw were ledgers, a pile of letters. Tradesmen's bills and several rolled canvases piled in a crate on the floor. She glanced at the letters, holding one to the light of a candle. She couldn't make it out and set it to the side.

She toed the edge of the crate, then lifted one of the canvases and unrolled a corner. A painting. While the canvases in the crate hadn't made it to the gilded frames on Briarly's walls, she was certain they were worth something. Foxwald wouldn't sully his collection with anything insignificant. There were a dozen or more in the box. Would one be missed?

A noise sounded in the hall. She cocked her head and held her breath. A tap, then another. Steps approaching the study. She looked at the desk once more then the French doors behind her. The steps grew closer. She thought of her small bag of trinkets, barely enough to see them through a month or two. Sweat plastered her dress to her back. She re-rolled the canvas and slipped through the door with it, her heart racing.

CHAPTER ONE

"I T'S AMAZING WOT A YEAR can do to a place," Penny said. Regina, Penny and Tilda stood in the cottage's foreyard as the farmer's cart retreated down the lane. The rattle of the wheels faded, and stillness settled around them. Only the faint, rhythmic shushing of the ocean below the cliffs opposite the lane could be heard.

Penny's mother's small cottage squatted in knee-high grass. Large patches of white stucco had sheared off, revealing the fieldstone beneath. The front door hung crookedly, and a dark gap between the wood and the frame hinted at untold surprises awaiting them inside. A vine choked the right side of the structure, swallowing a chimney, and mullioned windows stared over their heads with disinterest.

"Mama?" Tilda's hand curled into hers, and she turned skeptical coffee-brown eyes on Regina.

Regina squeezed her daughter's hand and firmed her lips. "I know, poppet. What an adventure this will be!" Tilda's eyes widened then narrowed at Regina's bright enthusiasm.

A wuffling snort drew Regina's eyes to the piglet at her daughter's feet. The farmer who'd driven them from Brighton had been helpless to Tilda's dimples and polite manners. The piglet had been inevitable. That he was the smallest of the litter and likely wouldn't see tomorrow (given the farmer's empty grain sack and seaside destination) . . . well, that didn't help Regina's determination to resist.

She sighed. "Shall we go in?"

Salt crusted the door's metal hinges, and they moaned and cracked as Penny pushed the door open. The inside was as bad as the outside promised. The sea air had not been kind, leaving the walls stale and damp. Leaves and debris had blown in through the gap in the door, and a thick layer of chalk dust coated everything. Tilda squatted and studied a tiny skeleton in the corner—a mouse more than likely. Hopefully. Regina prayed it wasn't a baby rat. She pulled Tilda away as her daughter stretched a finger toward the small bones.

A kitchen and small parlor filled most of the main floor, with a dining table pushed against the parlor's front window. A tiny room at the back held a small bed on a drunken frame. All told, the main floor would have fit inside the drawing room at Briarly. The second floor contained two tiny bedrooms where low ceilings pressed from above, and cobwebs decorated the corners.

"It's not much to look at, is it?" Penny asked, toeing a clump of something on the floor.

"It's . . . charming," Regina assured her. "Or it will be, once we've cleaned it."

Yes, it would be charming, she assured herself. Regina was accustomed to making do with whatever life saw fit to set in her path. She forced herself to look beyond the grime as she went to the bedroom's small window and rubbed a spot on the glass. An endless stretch of shimmering blue ocean lay just beyond the cliffs at the end of the lane. That was promising.

She turned back to Penny. "Thank you, Penny. I don't know what we would have done without you and your mother's cottage."

Penny sniffed and said, "Well, it won't clean itself. I'll see what supplies there may be. Why don't you"—she looked around the room skeptically—"find a spot and rest a bit. You must be fatigued. Tilda and I will take the next room."

"Nonsense, Penny. I'll help you clean. We'll accomplish much more together."

Penny looked at her in shock. "No, my lady. It wouldn't be right."

"The activity will take my mind off the situation." Regina looked at the accumulated filth around them. "And it will take both of us to set things straight."

"Well, you may be right about that."

They spent a week scrubbing and cleaning. Laundering and sweeping. For such a tiny space, the amount of dirt and grime that had accumulated over the last year was impressive.

Regina's back and arms ached, and her muscles burned, but the industry was satisfying. She felt as if she was taking control of her life again. In the weeks since Anthony had died, she'd been a leaf tossed on the wind, awaiting the whims of Arnold and Chesterton. Of Lady Foxwald. Now, her future was still uncertain, but at least she was doing something about it.

She entered the chamber she'd taken for herself and eyed the bed with anticipation. Fresh sheets beckoned from atop a newly stuffed mattress. A soft rain fell outside the open window, carrying seaside scents of salt and grass. Then she heard it. Drip . . . drip.

She looked up and spotted the source: a leak in the corner of the ceiling where the roof met the wall. She pushed the bed against the interior wall, away from the leak, then she placed a chamber pot over the growing puddle. Drip, drip.

The drops grew louder and more frequent, metallic pings hitting the pot. She sighed. They'd have to hire out to have the roof repaired, but she was reluctant to part with the little money she had. She'd already sold the trinkets she'd brought with her to purchase food and supplies. She'd not counted on roof repairs.

Her eyes landed on the rolled canvas atop her vanity. She pressed a hand to her forehead and wondered at her idiocy again. What had she been thinking, stealing the painting? What good would the canvas serve? While it might be worth something, it would take some time to find a buyer, and they needed currency *now*. She could hardly pay for a roof with a painting.

She pushed the pot with her foot, tucking it more firmly under the leak, then she unrolled the canvas. The style was not one she recognized, and she wondered about the artist. A bold signature marked the bottom. "Alexandre Marchand." The artist was unknown to her. That didn't mean much, though, as Foxwald's collection was extensive.

The painting depicted an idyllic landscape in unexpected shades of brown and amber. Gold and umber. A woman stood to the side, facing away from the artist, golden hair waving in a breeze. She didn't fit the painting. Regina couldn't identify the discord, but the woman seemed out of place, disconnected from the lovely scene before her.

She ran a fingertip over the surface, feeling the texture of the paint, the dips and peaks where the artist's brush had lifted and pressed the canvas.

Drip, drip. Water splashed in the chamber pot.

She found herself oddly reluctant to sell the painting. Exchanging it for money seemed to further her criminal activity, although she recognized the fallacy in that logic.

She had stolen it, pure and simple. Whether she sold it or not didn't change that fact, and they would need money eventually. They couldn't continue to live off her small savings, much less hire out for needed repairs on the cottage. She would need to sell it. Soon, but not yet.

———

ONE MONTH LATER, BRIGHTON

ALEXANDRE MARCHAND CROSSED THE HILLS and dales of Lewis, Ashcombe and Falmer before arriving at the top of Brighton's busiest street. The white town sparkled with light and energy, and he inhaled. Warm scents of fish and brine floated on the early autumn air.

The Steine, Brighton's main thoroughfare,

followed the valley's seam to the sea and divided the village between east and west. It provided a fashionable promenade where elegant ladies and gentlemen strolled while the fishermen stretched their nets to dry. Skiffs nodded on the sea, and the gentle breeze ruffled the ladies' hat feathers.

Stretching east to Alex's left, pristine chalk cliffs towered from the seabed. Fine establishments, newly constructed and freshly painted, offered prime views of the water. To his right, the picturesque bay shimmered, and lesser establishments offered economy. Alex mentally counted the coin in his purse and turned right.

The White Stag Inn was one such establishment where a man could be sociable (or not) for an affordable price. The inn, with its shake roof and crooked limed facade, squatted between newer buildings, a staunch sentry guarding against encroaching commerce. The distinctive smells of mutton and ale greeted him as he opened the door. The clientele in the taproom eyed his tailored attire and polished boots with suspicion. When it was clear he was just a man looking for a meal, they resumed their conversations.

An hour later, Alex lifted his second pint and wiped a spot on the scratched and scraped table. He sat in a darkened corner, his back to the wall, distanced from the droning hum of conversation. He was more accustomed to wine and brandy, but the ale wasn't bad. The fish pie, however, could use some seasoning. With luck and perseverance, perhaps he wouldn't need too many more bland meals.

After a failed courtship in Kent, he'd debated returning to Paris (and his creditors) or journeying to Brighton. It hadn't taken considerable thought to choose the seaside.

Heiresses were thick on the ground at the bustling resort, and he could use a change of scenery. His funds had grown distressingly low, and Paris had grown more expensive since the end of the war. He eyed his boots. As much as he admired the supple leather, he conceded that—perchance—they'd been an unnecessary expense. At least until his pockets were heavy again.

Perhaps he needn't marry but could find a wealthy widow. A pretty, flirtatious lady interested in funding a talented artist. A lady unencumbered with astronomers.

He frowned and reflected on his mistakes with Lady Celeste St. James. He'd enjoyed her company, and her dowry had been attractive as well. They'd shared a common interest in art, which had led to pleasurable conversation. And she seemed an independent sort, not one to place too many expectations upon a man.

But Lady Celeste was not the type with whom one dallied. She was the type one married. Dalliance or marriage, it didn't much matter one way or the other to him. As long as he could keep his creditors happy, he was agreeable either way. So, he'd courted Lady Celeste. Had followed her from Paris to Kent, in fact, when his creditors had grown tiresome.

He snorted to himself in disgust. That endeavor had turned out to be a tremendous waste of time, as Lady Celeste had developed an unaccountable affection for a scientist of no fortune. What she saw in the serious astronomer, he couldn't say, but he knew even his charms couldn't overcome that depth of feeling.

A pretty barmaid approached his table and offered another pint. She gave a broad smile and a wink, hinting that she was offering more if he was interested. She was pretty and willing, so of course he was. But he was more interested in saving his coin for a full belly and a soft bed. It wasn't the first time he'd been low on funds, and it probably wouldn't be the last, but it was a bloody nuisance.

"M'name's Betsy," she told him with a saucy grin. "Are you enjoying the sights?" she asked. She leaned over his table and offered a tempting view.

He smiled, taking her meaning. "Indeed. But I'm afraid this town is too rich for my purse." He let his brows dip in a deep V of regret.

She turned away with another wink and a twist of her hips.

He settled back in his chair to observe the pub's patrons. As an artist, observing was one of his favorite pastimes. Three tables over, an old man entertained several younger lads—men in their fourth or fifth decade—with boisterous tales. He laughed loud and deep at his own jokes, his chest rattling on a cough. Alex smiled. He'd like to be that old—and that amused—someday, but he doubted he'd be so fortunate.

The door opened and admitted a narrow beam of sunlight before slamming shut behind two men. They doffed their caps, blinking at the room's dimness. The first had a jagged scar that twisted one eyebrow, visible even from Alex's corner table. The other was taller, with a large nose. Crooked and off-center, it looked as if it had been improperly set more than once.

The men greeted familiar faces and moved toward the bar. The one with the puckered brow pinched Betsy, and she swatted at his hand playfully. Alex smiled to himself.

Bent-nose looked in Alex's direction, and his woolly eyebrows flew to his hairline. Alex narrowed his eyes, alert. Did he owe the man money?

The man elbowed his companion and pointed in Alex's corner. Alex sat straighter as the two neared his table and their grinning faces became clearer. The taller man with the broken nose spoke first. "Nicky March! As I live and breathe!"

Recognition flashed in Alex's mind before evaporating. Like an early morning dream, memory slid through his grasping fingers. Clearly the men thought they recognized him, but he couldn't place them. Confusion and anxiety, frequent companions of late, raised their heads. He threw a coin on the table, grabbed his hat and stood.

"I'm afraid you've mistaken me for someone else," he said as he brushed past them. They looked at him in surprise but didn't move to follow him.

Brighton was fast losing its sparkle.

CHAPTER TWO

ALEX PAUSED AT THE BOTTOM of the Steine, trying to collect his bearings. The encounter with the men in The White Stag had shaken him, but he couldn't say why. It had merely been a case of mistaken identity, he was certain, but he couldn't deny the jittery anxiety that seemed to plague him more and more these days. He should probably go easy on the spirits.

He inhaled slowly and surveyed his surroundings as he waited for his nerves to settle. The sea rolled in a smooth rhythm, rocking the skiffs off the shoreline. A line of darkening clouds smudged the distant horizon, promising a stormy night ahead. He rubbed a hand along the back of his neck, willing the tension from his muscles. Storms usually brought headaches, so he was in for a miserable evening, if experience was anything to judge by.

A signboard swayed and creaked on the whitewashed building next to him. *Lafontaine.*

Purveyor of Fine Art and Antiquities. He thought of the rolled painting in his bag. He was reluctant to sell his last one, and he almost turned away, but the dwindling jingle in his coat pocket reminded him again that he couldn't afford vanity. He thought there might be a moral lesson in there somewhere, were he inclined to heed it.

A bell rang above the door as he entered the establishment. A toy spaniel with a pink ribbon cocked her ears and watched him from a worn wool blanket. Thick carpets layered one atop the other muffled Alex's fine boots as he crossed the plank floor. Paintings in fancy frames filled every inch of wall space, and dark oak cabinets housed trinkets and what he assumed were Lafontaine's "antiquities."

A large man with dark hair, a bulbous nose, and a dreadful French accent greeted him. The man straightened the blond lace at his cuffs and stood taller on hearing Alex's own French vowels. Alex explained he had a painting to sell and unrolled his canvas on Lafontaine's table.

The dealer watched with interest. "A Marchand? Hmm." Alex was always surprised and not a little gratified when dealers recognized his work. Lafontaine lifted a loupe from around his neck and studied the canvas, his head moving from side to side. Alex crossed his arms and stroked his bottom lip as he watched the man study the painting.

A steep cliff dominated the canvas as it rose from a turbulent sea, jagged and stark. The piece was dark and moody. Unsettling. He'd painted it in somber shades of gray and umber beneath blackening clouds. A giant bird winged over the sea, caught mid-swoop as it dove toward the water. He'd never gotten the wings right. The angle was off, and the bird appeared to be falling rather than diving.

When he'd first set out to paint the scene, the dark landscape wasn't what he had in mind. But then he'd stepped back some hours later and was surprised to see what his brush had wrought. He'd quickly tucked the canvas away to be ignored and forgotten, but instead he found himself compelled to paint and re-paint the same scene. Despite the fact that the landscape caused icy fingers to march up his back, he couldn't dispel the need to render it on canvas again and again.

When he should have been painting portraits and still life studies, he'd been drawn instead to the moody cliffs. He'd painted tens of them, to his great frustration. He hadn't, in fact, painted much of anything else in nearly two years. Not since—well, not in a long time. He'd sold the cliffs off as fast as he could to cover his expenses, and this was the last one. If he sold this today, he'd have no more paintings left, which was a sobering thought.

Lafontaine concluded his study and lowered the loupe. "It's the second Marchand I've had this week," he said, rubbing his chin.

"What's that?" Alex asked, taking his hand from his lip. "You've had another?" He looked about the shop's walls again, but he didn't see any of his other works.

"Well, the first was a forgery. And a poor one at that. But yes."

Bloody hell. Who was selling forgeries of his work? And—more perplexing—why? Alex had enough vanity to realize he was talented, but he'd not yet reached forgery-level talent. Typically, one had to be dead first. Not always, but it certainly helped. And the last Alex checked, he was still breathing. He scowled and reached for the canvas.

Lafontaine stopped him, his lace cuff trailing across the painting as he held his hand over it. "This one is unique, not in the artist's usual style. I'll give you twenty pounds."

Alex studied the man through his lashes. Twenty pounds. The amount was tempting. With twenty pounds in his pocket, he could afford a room on the *east* side of the Steine. A new waistcoat and fine wine with his dinner.

But still he hesitated. The piece, dreadful as it was, was worth twice that amount. He knew impoverished artists couldn't be selective, but he was oddly reluctant to let the painting go, and for a mere twenty pounds at that. What if he sold his last painting and never painted again? If he was no longer a painter, then what was he?

The bell over the shop door rang, and the spaniel cocked her head at a newcomer. Lafontaine looked up, eager to greet his next customer.

"Thank you, but no," Alex said, deciding. He rolled the canvas and started to turn away, then stopped. "The gent who brought the forgery. Did you get his name by any chance?"

"Oh, it wasn't a gentleman, but a woman. A comely, dark-haired one, at that."

"Do you know her direction?"

"I didn't recognize her, and I know most of the local folk. She may have been a tourist passing through, or she may be staying along the cliff road past the tollgate. There's a cottage or two toward Rottingdean. I couldn't rightly say." He pulled on his ear as he remembered. "She had pretty green eyes, if I recall. But I'm not one to have my head turned by a comely face, especially one that's trying to pull one over on me."

"Did you inquire about the painting's provenance?" Alex asked.

"No, it was clearly an imitation, not worth my time. I just told her I didn't need more Marchands and sent her on her way."

He motioned to the canvas in Alex's hand. "Twenty-five, but I can't go any higher than that. You'll not find another dealer from here to London offering as much."

"I've changed my mind," Alex said, surprised by the relief that flooded him when he tucked the canvas back into his bag.

"If you change it again, come to me first," Lafontaine said. He turned to his customer, and the spaniel wagged her hind end as Alex left the shop.

Anger clenched his jaw as he thought of the unknown forger. The thieving baggage. Who did she think she was? If anyone was going to profit from imitations of *his* work, it would be him. He acknowledged the absurdity of that thought as he looked up and down the street, pondering.

There was still daylight left, and the clouds were some distance offshore. He had time to do a little investigating, but he could hardly go from door to door through the streets of Brighton seeking "a comely, dark-haired" woman. He might not have anywhere to be, but he knew the futility of trying to search the entire town. The cliff road it was.

———

AT THE END OF THE Steine, Alex turned his horse to the Marine Parade, which wound above the shingle beach toward Rottingdean. As he left Brighton and approached the tollgate, the crowds thinned, until he was on the empty cliff road. The route climbed and edged the bone-white cliffs that divided the rolling plain above from the sea below.

The green grass along the chalky path was fading to shades of brown with the arrival of autumn. Away from the buffering buildings and trees, the wind curled over the cliff's edge, and the tall grass waved.

The path was longer than he'd anticipated, with little to break the empty landscape. The sun began to sink, and the afternoon's warmth fell away quickly. Iron-gray clouds tumbled over the sea on his right, rolling one atop the other to reach the shore, and the heavy, damp scent of rain settled in the air.

Alex pulled his collar against the growing chill and fantasized about a warm, dry fire. Even the dubious culinary offerings of The White Stag appealed. Perhaps he shouldn't have been so eager to find the woman-thief. He debated turning back, but then he'd have wasted all this time. How far was it to Rottingdean? Lafontaine had said there were cottages past the tollgate. It couldn't be much further.

Lightning flashed in the distance, piercing the sea, and the wind picked up. The back of Alex's neck tightened and tingled, an ominous sign one of his headaches was imminent. He pressed his hat more firmly onto his head, as if it would protect against the pain to come.

It was a futile effort, he knew, as nothing could guard against the intense, bone-crushing agony. Certainly nothing so simple as a hat. The headaches had begun two years ago, usually in concert with a storm. He couldn't prevent them; he could only endure them. The episodes were thankfully brief, but crippling.

He waited, tense. His horse shuffled to the side, and he forced the tension from his legs. The first stab speared him behind his right eye. A pulsing staccato settled at the top of his head, keeping time with his heart, nearly blinding him. Nausea flooded him in a warm rush. Lightning flashed behind his eyelids, and the horse pranced beneath him.

He forced his breathing to calm and relaxed his hands on the reins. In. Out. He puffed his cheeks as he breathed. The rhythm of the horse's gait punctuated each drumbeat.

He pictured a hand reaching into his head and drawing the pain out. Long ribbons of agony unfurling from the crown of his head. It was a trick the monks of St. Augustine had taught him. A way to endure the pain until it passed.

He lost track of the minutes, but eventually the stabbing retreated to a bearable throb, ebbing as quickly as it had arrived. He forced the muscles in his shoulders to relax and opened his eyes on an exhale. His neck was clammy, his eyes stiff, but the worst had passed. He flexed his jaw and looked about to get his bearings.

He'd reached a small lane marked by a ragged copse of small trees and shrubs. Through the trees, opposite the cliff's edge, sat a shabby cottage. More brush and tall grass crowded the structure, and vines were swallowing it whole. It appeared vacant, and he almost turned back, until he spied the thin ribbon of smoke curling from a chimney.

It was an unlikely abode for an art forger, but as he studied the place, the first fat drops of rain splattered his sleeve. The clouds had reached land and now squatted over the tiny house. He looked up and down the cliff road, but he didn't see any other homes. He was shaky and his head still ached, but the rain would arrive in earnest soon. This was as good a place as any to begin his search.

———

"Penny, I think you're supposed to add the milk next."

"No, my lady, I'm fair certain that comes last."

Regina pressed her lips together. Penny was an excellent nurse to Tilda, but skilled in the culinary arts, she was not. They'd all learned this lamentable fact over the last weeks.

Now Regina watched as Penny attempted to make Bath buns with their precious flour and milk.

Briarly's extensive kitchens and staff had made cooking seem so effortless, with delectable options laid out at each meal, but Penny's flat, sticky dough clods didn't hold much promise.

Regina had relented and taken Foxwald's painting to Brighton this week, but she'd been unsuccessful in selling it. It wouldn't matter that the large proprietor with the false accent had turned her away, though. At this rate, they'd starve to death before they ran out of funds.

"Mama!" Tilda raced into the kitchen from where she'd been playing in the parlor. "Robert's out again!"

Robert. The blasted pig. Tilda had insisted on naming him after a kindly groom at Briarly, on account of them both being smallish. Regina pulled the apron from around her neck and hung it on a peg. If that pig trampled her cabbages again . . . For a small thing, he left a wide swath of destruction. Tilda should have named him Napoleon, she thought, and not for the first time.

"Come, poppet," she said with a hand on her daughter's hair. "Let's collect the scamp before he destroys the cabbages again."

The afternoon had been warm and humid but was cooling quickly. Another storm would arrive soon, to judge by the scent in the air and the fat clouds forming off the horizon. As she opened the cottage door, a small pink blur with dark spots raced across the foreyard. She looked to his pen and groaned at the small hole he'd dug under the bottom rail. Again. The tender cabbages in their small garden lay upturned, evidence of Robert's perfidy. She ran a hand over the top of her hair, smoothing a stray curl from her face.

Tilda squeezed past her and went to his pen. She began pushing dirt back into Robert's hole with her small hands, and Regina bent to help her. Chasing the piglet would serve no purpose other than to frustrate all involved. She'd learned to wait him out, and he'd return shortly.

A fat drop of rain stained the ground, then another. Regina thought again of the leaks in the house, which seemed to multiply each day. Indeed, they were running out of pots and buckets.

A horse whinnied, startling her from her thoughts. She looked from where she knelt in the dirt next to Robert's pen. They'd not had any visitors since they'd arrived, which suited her perfectly, but now a large chestnut approached from the end of the lane. A man in a dark coat sat atop the horse, a slight scowl on his face. She couldn't see his eyes beneath the shadow of his hat, but his jaw was set in a firm line. The cut of his tailored coat was elegant, and his boots appeared to be quality.

Had Foxwald found them then? Sent this man to

take them back to Briarly? What if Foxwald had discovered his missing painting? Regina's heart skipped, and her palms grew damp. She gripped Tilda's hand and held a finger to her lips. Her daughter's forehead wrinkled as she looked at her in confusion, and Regina tried to reassure her with a soft hand on her curls.

The man drew closer, surveying the cottage. He hadn't seen them by Robert's pen yet. If they were still, remained silent, would he go away? Even as she had the thought, she knew it was ridiculous. Her legs were cramping as it was. She'd have to reveal herself soon.

As his horse paced toward the cottage, a pink blur streaked from the underbrush and ran between the horse's hooves.

"Robert!" Tilda shouted, jumping up. Regina stood and gripped Tilda's hand to keep her from racing forward. The horse's eyes widened at the pig skittering beneath him, and he reared onto his hind legs, forelegs pawing the air. The man's hat fell to the ground and was trampled as he fought to control the horse.

Robert raced toward Tilda, away from the pounding hooves, and the man flew from the back of the horse. Regina held her breath as he was motionless, suspended in the air, for two heartbeats. Then he hit the ground with a sickening thud that echoed along her spine. The horse stomped the earth once then tore down the lane, and a cloud of dust settled over the man as the sound of galloping hooves faded. Regina waited, watching, but he remained still.

CHAPTER THREE

ALEX'S LUNGS HEAVED, AND HE sucked in a loud breath. It took a moment to realize he'd been unseated from his horse. That hadn't happened in . . . well, he couldn't recall that ever happening. It was a decidedly uncomfortable experience.

He forced his eyes open, and a raindrop landed on his nose. An upside-down cherub stared back at him. Pink cheeks, dark curls, brown eyes fringed with black. A tiny nose and full cherub lips. Had he died? Was this heaven? No, he was pretty certain heaven wasn't the direction he was heading.

A hot rush of pain quickly set his angelic illusion straight. It lanced through his shoulder, sharp and fiery like a brand, and the back of his head pounded once again. He gritted his teeth against the onslaught before his eyes fluttered shut.

A whisper of warm breath fanned his face, then a cool, soft kiss landed on his cheek as he fought for consciousness. Maybe this *was* heaven, then.

"Robert, no," the cherub spoke above him.

Who was Robert?

A snort brought his eyes open again and he turned, then recoiled. A pink snout pushed against his cheek. He'd been right. This was clearly not heaven . . . but not quite what he'd imagined hell to be, either. He shifted to rise, but the pain stabbed his shoulder again. Darkness edged his vision like the sea, rolling over him until he went under.

———

"DID HE DIE, MAMA?" TILDA asked with wide eyes.

"Oh, lud, is he dead then?" Penny's strident voice pitched over the growing wind.

"No, poppet, he's not dead." At least she didn't think so. Regina nudged his boot with her foot, but he didn't move. His arm lay at an odd angle, and the shoulder beneath his coat looked . . . well, peculiar. Squared instead of rounded. That couldn't be good, could it?

More drops of rain fell, beading on the dust in the foreyard. The clouds overhead were black and pregnant. A downpour would be on them soon.

She chewed her lip then sighed. There was no help for it. Apparently, life had seen fit to set an injured man in her path. "Penny, we need to get him inside."

"Inside? But my lady—" Penny motioned with her hand at the stranger sprawled in the dirt.

"He's injured, Penny. We can't leave him here. He'll catch his death in the rain." *If our pig hasn't already killed him.*

Penny remained skeptical, but Regina had no wish to add murder to her list of crimes. She went to the dilapidated stable beside Robert's pen, and eventually, Penny and Tilda followed her. She eyed the stable's contents: a scythe, a saw, some small tools, a few lengths of rope.

"There's not much to work with, my lady. And he must weigh twenty stone," Penny grumbled.

"Not so much, Penny. Fourteen, at most," Regina said. She tapped her chin and looked back at the stranger, hoping he'd risen on his own to go about his way. He hadn't moved.

Robert stood at her side, watching them with his dark piglet eyes. His pen had proved useless to keep him contained, but perhaps . . . She bent and pulled the bottom rail off and set it aside.

"Mama, what are you doing to Robert's pen?"

"Robert will have to sacrifice his pen, at least for the moment."

"He can sleep inside with me," Tilda said helpfully.

"No, poppet, Robert can't sleep inside, but we need to borrow his pen for a bit. Can you bring a blanket from the house? Penny, help me pull this rail off."

They removed three wide slats from Robert's pen and dragged them next to the stranger. Regina found two lengths of rope in the stable and laid them on the ground, then they placed the rails on top of the rope to create a pallet of sorts. When Tilda returned with a blanket, the end trailing in the dirt, Regina laid it across the rails. Then she turned to the man and drew a large breath.

There was no way this was going to work. Penny and Tilda seemed to be in silent agreement as they both looked at her skeptically. She shrugged her shoulders. What choice did they have?

"Help me get him onto the rails, Penny."

"Beggin' your pardon, my lady, but there's no way this will work," Penny said.

All right, so maybe Penny's agreement wasn't so silent. The rain picked up, and Regina brushed a damp lock of hair from her eyes. "Well, unless you've a better idea, this is what we're working with," she told Penny.

Penny opened her mouth then closed it again and nodded. With Penny at his head and Regina at his feet they managed to roll the man onto their makeshift litter.

Regina was thankful he'd not awakened, because their efforts were far from graceful. More than once his head bumped the ground as they pushed and shoved at him.

"He's got quite the egg starting on his head," Penny said.

"Let's not give him any more," Regina added. "So much as we can help it, anyway."

When all was said and done, he lay face down on the blanket, his arm still twisted at an unnatural angle. Bits of grass and twigs clung to his backside and coat. His legs, which Regina now knew all too well to be firm and muscular, hung off the end of the litter. Tilda, ever helpful, grabbed his hat and bag and placed them on top of him. Rain was falling in earnest, soaking them and turning the chalky dirt to slippery mud.

Penny eyed the distance to the cottage then the heap of stranger before them. "Now wot?" she asked.

"Now we lift." Regina bent and picked up the two ends of rope at the man's feet. Penny did the same at his head, and they both lifted. To be fair, Penny lifted, and Regina guided his feet at her end. His head was only a couple of inches off the ground at Penny's end, but it was enough to move him. The rails shifted and gapped beneath the blanket, but the ropes held everything together. Mostly.

Inch by inch they moved toward the door, pausing every foot or so to rest their hands and arms. Twenty stone or fourteen, it didn't matter. He was heavy indeed. Lift, shuffle, down. Repeat. The toes of his boots dug in the mud where they trailed off the end of the litter.

Once they reached the door of the cottage, the smell hit them. Burning Bath buns. Penny dropped her end of the litter, and the man's head bounced with a thump. Regina winced, maintaining hold of her end of the ropes while Penny ran to the kitchen. "Penny!" she called.

Penny appeared at the door a moment later, sweat beading above her lip. "Sorry, my lady, but those buns won't be any good, I'm sad to say. Lumps of coal, they are."

Regina thought burnt buns were the least of their problems. "It's all right, Penny, let's just get him inside."

They navigated the parlor to the small room at the back of the cottage. Regina surveyed the little bed and the man's large frame. He wouldn't fit, but there was no help for it. With one last effort, they half-rolled, half-dumped him from the litter onto the low mattress.

The bed's ropes creaked and groaned beneath his weight, and Regina sucked in a breath, but the bed held. She stretched her arms, then rubbed a hand over her belly to soothe the tumbling inside.

"Mama," Tilda said from the doorway where she held a placid piglet. "Robert likes it inside the house."

———

REGINA AND PENNY STUDIED THE stranger on the bed. It had been an hour and still he hadn't moved. Regina checked the back of his head and confirmed he did indeed have quite the egg growing.

The acrid scent of burnt Bath buns hung in the air. The rain had come, lashing the cottage from the sea-facing side before moving further along the coast. Water dripped from the eaves outside the room's small window and from a spot to the left of the bed. The room was a far stretch from the elegant guest chambers at Briarly, but then, they'd not been expecting guests.

Regina looked out the window and across the lane to the cliff's edge, where more clouds gathered above the sea. It promised to be a wet evening. She replaced the pot on the floor with an empty one to catch the drips, the metallic *tink, tink* ticking off the seconds.

"Who do you think he is?" Penny asked. "He seems fine enough. Or he did, before we dragged him through the mud."

Regina eyed the scuffed and muddied toes of his boots with a grimace. He did indeed appear to be a gentleman. She didn't voice her suspicions that Foxwald had sent the man. Her thoughts were merely idle speculation, fueled by her momentary panic on first seeing him at the end of their lane. Given her fear of Foxwald finding them, her alarm had been a natural reaction. The man was probably nothing more than a lost traveler, and rousing Penny's hysterics wouldn't help.

"Oh, lud," Penny said, breaking into her thoughts. "Do you think Foxwald sent him?" Her eyes widened and she gasped, clutching the edge of her apron. "My lady, what have we done? We should have left him where he lay and locked the door! He'll drag us back to Briarly. Or worse, he'll murder us in our beds."

"Hush, Penny. No one's murdering anyone. But the sooner he's up, the sooner he can be on his way." And the sooner she could relax. "We should summon a doctor, though. That's quite the lump on his head, and his face seems too pale. I don't like the look of his shoulder, either."

"Maybe he always looks like that," Penny said.

Regina studied him from the foot of the bed, doubting the truth of Penny's words. Despite his waxen complexion and misshapen arm, he was, quite simply . . . beautiful. She could think of no other word to describe his appearance.

High cheekbones, wide forehead. Wavy hair in ten shades ranging from light brown to burnished gold. But his lips . . . She'd never seen lips that perfect before. Smooth and sculpted, the bottom one full and soft-looking. A small divot above where the top one dipped in. Light brown stubble framed them and outlined his jaw, and Regina pressed her own lips together.

"I'll go," Penny said.

"Go?"

"For the doctor," Penny reminded her, studying the clouds beyond the window. "If I leave now, I should return before the next storms arrive."

Regina nodded. She didn't relish being alone with the man, but he was unconscious, and it was the most sensible plan.

______

TWO HOURS LATER

After Penny left, Regina remained by the stranger's side in case he should wake. He was uncomfortably still, with only the slow, shallow rise of his chest to reassure her that he still lived. What would they do if he died? She didn't wish such a fate on anyone, and they certainly didn't need the attention that a death on their doorstep would claim.

She paced the little room while she waited for Penny to return and found her attention drawn back to him. He was nicely formed. Not too thin or too fat. He appeared to be tall, although from this perspective it was hard to tell. Judging from the length of his legs hanging off the end of the bed, though, she estimated him at six feet or more.

She bit her lip and moved closer for a better look. Yes, he was just as beautiful up close, but now she noticed thick lashes fanning his cheeks and faint lines etching his forehead and the corners of his eyes. He looked worried, even in sleep. Pinched. She wondered what color his eyes were.

He had a warm, citrusy scent at odds with the poor muddy state of his attire. Then she sniffed again and through the citrusy scent, she detected . . . mildew?

They'd closed the door on this tiny back room and hadn't cleaned it yet, focusing first on the spaces they planned to use for their temporary stay. The linens hadn't been changed and were likely infested with . . . things. Regardless of who the man was, common decency made her cringe at their poor hospitality.

She leaned over the head of the bed and inhaled again. Yes, definitely mildew. A loud inhale interrupted her investigation, and she looked down. A smile teased the corner of his lovely lips. His eyes fluttered open, and he stared at her chest, his perfect lips lifting in a one-sided grin.

"Oh!" She straightened and backed away from the bed.

———

ALEX WAS IN A FIELD of waving lavender. The fragrance tickled his nose and calmed his mind.

Maybe this was heaven after all. He smiled and his eyes drifted open.

The lavender "field" turned out to be a female. She was slight, but soft and plump in the best places. Yes, this was most definitely heaven.

He lifted his gaze, and green eyes stared back at him. He had an impression of a small, upturned nose, thick black lashes and lush, kissable lips. Heaven was very fine indeed. He took a moment to regret his early death, but if this was heaven, it was worth it.

"Oh!" His vision jumped and backed away, and he turned his head to follow her movements. She faced him fully, and he stared at her rounded belly. Disappointment jolted him. Not heaven, then, for surely heaven wouldn't tease him so. Pain returned to slam through his hazy mind.

His head throbbed a steady beat, but it was nothing to the pain in his arm. His shoulder was in fiery agony. He glanced to the side and was alarmed to see the joint protruding unnaturally. His stomach turned violently, and his vision darkened at the sight.

Don't faint, he told himself. He forced his mind to remain alert. He'd never been good with gruesome sights—he would have made a terrible soldier or surgeon, in fact. He closed his eyes to the image of his shoulder and imagined a hand drawing the pain from him in one long ribbon. Except the ribbon never ended. It just kept coming, yard after yard of red silk.

The darkness at the edge of his vision beckoned, and he resisted. Forced his mind to focus. To pack the pain in a box and set it aside. Another trick from the monks of St. Augustine. The lid kept sliding off the box, but he slapped it back on. Off, then on, went the lid. Back and forth, until Alex slipped and dropped the lid, and the pain escaped to coat everything.

When next he woke, it was to the cherub's face. She stood beside the bed and studied him with a disconcerting stare. Had he dreamt the lavender angel then? The sky beyond the room's grimy window was darkening, and he wondered how long he'd lain there.

"You're going to be all right," the cherub assured him on a whisper. "I hurt my arm too. Last summer I fell off my bed. Well, I was jumping, but only a little. But Mama told me it would be all better, and it was." She showed him a minuscule scar on her arm and waited, expecting a response, so he nodded at her.

She smiled, a broad grin with little white teeth, then bent to scoop something off the floor. "This is Robert," she confided, holding the "something" to face Alex.

Robert was pink, with brown-tipped ears, as if they'd been dipped in mud. Alex's memory recalled a pig's kiss. His forehead wrinkled; that couldn't be right.

"He's not supposed to be inside, but we used his pen to get *you* inside, so now he's here. He gets lonely outside." He tried to follow her logic and failed. He was brought in on a . . . pig pen?

"Tilda?" A voice called from outside his room.

The cherub looked over her shoulder then back at him. "I have to go. You're going to be all right," she assured him again, then she spun and left in a cloud of dark curls. The pig watched him from over her shoulder before Alex let his eyes drift shut again.

CHAPTER FOUR

THREE HOURS LATER

REGINA PACED THE SMALL PARLOR. Penny still hadn't returned from retrieving the doctor, and the longer she was gone, the more nervous Regina grew. It simply wasn't done, having a man in the house with just her and Tilda. At least he'd been unconscious for the most part. That had to count for something, didn't it?

The clouds that had been gathering as Penny left were now upon them, and the rain began again. Regina went in search of something with which to occupy her time and surveyed the larder. They needed to eat, and there was no sense waiting for Penny to return. Penny's meals were rarely edible anyway.

Their patient would likely need a broth of some sort if he ever woke. Isn't that what Briarly's cook always prepared when someone fell ill? Despite her suspicions about the man, she was determined to feed him. The sooner he recovered, the sooner he could be on his way.

She pulled an onion and some carrots from the larder and began chopping. Everything went into a pot with stock from a chicken Penny had stewed the day before. She shivered as she recalled the dreadful concoction Penny had served up. Tilda had found a *feather* in her bowl. When she pulled it out, eyes wide, Regina had delivered both of their bowls to Robert. Penny had merely soldiered on with stubborn cheer, insisting, "It's quite good, actually."

Regina added a dash of salt to the stock and set the pot over the fire. While it simmered, she went to check on their patient again. He still slept, his distorted shoulder silhouetted in the fading light from the window.

She surveyed the man's belongings. His hat, sadly crushed, hung on a peg by the door. She tried to brush the leaves from it, but she didn't think it was recoverable. She returned it to the peg.

His canvas bag lay on the floor in shadows. She debated for a moment then picked it up, watching him for signs of movement. If Foxwald had sent him, she wanted to be forewarned. Perhaps his bag contained a hint as to his identity inside.

She undid the tie and peeked inside, but it was too dark in the little room to see much of anything.

She glanced at him once more then took the bag to the kitchen. One by one she removed his things and examined them in the candlelight.

An unmarked silver flask. She unscrewed the top and sniffed. Brandy, if she was any judge. A case of cheroots, although she'd not smelled tobacco on him, only pleasant citrus. The spicy-sweet tobacco scent floating from the case reminded her of Foxwald's tobacco, and she wrinkled her nose before snapping the case shut.

Next, a small amber bottle. She untwisted the cap, and a light scent drifted to her nose. Ah. Cologne, the source of his citrusy scent. Next, she found a straight razor, tooth powder. Shirts, cravats, smallclothes. She brushed aside her guilt at invading his privacy. Needs must, and all that.

From the bottom she pulled a wooden box containing paints and brushes. A pencil and sketch pad, its pages curiously blank. Hmm. An artist, then, or at least a man who fancied himself an artist. He probably had a glib poet's tongue to go with his beautiful lips.

Next, she lifted a rolled canvas from the bag. She spread it across the kitchen worktable, held it flat and studied it. The style was remarkably similar to her brown painting, but more refined. This one lacked the discordant feeling of hers. "Alexandre Marchand" was inked boldly at the bottom, the final "d" curling in a flourish above the rest of the letters.

Marchand. The same artist as a similar painting she'd taken from Foxwald.

Regina stared at the canvas and chewed her lip, thinking. She didn't believe in coincidence. Happenstance hadn't brought this man to their cottage with a painting by the same artist in his bag.

Did he know who she was, or was he just searching for the Countess of Foxwald? If he didn't know yet who she was, he mustn't ever learn her identity. Regardless of what he knew or how he knew it, he needed to go. Soon. Regina refused to return to Briarly.

She reconsidered feeding their "guest." They didn't owe him any hospitality, and the thought of offering sustenance to a colleague of Foxwald's . . . well. She replaced his things in his room and paced the parlor, debating until her conscience finally won the battle. No matter how she felt about him, her upbringing would not allow an injured man to go without food. Grudgingly, she ladled a chipped bowl with broth and placed it on a tray.

Their guest's eyes were open when she returned to his room, and he stared at the ceiling. Good. She could learn more about who he was and how he'd come to be on their little lane.

"You're awake," she said. "How do you feel?"

He turned toward her, candlelight lining the side

of his face. He still had a pinched look, more so now that he was awake, and pain glazed his eyes. They were a rich brown topaz, she noted, like a lovely choker she'd had at Briarly. Velvety brown with shimmering gold flecks. With effort, he levered to an upright position, a grimace marring his face.

"How do I feel?" he asked. "Like I've been run over by a cart full of boulders."

Or dragged through the mud on his face, she thought, wincing. Guilt flashed through her—it was their pig who'd startled his horse, after all—but she ruthlessly set it aside. Sympathy for this man would get them nowhere.

Then she took notice of his accent and frowned. His voice was rich and flowy, like melted chocolate, but it had a foreign lilt. A *French* lilt. Memories of the poet with the false French accent assailed her, threatening her composure, and she forced them down.

He watched her, and she was struck again by the smooth features of his face. The impossible perfection of his lips. He's an *artist*, she reminded herself, lest she refine too much on his physical attributes. A *French* artist. And he was probably— possibly—working for Foxwald. She wasn't sure which of his crimes was worse.

"I thought you might like something to eat," she said shortly as she set the tray beside the bed.

"Thank you," he said.

"It's broth," she added.

His face fell at her announcement, and she pressed her lips together. He was an *ungrateful* French artist, apparently.

He lifted his hand to reach for the bowl, then dropped it immediately. It was obvious his shoulder pained him. With a grudging twist of her lips, she passed the bowl to his good hand and settled the spoon in the other.

"What's your name?" she asked.

His brows lifted at her question. He may have been scandalized by her bluntness, but how else was she to know his name? It wasn't as if they had an acquaintance to introduce them. After a moment, he replied. "Alexandre Marchand."

Alex—Alexandre Marchand. Did he truly expect her to believe he was a French painter? Her eyes narrowed as she thought of the artist's supplies in his bag. The used paints and his—conspicuously blank—sketch pad. Anyone could have acquired secondhand paints—she'd seen them in a shop in Brighton, in fact—but she was no one's fool. A true painter would have had true sketches. She wasn't certain why he would pretend at being an artist, but at least she had his measure. She could play along until she learned more of him.

"And where do you hail from, Mr. Alexandre

Marchand?"

"Paris. I'm in Brighton taking in the sights." He gazed impassively around the room as if to say the sights weren't that impressive at the moment.

She crossed her arms as she recalled the poet and his false accent. This man was probably no more French than she was, although she had to admit his accent was very nicely done. Was she fated to be plagued by lying artists? Fine.

"Why were you coming to our cottage, *Mr. Marchand*?" she asked.

He stared at her, the spoon still resting in his hand. "I'd become lost and thought to ask for directions."

She refrained from rolling her eyes, but only just. "You're on a cliff," she said shortly. "Keep the sea to your left and you'll reach Brighton. You can't miss it."

He nodded, a small smile tilting the corner of his mouth. He lifted the spoon to dip it into the broth, but his hand shook, and soup splashed onto the bedclothes.

She sighed and took the spoon from him and dipped it in the bowl. As she raised it to his lips, his brow furrowed.

"You don't need to feed me," he said. "I assure you I'm perfectly capable." He held his hand out for the spoon, then dropped it on a wince. He seemed as reluctant to be fed as she was to do the feeding, but they'd be here all night if she left him to it.

"I can see that. However, humor a lady."

He studied her a moment longer, then opened his mouth. Before she could insert the spoon, though, he spoke again. "I should at least have the privilege of knowing who feeds me." He smiled, his beautiful lips tipping up at one corner.

She put the spoon back in the bowl. "You may call me Mrs. Townsend." She couldn't give him her married name, but too late, she wondered if her maiden name would be known to him. She watched for signs of recognition, but his face remained impassive.

He was silent for a few moments, watching her. Then, "Is there a Mr. Townsend?"

He looked at her rounded belly, and a blush climbed her chest and neck at his implication. The impudence!

"Of course there's a Mr. Townsend," she said with frost before she realized her error. Now how was she to produce a Mr. Townsend?

She chewed her lip and considered admitting that poor "Mr. Townsend" had left her a widow, but she still didn't know who this man was or why he was here. His answers thus far had been resoundingly *un*helpful.

If Foxwald had sent him, then he already knew she was a widow. But, on the chance that he *wasn't* working with Foxwald, then he was just a stranger. And Penny had the right of it. He could murder them in their beds, and no one would ever be the wiser. She didn't think it prudent to tell him they were alone at the cottage, without male protection.

But perhaps more importantly . . . the less her story resembled that of the Countess of Foxwald, the better. If he didn't know who she was, then she needed to keep it that way. So, she scrambled instead for an explanation for the absent Mr. Townsend.

"Mr. Townsend has gone for the doctor." There, that should suffice. "Now, open up," she said.

He did as she commanded, and she drove the spoon into his mouth. He swallowed, and a funny look crossed his face. She waited, but he said nothing. Before she could shove another spoonful into his mouth, he took the utensil from her with another wince.

She watched him with arms crossed while he took another sip. The spoon shook in his hand, dribbling soup onto his lap. She handed him a linen from the tray, and their fingers brushed, making her jump.

"I've had enough, thank you," he said, handing the bowl back to her.

She nodded and looked out the window. Where was Penny? "The storm has returned, but your horse hasn't," she told him. "I'm afraid you're stuck here for the night."

He nodded.

She looked at the room again, tempted to apologize for the poor accommodations, but refrained. "Do you need anything . . . You must . . ." Her face burned.

"What?"

"The necessary. Do you need any help?"

Now his face was as red as she imagined hers to be. He coughed. "Do I need any help in the necessary? No, I think I can manage." He smiled at her discomfort.

She pressed her lips together. "I meant, do you need help *getting to* the—"

"Mama?" Tilda spoke from the doorway. "Robert wants to know where he's to sleep."

Blast! She'd forgotten about Robert's pen. She rubbed her forehead. "Robert can sleep in the parlor for tonight. But just for tonight. Let's get you some broth, and you can both go to sleep." She gathered the soup things and hustled girl and pig from the room, shutting the door behind her.

———

ALEX HAD LEARNED THREE THINGS from his supper with Mrs. Townsend, none of them good.

One: Mrs. Townsend, if indeed that was her name, was an abysmal cook. The broth, which she'd seemed inordinately proud of, was both horribly bland and salty at the same time. He was fairly certain she hadn't removed the skin from the onion. He took a moment to pity Mr. Townsend. Alex had swallowed as much as he could stand before putting an end to *that* torture.

Two: Mrs. Townsend was in over her head. When he'd told her his name, he watched for a reaction. Her eyes had widened before narrowing on him. If he hadn't been looking for a sign, he might have missed it, but she recognized his name, that much was certain.

He'd bet his last canvas she was the "comely, dark-haired woman" he sought. But if she was the one fencing forgeries of his work, she was abysmal at that as well, at least judging by the condition of her cottage. He hadn't seen the rest of the place, but this room was no better than a stable. Well, perhaps that was a stretch, but he was in pain and not feeling particularly charitable.

His work, even forged, could afford a better life than the one she was living. *If* one practiced economy, which, admittedly, he had not. But that was beside the point. Surely a successful forger would have better accommodations. To punctuate that thought, rain dripped into a pot with a soft splash. What game was Mrs. Townsend playing?

She'd asked why he was at their cottage. He'd almost come right out and accused her, taken her to task for her scheming thievery, but then he'd seen her rounded belly again and hesitated. He'd not seen this forged painting for himself. He needed to know more. And so, he'd given the ridiculous explanation that he'd become lost and was seeking directions. Ridiculous, because he didn't get lost, and he bloody well wouldn't ask for directions if he did.

Three (and by far the most troubling): Mrs. Townsend was oddly immune to his charm. She'd fussed and frowned at him, but not once had she smiled. Widow or no, she'd neither blushed nor looked at him through her lashes. Granted, he wasn't in top form at the moment, but feminine reaction to him wasn't usually so . . . flat.

Clearly, the fall from his horse had broken something. He felt the back of his head where a large goose egg throbbed. He moved his hand around to the front where another lump was forming above his left brow. How did a man fall from a horse and hit both the front *and* back of his head? But more importantly, when would his charm return? It seemed his shoulder wasn't the only thing out of joint.

He looked at the door frame curiously. He'd known a man once who'd achieved a similar injury, albeit in a much more interesting manner—he'd fallen while escaping from a third story bedchamber window. His acquaintance had manfully reset the joint himself against a sturdy oak timber.

Alex couldn't even look at his misshapen lump of a shoulder without nausea rising in his throat, but he preferred two arms to one. He climbed from the lumpy bed and tested the joint, shrugging and pressing it against the door frame, but the agony nearly brought him to his knees. He was a coward, that much was clear.

Night had fallen, and he wouldn't be leaving anytime soon. He would practice his mind tricks to keep the pain at bay, then he'd address the problem of his shoulder on the morrow. With luck, Mr. Townsend would return with the doctor, who would know best how to set the joint. There was no point in rushing things and making it worse. He was in no hurry, although another meal of Mrs. Townsend's cooking was likely to put him in an early grave.

He found his bag near the door and brought it into the room. He pulled out a nightshirt and wrestled with it briefly, then surrendered and tossed the garment onto a chair.

It was clear he wouldn't be able to don the nightshirt in his current state. He returned to the bed in his clothes and his boots and tried to settle the lid back on his box of pain.

———

THAT NIGHT, ALEX DREAMED. Horrific dreams of falling and water and darkness. Of searing pain in his chest, an unbearable pressure holding him down, choking the breath from him.

It was as if he was suffocating all over again. Desperate to breathe, he thrashed, heedless of the agony in his shoulder, until a soft touch penetrated the fog in his mind. The nightmare was a frequent one, and he climbed from the depths of it with a low groan.

Cool fingers stroked his brow, and his eyes regained their focus. Mrs. Townsend stood over him, her dark hair twisted in a long braid over her shoulder. Her rounded belly was obvious in her nightrail and dressing gown.

The cherub—Tilda, he remembered—held the pig and watched from the doorway. Outside, rain beat against the dark window, while inside, the ceiling dripped. He'd left his candle burning, and the flame flickered on the tallow stub, casting long shadows on the narrow walls.

"You were dreaming," Mrs. Townsend said with a scowl, pulling her hand away.

He nodded. "Sorry to have disturbed you."

She nodded and turned to leave. "Come along, Tilda," she said softly. "Let's get you and Robert back to bed. Robert needs his sleep."

Tilda looked at his candle and approached the bed while the pig gazed at him with a slow blink. "Are you afraid of the dark too?" she whispered.

He almost denied the accusation, but the earnest look on her face stopped him. "Sometimes," he confessed.

"Mama says there's nothing to fear. The dark is when the fairies come to watch over us, so we have to let it happen."

Fairies. Wonderful. Something new to fill his dreams. "Thank you, Tilda. I'll keep that in mind."

She followed her mother and looked at him once over her shoulder. Her grin was blinding as she left, and he found himself smiling back.

Only children were afraid of the dark, but Alex admitted the horrible truth. The dark terrified him. Horrible things happened in the dark. Things one couldn't control. His candle eventually sputtered and went out, taking its meager comfort.

He passed a fitful night after that, waking and dozing only to wake again to the never-ending darkness. Would morning never come?

At last, clear light pushed through the holes in the dingy lace curtain. Water dripped from the eaves outside the window and splashed in his corner pot.

A soft snuffling from the corner of the tiny room disturbed the early morning silence, and he turned his head. The pig lay stretched on the floor, his head on Alex's nightshirt, his back leg twitching. At least someone enjoyed pleasant dreams.

CHAPTER FIVE

THE MORNING BROUGHT CLEAR SKIES, but still no Penny. Regina assured herself she had likely gotten caught in the storm. She had probably taken shelter in Brighton, or with a neighbor. Regina chewed her lip, hating how anxious their flight from Briarly had made her.

She put on a pot of porridge and then, to distract herself, she went to survey the repairs needed to Robert's pen. They did *not* need a pig sleeping in the house.

A cart rattled down the lane as she inventoried the tools in the stable. She shielded her hand against the rising sun, relieved to see Penny with the midwife.

"My lady," Penny said breathlessly after she climbed from the cart. "It's that sorry I am that it took me so long. The doctor is down with the ague, so I went to fetch Mrs. Simmons, and then the storm . . ." She paused to draw a breath.

"It's all right," Regina said. "But I don't think Mrs. Simmons can help Mr. Marchand's shoulder. Good morning, Mrs. Simmons," she said to the older lady.

"Good morning, Mrs. Townsend. I thought it was time for another visit to see how you're getting on, and perhaps I can help your young man while I'm here," she said.

Mrs. Simmons was in her seventh decade, so anyone below fifty was considered "young." Regina estimated their guest to be around thirty, though, so he certainly qualified. Having delivered her own seven children plus hundreds of others in the vicinity, Mrs. Simmons was fully qualified to deliver Regina's babe when the time came. But setting a shoulder? Regina wasn't so sure.

"How's the patient?" Penny asked.

"Well enough. He passed a rough night, but he was still sleeping when last I checked." A "rough night" was an understatement. She'd awakened to sounds of distress coming from his room. Unsure what she would find, she'd entered. His candle had still burned, and he'd tossed about on the small bed. Sweat dampened his hair, and a deep wrinkle furrowed his forehead. He'd choked and gasped, clawing at his collar as if he couldn't breathe.

It had been natural to press a soothing finger over his brow, much as she did for Tilda when she had a bad dream. And that was the problem: caught in his nightmare, he'd reminded her of a child in distress. She'd been helpless to ignore his pain, but she preferred to keep him and his lying French charm at a distance.

"I'm sorry to have left you alone with him for so long," Penny said, pulling Regina's thoughts back.

"He asked about Mr. Townsend," Regina said. "He thinks Mr. Townsend went for the doctor," she added meaningfully.

Mrs. Simmons, who was aware of Regina's widowed status, nodded approvingly. "It's just as well you've outgrown your widow's weeds then, and you can rest assured I won't reveal your secret," she said, patting Regina's hand. "A lady can't be too careful in this day."

"If he's expecting Mr. Townsend, we'll give him Mr. Townsend," Penny said, nodding her head.

Regina and Mrs. Simmons eyed her skeptically. "What do you mean?" Regina asked.

"Just you watch."

Regina shook her head but followed Penny into the cottage. She poured a cup of tea for Mrs. Simmons while Penny hurried upstairs. When Penny returned, she carried a large pair of men's boots from the attic. She held a finger to her lips as she pulled them on over her own smaller boots.

Regina pressed a hand to her mouth and stifled a

laugh as Penny marched about the parlor, taking long, man-sized strides. Their patient would have to be daft indeed to fall for the sound of Penny's manly stomping, but she couldn't fault her creativity.

"Mama, what's Penny doing?" Tilda asked.

"She's playacting," Regina responded.

"Playacting at what?"

"I'm not sure, poppet." She shook her head and returned to the kitchen while Penny continued her charade.

The porridge looked to be finished, and she poked it with her spoon. It was a little thick, but some liked it that way. Although why she should care what a lying artist thought of her porridge she couldn't say.

Distance, she reminded herself. *Alexandre Marchand*, indeed.

She set a bowl of porridge on the dining table in front of Tilda, who eyed it skeptically. Tilda hadn't taken more than a few sips of the broth last night, and the curl of her lip didn't bode well for breaking her fast today.

Her daughter hadn't been such a fussy eater at Briarly, but then, she'd had the luxury of a lovely, *accomplished* cook to prepare her meals. Regina sighed. She was quickly finding that the domestic arts did not agree with her.

She placed a second bowl on a tray for Mr.

Marchand. Mrs. Simmons followed her, and she tapped at his door, listening for signs that he was awake. Footsteps sounded on the wooden floor before he opened the door. He was much more imposing when he was upright, and she stepped back.

Tall and long-limbed, she imagined he cut quite a swath through the ladies when he was in top form. He had the look of one accustomed to charming his way through life.

As it was, his shirt and hair were rumpled, and faint whiskers covered his cheeks. Rather than diminish his appeal, the roughness only accentuated the fine shape of his lips and jaw. She firmed her own lips against the flutter in her stomach—the flutter that reinforced why it was ill-advised to have a man in the house.

His color was improved, although his arm still hung at an odd angle. Regina cringed at the sight of the squared shoulder joint. Fine lines accented the corners of his eyes, and a sheen of sweat dampened his upper lip. Pain was a look she recognized well from her years with Anthony. Her husband had battled it daily.

Regina swallowed and looked down. His boots were scuffed and likely would never be the same again. She wondered how he'd managed them with one arm, then she realized he'd probably slept in them. In her concern for him last night, she'd not noticed his boots as she'd stroked his brow.

Guilt, for her poor nursing of him and for Robert's landing him in this position in the first place, niggled. Then she reminded herself he might be an associate of Foxwald. He wouldn't be *in this position* if he hadn't come looking for her. The sooner he could travel, the better.

She indicated the tray she carried. "I've brought you something to break your fast," she said.

He glanced inside the bowl and assured her he could manage it on his own. "Leave it on the table," he said shortly then added, "please." His tone was abrupt, bordering on rudeness.

She reminded herself he was in pain. Anthony had often been terse when he was having a particularly bad day. She set the tray down and turned to introduce Mrs. Simmons.

"Mr. Townsend returned and brought the midwife." She closed her eyes briefly on the lie. "Mrs. Simmons can assist with your shoulder, and then you can be on your way."

"A midwife?" he asked, eyeing them both.

"Mrs. Simmons is very knowledgeable," Regina assured him, although she too had her doubts.

He stared at her for a beat. "I've no doubt of that, *were I delivering a babe*. But I'm not. Thank you, Mrs. Simmons, but I'll manage."

Pain or not, Regina didn't think he needed to be

so curt about it. They were only trying to help him. "How, exactly, will you *manage*?" she asked. "How will you manage the porridge? How will you manage your shoulder? Have you done this before? Do you even know how to set your own shoulder?"

"How hard can it be? I just need to . . . to force the joint back into place." He looked at his arm, limp at his side, and his misshapen shoulder. He inhaled heavily.

"Very well. When are you going to do it? Because I'd like to make sure Tilda and I are away from the house."

He looked at her for a moment, then finally he said, "Now. I'll do it now, all right?"

Regina nodded and went to collect her daughter.

———

ALEX SHOOK HIS HEAD AS Mrs. Townsend left. Who did she think she was fooling? He'd risen when he heard commotion in the parlor and had peeked around the door frame.

He'd been surprised to see another woman stomping about in men's boots. As far as tricksters went, Mrs. Townsend was clearly a novice. An amateur. The image reinforced his thought that she was in over her head.

And a midwife? To set a man's shoulder? He realized pain, not to mention lack of sleep, was making him a poor guest, so he'd tried to temper his irritation. He didn't think he'd been very successful, though, judging from the pinched look on Mrs. Townsend's face as she left.

The midwife in question watched him from the doorway, her brows drawn in a steep V.

"You'll need to be direct about it, Mr. Marchand. Otherwise, you'll swoon from the pain before the thing is done, and then you'll have to attempt it all over again."

"I won't swoon," he bit off, although he wasn't so sure. He was feeling a trifle light-headed as it was. He eyed the door frame again.

"Be sure the muscles around the joint are relaxed. If they're not, it will be near impossible to reset. Have you any spirits?" she asked.

Spirits. That was a good idea. He nodded toward his bag. "Brandy, in my flask."

The midwife opened the bag, pulled out his flask and handed it to him. He took a lengthy swallow and started to hand it back to her. Before she could take it though, he pulled his hand back and drained the flask. Warmth flooded his belly but did little for the pain in his shoulder. And now he was out of brandy.

"Forget the door frame," she said.

"Pardon?"

"You're thinking to reset it by applying it to the door frame, correct?"

He nodded. How else did one go about this?

"Lie on the bed, and I'll walk you through it." He eyed her skeptically and thought about sending her away. He opened his mouth to do just that, but then he realized he was out of his depth, so he closed his mouth and did as she asked. Once he settled on the bed, he looked to her.

"Allow the muscles in your shoulder to relax. Are they relaxed?"

"Not yet." A beat passed.

"Now?"

"No, stop asking," he commanded. Then he closed his eyes and focused on releasing the pain to allow his shoulder to relax. The brandy flowed from his belly to his arms and finally helped ease his tension. "Now what?" he asked, lifting one eyelid.

"Slowly lift your arm above your head. It will hurt," she warned, "but you need to raise it above your head."

He did as she instructed, the pain tearing through him. He closed his eyes and exhaled, waiting for her instruction.

"Now, reach behind and scratch your neck." His eyes flew open then narrowed on her. "Just do it," she said. "Then reach for the opposite shoulder. Don't push or pull, just reach."

He inhaled and did as she instructed. Sweat beaded his lip. The pain burned white hot, tearing through flesh and bone. The movement was excruciating, wringing a groan from him, but nothing happened.

"Relax and try it again. Don't forget to breathe," she reminded him.

Rather unnecessarily, he thought, then he realized he was holding his breath. He let it out and tried again.

His heart beat rapidly in his ears. A low groan escaped him as the joint slid into place with a loud pop. The relief was immediate. He puffed out a long sigh and opened his eyes.

"Congratulations," she said. "You've birthed a lovely shoulder."

———

"Are you all better, Mr. Marchand?" Tilda asked, the pig close on her heels. She carried a late-blooming weed, which she handed to him with a grin. He took the purple flower and looked at it, then at her. She appeared so hopeful as she watched him. He'd never been one to disappoint a lady, although he'd never set out to charm one quite so . . . short . . . before. He tucked the flower in his buttonhole one-handed.

"I'm much improved, Miss Tilda, thank you." Mrs. Simmons had wrapped a wide strip of linen around his back, shoulder and chest to create a sling, her movements as quick and efficient as if she swaddled a newborn. He rotated his shoulder gently. It was still sore, shaky even, but at least the stabbing pain was gone, and it didn't look grotesque any longer. "See? Nearly good as new."

"Did it hurt? It must have hurt terribly." She looked his arm over, studying his sling. "Mama covered my ears, but I bet you cried. Did you cry?"

"I'm ashamed to say I did. Just a bit."

"Don't be ashamed. Mama says it's all right to cry. It helps the pain come out."

"She might be right about that. Your mama's a wise lady."

"Was there blood?" Tilda whispered, eyes wide.

She was a bloodthirsty little wench. "No, I'm sorry to say, there was no blood." He hid his smile as she frowned.

Ducking beneath the door frame, he followed Tilda and the pig to the parlor where he found Mrs. Townsend and the other woman. The one who wore men's boots. Mrs. Townsend clasped her hands before her, stretching her dress over her belly.

"Tilda, please take Robert outside." Tilda grinned at him again before skipping from the room, the pig in her wake. "Walk, please. And don't go past the privy," Mrs. Townsend said, although her words fell on deaf ears. She turned back to Alex.

"I'm glad to see your shoulder is better. I'm sure you'll wish to be on your way now."

He eyed her and the other female. If he left now, he'd not find out what they were up to. And truly, he had nowhere else to be anyway. He thought of his light purse, and the lodging options he could afford in Brighton. He wouldn't be missing much by staying an extra day or two. He rubbed his jaw with his good arm.

"I'm afraid I'm still without a horse, thanks to um . . . Robert," he added with a smile. "And Mrs. Simmons advised me to wear the sling for at least a few days, so I couldn't ride if I had one." He didn't miss the narrowing of Mrs. Townsend's eyes, but he pushed on. "I don't suppose you have need for a man of all work?"

The steady drip of water hitting the wooden bucket in the parlor's corner couldn't have been timed any better.

"No, we're fine," Mrs. Townsend said.

"Yes," the other woman said at the same time. Mrs. Townsend looked at her and shook her head slightly. The other woman acknowledged her with a brief nod and a curtsy.

"Perhaps I could speak with Mr. Townsend? I thought I heard him earlier this morning . . .?" He let his voice trail off in question. "I'd like to thank him for fetching the . . . midwife."

"He's gone out again," Mrs. Townsend said, squeezing her hands together.

"That's too bad. When do you expect him back?"

"Tonight."

"Tomorrow." This from the other woman. They truly needed to coordinate their story better.

"Mama, Penny," Tilda blew into the parlor. "Robert's in the cabbages again."

Mrs. Townsend closed her eyes for a beat and clenched her hands tighter. He could hear her soft sigh from where he stood, and he seized his opportunity.

"Why don't I fix the pig's pen? Then you can decide." He looked down at the floor, then up at her through his lashes. It was a look guaranteed to beguile and persuade. She narrowed her eyes at him again. Clearly, he'd miscalculated the depth of his charm. It was a lowering thought.

"How do you plan to do that with one arm in a sling?" she asked.

"I can help!" Tilda said in her child's voice.

What? No. She was adorable, but he didn't need her following him about all day. He worked best alone. Well, in truth, he'd never repaired a pig's pen before, but he suspected it was a task best performed alone.

"No, poppet," Mrs. Townsend said.

He smiled regretfully at the sprite with an I'd-love-to-have-your-help-but-your-mother-said-no look.

Mrs. Townsend frowned at him then said, "I

can't pay you." She nodded once at his silence as if she expected him to withdraw his offer . . . and was pleased.

"Room and board will be sufficient." He cringed inwardly at the thought of another bowl of her broth. Or porridge. It was all quite dreadful, and he was likely to starve, but some instinct was pushing him to stay, to learn more about this woman. And for a man who'd lost his charm, his funds and his horse, instinct was all he had.

She firmed her lips and stared at him, clearly torn. "Very well. But just until the pig's pen is finished."

CHAPTER SIX

"PENNY." REGINA RUBBED HER FOREHEAD once their new man of all work had left. "What was that about?"

"Wot was wot, my lady?"

"What happened to being murdered in our beds? Now you're inviting him to stay. We do *not* need him to stay. For all we know, he's here for Foxwald."

"Beggin' your pardon, my lady, but if he was here for the earl, wouldn't we know by now?"

"Unless he's merely biding his time until Foxwald arrives."

"Oh, well, there's that." Penny looked at the floor and pursed her lips. "But I don't think so. He seems like a good sort of fellow."

"A good sort? He's lying about who he is. He claims to be a fancy painter from Paris."

Penny crossed her arms. "Who's to say he's not? And the pen does need fixing." At Regina's continued silence, she added, "He's certainly fine on the eyes, don't you think?" Penny's own eyes took on an unfocused haze.

"Yes, but—No! He's not 'fine on the eyes.' And he carries on like a girl. I heard him all the way at the end of the lane when Mrs. Simmons assisted him with his shoulder. I had to cover Tilda's ears."

Regina ignored the irritating conscience that told her she was lying when she said he wasn't fine to look at. Even injured and scuffed, he was captivating. Compelling. And a *lying artist*, she reminded herself, which should have negated any attractiveness. If she'd learned anything in her foolish youth, she should find him wholly *unattractive*, but it seemed she had not learned a thing after all.

Penny was eying her skeptically, so she pulled her mind back to their conversation. "And how do we explain the continued absence of Mr. Townsend?"

"Oh, that's easy enough," Penny said, her face brightening. "There could be any number of reasons why Mr. Townsend doesn't show hisself. P'raps he's a sailor, or an invalid. Or a drunk, even. Maybe he's right this minute at the pub."

"Or perhaps he's *right this minute* seeking a new position for you."

Penny twisted her lips, thinking. "Well, there's no cause to be snappish about it."

Regina rubbed her forehead again and sighed. Penny was right. This entire situation had her on edge. "Of course, Penny. Where would we be without you? But we need to be careful. Even if he's not here for Foxwald, we don't need to give him any ideas about who we are. No *my ladys* while he's here. No curtsying. I'm just Mrs. Townsend."

"Yes, my la—Mrs. Townsend."

———

ALEX IGNORED THE RUMBLING OF his stomach as he surveyed the partially intact pig pen. After settling the question of him staying, he'd dipped a spoon into Mrs. Townsend's porridge, resolved to be optimistic. But when the spoon remained upright in the gray gruel, he'd grimaced and set the bowl aside.

Perhaps staying wasn't such a good idea after all. As any man, he enjoyed eating, but it didn't look like he'd be doing much of that here.

Tilda played in the dirt behind him, tossing a stick for the pig—Robert—and encouraging him to fetch it. Robert didn't seem like a fetching sort of chap. In fact, he seemed content to climb and waddle over Tilda's lap. Alex suspected there would be tears when the time came to take Robert to market. Not his problem, he told himself; he'd be long gone by then.

Mrs. Townsend fluttered between the cottage and the porch, watching over her daughter despite the nurse's presence.

He turned back to his assignment and studied the low structure. The pen had three intact sides. The fourth had been dismantled, presumably, to carry him into the house.

How two women had managed the feat, he couldn't imagine, but it did explain the purpling bruises blooming over his body and the lump on his brow. Not to mention the state of his boots. He stared at the scuffed toes with resignation. These were his favorite Hobies. Although, to be fair, being thrown from a horse could have done the same damage. Probably. Maybe.

He entered the small stable and took stock of the tools there. He found a hammer and some nails and carried them outside, then retrieved the slats the ladies had taken down. With his good arm, he held one to the pen's posts and braced it with his knee while he reached for the hammer. The wood tilted then slipped. He tried again and watched as it slid once more.

His head pounded from the beating it had taken yesterday from the earth. He raised his good arm and felt the lump on the back. Yes, it was still there, tender and throbbing. He looked at the hammer in his hand. It was incongruous with the image he was accustomed to seeing there—a paintbrush caressing canvas.

What was he doing? He was an artist. He imagined and created. He did not *build* things. Granted, he was an artist without a muse, a painter on extended holiday, but that was beside the point. Never mind that he'd asked for it, he didn't belong here, fixing a pig pen. *It's just until you find out more about Mrs. Townsend and her forgery game*, he reminded himself. But there had to be other ways to go about that.

He was about to set the hammer aside when two small, dirty hands appeared next to his. Tilda had abandoned her stick-throwing to hold the board. It looked like he was to have an assistant after all. She appeared so earnest in her attempt to help that he didn't have the heart to quit.

"Hold it steady," he said around the nail between his lips. She nodded, a serious expression on her face. He put hammer to nail and was amazed, and absurdly pleased, when it sank into the wood. They moved down the slat to the next post.

"What is Tilda short for?" he asked once the first board was complete.

"Matilda," she said, squinting up at him.

"Like the queen?"

"Yes, but Mama says I'm still a princess. Not a queen yet. Not like her."

"Your Mama's a queen?"

She nodded, her dark curls bouncing. "Regina means 'queen.' It's Latin. Do you know Latin?"

"Believe it or not, I do." Languages had always been easy for him. English, French, Italian. Latin.

"Say something."

"Pardon?"

"Say something in Latin."

He thought for a moment while she held the board with her little hands. "*Parum manus, sed sortem de luto.*"

"What does it mean?"

"*You have little hands, but lots of dirt.*" Or something along those lines. She looked at her hands and grinned her big, little-toothed smile.

When the three boards had been replaced, he studied the remaining gaps in the pen. Then he studied the pig. Robert was a little thing, so height wasn't important. But he could easily wriggle under the lowest rail if he dug just a bit. Alex had seen a saw and some old lengths of wood in the corner of the stable. He collected them and stacked the wood near an old stump.

"What are we doing now?"

"We need another row of rails along the bottom, so Robert doesn't sneak out. These are too long, so we need to cut them to size."

"Can I do it?"

Since the saw was not much shorter than she was, he thought perhaps another task would suit her better. "I've a better idea. Do you see that apple tree over there?" He motioned with his head, and she nodded. "Why don't you go find two of the biggest, juiciest apples for us to enjoy. No, make it three."

She looked at the tree some distance away. "I'm not s'posed to go past the privy."

"What? Even for the best apples?"

She shook her head.

"I won't tell anyone. It will be our secret."

She remained skeptical as she studied him, then the tree, then the cottage. Her inner debate was transparent as it played across her face. Was he a cad to tempt her into disobeying her mother? Yes, he feared he was. He almost told her to forget the apples, but then his stomach rumbled again.

"Are you trying to lead me astray?"

He choked back a laugh. "What do you mean?"

"Mama says when a handsome man wants something he shouldn't have, he'll try to lead the lady astray. Even queens and princesses."

Interesting. What was he to say to that? "Well, sometimes I suppose that may be the case," he hedged. "But sometimes a handsome man just wants an apple."

"I'll cut the board and *you* get the apples," she offered.

Hmm. She was a crafty negotiator. "Let's cut the board *together*, then I'll get us some apples," he bargained, and she agreed with a vigorous nod. He put the first board on top of the stump and motioned her over. She stood in front of him, and he placed his hands over hers on the saw handle.

Surely entire houses were built in the time it took them to cut one board. But she laughed and clapped her hands when the end of the timber dropped to the grass, and speed didn't matter so much. He was happy to see his charm still worked. Apparently, the short ones were absurdly easy to please.

———

HER DAUGHTER HAD A SHORT memory, Regina reflected. At four years of age, she supposed that was to be expected, but she distinctly recalled telling her to mind the pig, not the pig pen. And yet, as she watched from the window, Tilda stood in front of Mr. Marchand—or whatever his name was—and *sawed*.

A four-year-old had no cause to handle a *saw*. What was he thinking? He clearly had no experience with small children. She rounded the table and threw the door open and . . . the luminous look on Tilda's face stopped her.

She admitted to herself he was being more careful than she expected. His large hands guided Tilda's smaller ones, keeping her fingers far from the teeth of the blade. She forced her panic down. Robert would outgrow the pen before they finished, but she didn't have the heart to stop them.

When the end of the board dropped into the grass, Mr. Marchand looked up and spotted her in the doorway. He gave a little shrug and tilted a grin at her as Tilda clapped and bounced on her toes.

Anthony had never spent time getting to know his daughter. Between his illness and estate matters, he'd never made the time. Regina's own father had been distant, so she didn't know what it was like to have an attentive parent, but it saddened her to think Tilda would never know her father. That a stranger—whoever he was—had spent more time with Tilda in a few hours than her father had her entire short life. And that her new baby would have only Regina for guidance.

Panic fluttered in her chest whenever she thought of the future. She needed a plan for what she would do if she did indeed carry a boy. Foxwald would contest her custody, of that there was no question. He would demand guardianship if she tried to claim the earldom for her son.

If she carried a boy, the only way she could see forward was to disappear and make a new life for them. America, perhaps, or the Continent. But that would deprive her son of his rightful inheritance. Was it selfish of her to consider such a path? As he grew into a man, would he resent her actions?

She rubbed her forehead. Surely it was

premature to think of such things. With any luck, she carried a girl, and these musings would be irrelevant. She was worrying for nothing.

She returned to the small dining table and unfolded the financial papers. Several months old and curled at the corners, they were all she'd convinced the Brighton shopkeeper to sell at a discount, but they would serve.

She made notes in the margins with a small pencil, circling investments with promise, and marking through those that looked dubious. With the back issues she'd secured, she could track their performance over time. She was also able to note which enterprises were poised to be acquired by other, more stable firms.

As a plan, it wasn't much to work with, but it gave her a much-needed sense of control. With enough funds to start, she was confident she could make sound investments to support them in time. They couldn't hide at Penny's mother's cottage forever.

But "funds to start" was where she was stuck. Most of her jewelry had been entailed and now adorned the new Lady Foxwald. Her husband had not been a skinflint, but with his deteriorating health, lavish gifts had not been Anthony's priority.

He'd given her the occasional trinket for birthdays, a small pair of ruby earbobs when Tilda was born, but nothing extravagant. Certainly nothing to support them for longer than a few months. She'd sold his gifts when they'd first arrived at the coast, and the funds were dwindling.

She thought again of the rolled canvas in her room. She'd tucked it behind a loose board in the wall. It was disheartening to think a purloined painting was all she had left in the world. And judging by the proprietor's reaction to it, it wasn't even worth much. Not as much as she'd hoped, at any rate, knowing Foxwald's expensive taste in art. One would have thought her house guest could have chosen a more successful painter to impersonate.

She looked at her ever-increasing belly and rubbed a hand over the firm mound, considering their future. She'd been thinking of him or her as a little mouse, given the delicate flutters she felt. Tilda had been sharp elbows and knees inside her, but this one made his—or her—presence known with soft little taps. Like a mouse nibbling cheese.

The door flew open, and Tilda rushed in on a wave of energy. She crunched an apple and handed one to Regina. "Mama, Alex got us apples."

"That was nice of him, but you must call him Mr. Marchand." She closed her eyes at the words. They might not know his true name, but they could at least observe the proprieties.

"But he said I can call him Alex," Tilda said, "since we're friends."

How did one explain to a four-year-old when a man was being too familiar? That using a man's given name would only lead to further liberties? She opened her mouth, then closed it and glared at him instead. He would be gone soon, she reminded herself. Surely, Tilda using his given name was no different than her speaking to one of the grooms at Briarly.

Regina pressed her lips together and studied her daughter. "There's more dirt on your hands than in Robert's pen, young lady. Go wash up, please."

Tilda studied her hands, which were crusted with dirt on the backs and under her nails. Regina watched her expression, waiting . . .

"They're not *that* dirty, Mama."

Regina remained silent and lifted an eyebrow.

"Come along, miss," Penny said, guiding Tilda to the scullery. "Save your remaining apple for dessert. Your mama's making a stew for us tonight."

Regina didn't miss the look of trepidation on Alex's—Mr. Marchand's—face, but she chose to ignore it. The man was fortunate they were willing to feed him.

"I'll thank you not to be overly familiar with my daughter," she said.

"You can call me Alex, too, if you'd like," he

replied with a wink.

She scowled and turned back to her papers. He would be gone soon, she reminded herself again. The pig's pen was finished. She'd feed him tonight—provide the room and board she'd agreed to—but then he needed to leave.

He took a bite of his own apple, the crunch loud in the small space. She tried to ignore him, but he commanded her attention. Even as she gazed unseeing at her papers, she was aware of him from the corner of her eye. A trickle of juice appeared at the corner of his mouth before he wiped it away with his thumb. What must it be like to have such perfect lips?

"What are you working on?" he asked.

"Pardon?"

He motioned to the papers on the table.

"Oh! It's nothing. Just some notes," she said. She began gathering the papers into a tidy pile.

He lifted one and read her notes in the margin. His eyebrows arched. "Investments? Do you play the five percents then?"

She took the sheet from him and added it to her pile. "No. Not yet."

"But you've some knowledge of how they work?"

He pulled a chair out with his foot and sat across from her. A bruise purpled his forehead above one eyebrow, and she winced with guilt. Even with the bruise, though, his appeal was compelling. With his arm in a sling and his hair rumpled from the outdoors, he looked raffish. Dashing, even.

She felt another flash of irritation and pinched her lips. She wasn't an irritable sort, but that seemed to be her normal reaction to him. Which, of course, irritated her further. He took another bite of apple while he awaited her response. What had he asked her? Oh, yes. Investments.

"I've followed them for some time." She shifted in her chair, bracing for his scorn and condescension.

He nodded at her response, thinking and chewing. She watched him as he leaned back and crossed his good arm over the sling, his apple dangling from long fingers. "What are your picks? Who do you favor?"

Surprised at his interest, she swallowed. "Well," she began, folding her hands atop her papers. "The war will have far-reaching impact that we're only just beginning to understand." Did he truly want to hear her thoughts?

At his encouraging gaze, she continued. "I'm avoiding enterprises that don't have a clear plan to discharge their surplus supplies. And firms that have the ability and fortitude to import staples from America are at the top of my list." She waited for his reaction.

"Why the American imports?" he asked.

She studied him for signs of skepticism, but he only appeared . . . curious. She continued hesitantly. "Cotton, wheat and corn are already in short supply due to the war. That shortage is only going to grow. The firms that manage the supply well, with American imports for example, will succeed." She tapped her pages with a finger. "Some are already showing promise."

He nodded again and looked at the cottage around them. "Investing requires funds. Where will you get the money to start?"

She drew a breath and blew it out, her cheeks puffing. She thought about pulling the fictitious Mr. Townsend into the discussion. Perhaps Mr. Townsend had a long-lost aunt who'd left a small inheritance . . . .? But no, she didn't have Penny's flair for the dramatic. Or her penchant for subterfuge, it would seem. "I have some . . . things to sell." *One thing* to sell.

"Things? What sorts of things?" Well, now his questions were making her nervous. Why did he want to know? Did he think to steal from them? He'd be sorely disappointed if that was his plan.

She stood and tapped the pages on the table. "Nothing of any import. You should wash for supper. We'll dine shortly."

CHAPTER SEVEN

ALEX DUCKED AND ENTERED HIS tiny bedroom to wash. He unwound the sling and pulled his shirt over his head, favoring his bad arm. What he wouldn't give for a proper bath, but he didn't think a tub would fit through the narrow doorway. Even if he could somehow manage it, the small bed and table took up all the floor space. He vowed tomorrow he would find a way to bathe. Tonight, a square of linen dipped in a basin of cold water would have to suffice. He grimaced.

As he went through his chilly scrub, thoughts of Mrs. Townsend plagued him. Regina. The name suited her. Regal and earthy at the same time. He'd seen her through the window as he and Tilda returned to the cottage, and the image remained imprinted on his mind: Regina, seated at the dining table, sunshine lighting one side of her face. Regina, rubbing a hand over her swollen belly.

A portrait began painting itself in his mind,

elements shifting and snapping into place. He could picture the contours, the light and shadow, the smooth creamy palette of her face and lips touched by light. If only he could translate the image from his mind to canvas without the intrusion of gloomy cliffs and stormy seas . . .

Regina would make a sublime madonna, soft and glowing, and his stomach twisted and tightened at the image. He drew up short. He'd not felt such a reaction to a lady before. Certainly not on such short acquaintance. It unsettled him. He had experience with all sorts of ladies, but rarely did he feel *twisty*. He was not the twisty sort. And she was hardly the sort he normally pursued.

While many men had a distinct preference for short women, or red-haired women, or women with curves, he wasn't choosy. He enjoyed all types. Short, tall, thin, not-thin, dark, fair. But he'd never been drawn to an *enceinte* lady.

The idea of babies somewhat terrified him. No, he corrected. Not *somewhat*. They petrified him, pure and simple. He enjoyed a life free of responsibility. No one depended on him for anything, and that was the way he preferred it, as there was no one to disappoint.

But nothing and no one could be more *dependent* than a baby. So why he found Regina so compelling, rather than *repelling*, was a mystery. It would be better if there *was* a Mr. Townsend, to set her safely out of his range and his thoughts.

He splashed cold water on his face as if that would wash away her image. It didn't. He dried his face and neck and pulled on a fresh shirt. Ran a hand through his hair then cleaned his teeth.

Why did he feel like he was calling on a new lover? It wasn't as if he was courting the lady, but he had to admit it would soothe his vanity if she would respond to his charm just a bit. He forced his nerves to settle and focused on the smells coming from the kitchen.

They were actually . . . promising. His mouth watered and his stomach rumbled. He'd eaten three apples, and they'd long since left his belly. While he didn't miss his creditors, he did miss fine Parisian food. Bloody hell, he missed *edible* food.

He enjoyed a tantalizing fantasy about a nice *boeuf à la Bourguignonne*, with crusty bread and a rich red Carménère. He'd even settle for a savory *blanquette de veau* with tender mushrooms simmered in a creamy white sauce. Or *coq au vin* with a delicate Beaujolais . . .

The plop of water in his corner pot jolted him from his reverie, and he reminded himself to be realistic. One didn't rise from the depths of tar-thick porridge to coq au vin overnight, but one could dream.

Tilda was already at the small dining table when he arrived, freshly scrubbed and dressed in a frilly pink frock. The pig dozed in a corner, cushioned by Alex's nightshirt. His forelegs embraced a . . . doll? Poor form, Robert. Poor form.

Recalling Regina's admonishment, he strove for a less familiar approach. "Good evening, Miss Tilda."

Tilda giggled at his formality. "Mr. Marchand." She nodded at him as if she truly was a queen, then she spoiled the effect with another giggle behind her hand.

Penny came and scooted Tilda's chair closer to the table. "Sit up straight, Miss Tilda," she reminded her.

Regina entered from the kitchen. She carried a heavy iron pot with a thick linen towel wrapped about the handles. He rushed to help her, reaching for the pot with both hands.

"Bloody hell!" he muttered, pulling his hands from the fiery iron.

She scowled at his language. "It just came off the fire," she told him unnecessarily. She looked at his hands, now red and preparing to blister, he was certain. "Are you all right?"

"Fine," he murmured. His efforts to be polished and charming were not off to a good start.

She set the pot on a linen in the middle of the table and stepped back. He pulled her chair out and smiled, ignoring the raging burning of his hands and imbuing his expression with every bit of dash and sophistication he could muster. She hesitated before sitting, her lips pressed in a firm line. Yes, his polish was definitely tarnished.

"Mr. Townsend doesn't dine with us?" he asked.

A pause. "No, he's otherwise engaged."

"Who's Mr. Tow—

"Don't talk with your mouth full, poppet."

"But it's not—"

"Shall we say grace?" Regina asked, directing an expectant look toward Alex. He blinked in surprise.

All right. He could do this. The three ladies bowed their heads and closed their eyes, waiting. "Um . . . Dear Lord. Thank you for Miss Penny and Miss Tilda and Miss Regina. Mrs. Townsend, that is. Thank you for providing food for us to eat. Even this food. Especially this food," he corrected. A sleepy snort interrupted from the corner. "And thank you for Robert. Amen."

"That was . . . nice," Regina said. She lifted the top off the iron pot and steam curled above it. Alex's mouth watered as she began ladling stew into bowls. He felt a trifle faint.

"I'm sure Robert will enjoy his new pen tonight," Regina said to Tilda. "You did a fine job repairing it."

"Alex did most of it," Tilda confessed. "But I

held the wood. And I got to saw. Then Alex tried to lead me astray, but I said no."

Silence settled on the table. Alex thought he could hear his own heartbeat in his ears as Regina's ladle hung suspended over the pot.

"Apples," he muttered.

"What was that?" Regina asked.

"I asked her to fetch the apples. I did *not* try to lead you astray," he directed at Tilda with a glare.

"I didn't go past the privy," Tilda assured her mother.

"I'm proud of you, poppet," Regina said, the corners of her mouth twitching. She handed Alex a warm bowl. He looked at the contents. And scowled. The stew was . . . gray. Watery. A film of something floated on the top. Not coq au vin then.

She passed him a thick slab of bread to dip in his stew. At least, he thought it was bread. He watched the ladies dip their spoons into their bowls and waited. Penny smiled around a mouthful of stew. Alex took a tentative bite and chewed. And chewed. She'd served them . . . leather boiled in . . . ditch water? He coughed.

"It's quite good, my la—Mrs. Townsend," Penny said, still smiling. Was the woman daft or just excessively loyal? Alex's bet was a little of both.

Tilda had one elbow on the table as she stirred her spoon in her bowl. He noticed she'd not yet taken a bite. She watched him out of the corner of her eye, waiting. He was still chewing. He finally just swallowed it whole. And gagged.

"Sorry," he muttered when he could catch his breath. Regina narrowed her eyes at him.

Madonna or no, this was a travesty. They'd starve if they had to endure much more of this. How the ladies had survived as long as they had was a mystery. Perhaps this explained Mr. Townsend's absence. The man had died from a virulent case of bad stew.

"Mama, I'm not hungry."

Regina gazed at her daughter then at her own bowl, and her shoulders rounded. He detected a slight tremble to her chin. He much preferred her scowls, and he spoke without thinking. Anything to forestall tears.

"Perhaps it just needs a little roux," he began, "to thicken the broth." It would take more than a little roux, but they had to start somewhere.

"It's quite good," Penny repeated, and Regina gave her a shaky smile.

"Is it . . . beef?" he asked, poking a gray lump.

"Chicken." Regina's head came up and she firmed her chin. Her shoulders straightened, and her nostrils flared as she narrowed her eyes at him. How did she do that, the narrowing and the flaring at the same time? Still, it was better than the trembling. He'd gladly take anger over tears.

In hindsight, he realized a prudent man would have stopped talking, but he'd never been prudent. "Oh. Well. Maybe a little parsley or tarragon. To bring out the potatoes."

"Those are carrots."

His collar felt tight. He tugged on it. "It's not that bad," he said with more forced cheer. "I'm sure I've had worse," he assured her, smiling through the lie. No. No, that was the wrong thing to say. He saw it immediately in the set of her jaw. Time slowed then stopped as she calmly rose, lifted her bowl, and emptied it in his lap.

Tilda gasped and looked at him, her mouth a round O. Penny's head was aimed at her own bowl, but Alex thought he detected a smirk. Regina rounded the table and returned to the kitchen, her back straight. He forced his mouth to close. Yes, he definitely needed to work on his polish.

"What's roux?" Tilda asked.

———

LATE THAT NIGHT, REGINA BRUSHED her hair and cringed as the evening replayed in her mind. After letting her temper cool, she'd cobbled together a meal from apples, biscuits and wedges of cheese, so at least they hadn't starved. Yet.

Her stew had been abysmal. As annoyed as she'd been with his critique, Mr. Marchand had been correct about that.

But ever since the poet's departure, she'd been a model of unimpeachable propriety. She'd restrained every thought, every action until sometimes she didn't even recognize herself. But as her irritation with Mr. Marchand—and frustration with her life's path—had grown, so too did her desire to simply . . . let go.

All of her lessons in proper etiquette told her it was not appropriate to empty a bowl in a man's lap. But oh, the freedom of not being Lady Regina, of being an anonymous widow with no expectations or scrutiny, had been . . . intoxicating.

She grinned, recalling the look on his face as she'd shaken the last drop from her bowl. Then she sobered as she recalled how handsome the man was. At least until he opened his mouth and tried to charm her.

She'd almost dropped the pot when she left the kitchen and saw him standing there, filling the room. Tall, broad. Golden. Hints of warm citrus wafting from him as he held her chair. Even with the sling wrapped about his shoulder, he exuded strength.

Stop, she told herself. He'd only been here two days, and he'd been unconscious for some of that time. It had taken at least a week to lose her mind over the poet.

Perhaps it was Mr. Marchand's vulnerability. He'd seemed nervous when he entered the parlor.

She saw it in his eyes and the rounded set of his shoulders as he approached her. And now his poor hands, which surely must have blistered from reaching for the pot. She should have warned him, but her brain didn't work properly in his presence. *Artist,* she reminded her brain in a futile attempt to set it straight.

But her brain wouldn't heed her. She thought again of his burned hands and gave in to her sympathy. She went to find Penny. "Where do you keep the salve?" she asked, careful not to wake Tilda.

"Whatever for?" Penny said as she rummaged in a box.

"Mr. Marchand's hands."

Penny stopped rummaging and looked at her.

"He burned them on the pot," Regina reminded her. "I don't want them to become infected. Then we'll never be rid of him."

"Mmm hmm. Here we are." Penny handed her a small jar.

"Thank you," Regina whispered.

Dim light shone around the door frame of his room. He was awake, good. She hesitated then knocked softly. A minute or two passed before she heard noise on the other side of the door. Another minute after that before the door cracked open.

Her eyes widened at his appearance. He looked like he'd been asleep, despite the light she'd seen coming from his room. His hair was rumpled, his shirt open at the top. Her palms dampened while her mouth went dry. She looked down and saw her rounded belly. What was she doing, she wondered, feeling such things in her condition?

He looked at her expectantly. *Say something.* But it seemed her traitorous brain had disconnected from her mouth. "Here," she offered brilliantly. "It's a salve. For your hands." She handed him the jar and turned to go.

"Wait." He pulled the door wider and stepped back.

Artist, she reminded herself, but her self didn't listen. Her feet were across the threshold before she could stop them. He left the door open, which soothed her anxiety a fraction.

She looked at the room through his eyes and fresh mortification washed over her. Cobwebs clung to the corners. The ceiling was brown in places, the plaster shiny where the roof leaked. Dust coated the small table next to the bed, and footsteps could be seen in the layer on the floor. His mattress still needed an airing, but he'd not complained. Just as he'd not complained as she'd emptied her stew in his lap. He hadn't said a word, in fact, just watched her and accepted it as his due.

He was leaving soon, she reminded herself. Tomorrow. The room didn't matter.

"Do you need assistance with the salve?"

He turned the jar in his hand, and she followed the movement. His palm was wide, the fingers long. He nodded. "If you would."

She took the jar and urged him to sit on the end of the bed. The frame creaked under his weight but held.

His clothing was stained from her stew. His shirt gapped, and she stared at a sliver of his bare chest. It was firm and muscled, dusted with light brown hair. Nothing like Anthony's thin frame had been. Like his lips, Mr. Marchand's chest was beautifully sculpted. She forced her breathing to slow, then she narrowed her eyes on a puckered scar near his heart.

He followed her gaze and pulled the edges of his shirt together. "It's nothing."

She looked in his eyes, but he seemed self-conscious, so she shifted her focus back to his hands. She spread the fingers of one hand flat. His palm bore shiny red streaks where it had come into contact with the stew pot.

She dipped a finger into the salve and smoothed the ointment over his warm skin, just below where his palm met his fingers. His hands were beautiful like the rest of him. Not soft, but not calloused either. They seemed capable. Citrusy heat radiated from him, warming her from head to toe.

Her gaze was fixed on her ministrations, so it

was some time before she saw that *his* was fixed on her belly, positioned as it was before him. She inhaled at the rough expression she saw there and started to step back, but he curled his fingers around hers and held her still.

"I know there's no Mr. Townsend," he said, looking up.

"What—what do you mean?" she asked, pulling her hand from his and stepping back as far as the little room would allow. She'd forgotten about Mr. Townsend, her supposed husband, and her face flamed.

"I saw Penny in her boots."

"Ah." She turned from him, replaced the lid on the salve and set in on the little table. She thought of fabricating another lie, but in the end she said simply, "She means well, but it was a silly ruse, I suppose."

"Was there ever a Mr. Townsend?" he asked.

There was no censure in his voice, just curiosity. She knew she shouldn't care what he thought of her, but she did. She also knew she shouldn't trust him with her secrets. She didn't know him, still didn't know his purpose for being there, but she found herself turning back to him and confessing a little of the truth. "Yes, there was a Mr. Townsend, until recently. I'm a widow."

He nodded and stood. "You've no other family?"

She shook her head. His questions were getting too personal. Too close to the truth. "The pen is finished. You need to leave tomorrow."

The ceiling drip echoed in the small room. She firmed her lips at the reminder of the sorry state the cottage was in. The sorry state *she* was in. He took advantage of the opportunity to say, "Let me fix the roof."

His offer was tempting. They couldn't afford to hire someone, and the leaks were growing. *Artist*, she reminded herself. She stood straighter, impenetrable, and shook her head.

"Let me cook."

Her head came up at that. "You can cook?"

"No, but neither can you. Let me try."

"I can make a nice cheese toast," she protested. And she could. Probably.

He lifted a brow. His doubt was lowering, but she thought again of the leaking roof, and the tasteless meals they'd endured. If she only had herself to worry about, she could persevere. But then she thought of the life inside her, and Tilda. They were growing babes and deserved better. Penny, who'd fled in the night with her, deserved better.

"Why?" she asked.

"Why?"

"Why are you here? And don't tell me you were lost. Why are you *still* here?"

He was quiet for so long she thought he wouldn't answer. Then he said with a shrug, "I've nowhere else to be."

The words were spoken casually, but she stared at him. Was he so alone then? Was there no one waiting for him somewhere? No one wishing for his return? Like her, he seemed adrift, anchorless. She shushed the ever-present suspicious whispers in her mind. They wouldn't quiet entirely, but perhaps they'd settle enough so she could think.

Finally, she nodded in response to his offer. "You may try."

She swallowed before speaking again and motioned to his shirt. "Tomorrow is wash day. I'll see that your things are cleaned. The previous tenant left some clothes in the attic if you wish to find another shirt or . . . something."

He smiled, and she smiled back before she caught herself. At this close distance, his warmth folded around her. Male and earthy. When was the last time she'd felt cocooned? Had she ever? She watched the curve of his beautiful, sculpted lips, wishing . . . Her heart skipped and the babe kicked. She pulled away and he dropped his hand.

"May I call you Reggie?"

She frowned. "You may call me Mrs. Townsend."

"Regina?"

"Mrs. Townsend."

"We'll see."

———

THERE WAS NO MR. TOWNSEND. He'd suspected as much, but to hear her confirm it . . . well. He smiled.

But why all the secrecy? Why the forgery? He couldn't put his finger on it, but Regina didn't belong in this dilapidated cottage any more than he did.

He turned the problem over and studied it from various angles. Wondered why she couldn't—or wouldn't—just tell the truth. Then he tried to see himself through her eyes, and he wasn't sure he would trust himself either. But clearly, she was running from something, or someone.

It was not his concern, he reminded himself. He made a habit of staying well out of other people's business, but whatever her story, it seemed he'd be allowed to stay a bit longer.

He wasn't sure she'd accept his offer to fix the roof or to cook, never mind that she desperately needed both. He'd fully expected her to refuse him out of hand, and then she'd asked why he was there.

He'd almost redoubled his efforts to charm her. Prepared a wink and a smile and a glib response but stopped. Every time he tried to charm her, she stiffened, so he'd given her the truth instead. *I've nowhere else to be.* Surprisingly, it had worked.

He put his good arm behind his head as he lay

on the bed, his feet hanging off the end. His hands throbbed where he'd burned them on the iron pot. Rather than soothing him with the salve, though, her touch had sharpened his awareness. He felt each heartbeat in his palms.

Above his head, the drip had spread, dark and blooming across the plaster. A spider watched him from a gauzy web above the washstand. Light from his shrinking candle reflected in the grime on the window. He was pretty sure there was something crawling in his mattress. His stomach growled its displeasure, and somewhere a pig slept on his nightshirt. But for some reason, he was pleased.

Then he recalled the image of Regina's rounded belly and his smile fell. How much longer did she have until her confinement? How did these things work?

He knew nothing about childbirth, as he suspected few men did. He didn't *want* to know about childbirth, but he couldn't help the questions running through his mind. Was she getting the care she needed? Shouldn't she be eating more? Was it safe for her to be up, or should she be abed?

As she'd stood before him, soothing the salve over his hands, he'd been captivated by her roundness. His mind grappled to accept the wonder in her belly. There was a tiny person in there.

Another little human.

There hadn't been four of them at table tonight, there had been five. And when the fifth one arrived in the world, he—or she—would need . . . things. A home. Family. Stability. Love. Honor. Things Alex was pretty sure he knew nothing about. His pleasure evaporated, and he laid his arm across his eyes. It would be best for everyone if he was gone when that time came.

CHAPTER EIGHT

A NOISE WOKE REGINA BEFORE the day lightened. Indeed, the faded half-moon was still visible beyond her window. She pulled a pillow over her head and turned, but the noise came again. Someone was in the kitchen.

She sighed and crawled out from under the thin counterpane. She washed and dressed in a pale blue gown that tied in the front. There was a distinct freedom in shedding her upper-class identity. She never could have dressed herself as Lady Foxwald, with all the layers that tied in the back. Who knew something as simple as dressing oneself could be so liberating?

She put her hair in a simple twist, cleaned her teeth and slid her feet into half-boots. Tilda and Penny were still asleep in the room next to hers, and she cracked the door open to watch her daughter. Tilda curled on her side, a soft blanket bunched around her waist. She was a heavy sleeper and didn't flinch when Penny's loud snore echoed off the low ceiling.

Pulling the door closed, Regina descended the stairs. The sun was breaching the horizon to illuminate the low morning fog, and its misty light angled through the front windows to pool on the wooden floor. She caught tiny glimpses of the sea through the scrub at the end of the lane. With luck, they'd have a brilliant blue sky by midday—the sharp, vibrant sort only seen in the cooling months between summer and winter.

She entered the kitchen and stopped short.

Mr. Marchand stood behind the worktable, one hand in his hair and the other hanging from his sling. He surveyed the surface before him. It looked like he'd removed every item from the larder and laid it out for inspection.

His rough linen shirt was about two sizes too small, and the cuffs were tight around his forearms. He'd found the clothing in the attic then, although he still wore his own trousers. He looked up and his face cleared on seeing her.

"What are you doing?" she asked.

"Taking stock. How long have these items been here?" He hefted a bag of flour to the table and sniffed the contents.

"Most of them were here when we arrived. Except for the vegetables, of course."

He was still for a moment. "When you arrived. When did the previous tenant leave?"

She thought back to her conversations with Penny. "A year ago, maybe two?"

He moved the flour to a pile on the right. A smaller pile on the left contained salt, dried beans and some seasonings, but most everything else was in a haphazard collection on the right. He sighed. "There's nothing here to work with."

"What do you mean, there's nothing? There's flour and barley. Lard. A joint of dried beef. There's plenty here."

"The flour smells rancid, and I'm fairly certain I see bugs in the sack."

Regina's stomach turned and she pressed a hand to settle it. "Bugs?" she whispered.

"Yes, weevils if I'm not mistaken." He lifted the grain sack again. "You can tell a weevil from a beetle by the snout. See?"

He angled the flour toward her, but her vision blackened. She inhaled through her nose. Her head felt fuzzy, the back of her neck clammy. She'd not felt ill from the baby since the first months, but nausea now climbed her throat. Weevils. She'd served them bugs.

"I served us bugs," she said on an exhale.

"Not to worry," he said with a grin. "I'm sure they were dead."

She closed her eyes, inhaled through her nose and exhaled.

"Reggie?"

"Mrs. Townsend," she reminded him, pressing a hand against the wall behind her.

He came around the table and guided her to a chair. He rubbed her hands between his, awkward in his sling, and she eased her eyes open. Darkness edged her vision, and she forced herself to breathe. She didn't faint. She wasn't a fainter.

A small V creased his forehead as he watched her. At this close distance, she could see the faint lines fanning out from the corners of his eyes. His eyes, with their intriguing blend of dark and light, captivated her. Coffee-brown irises, accented with tiny chips of gold and amber.

She realized he still held her hands between his, and she pulled away.

"I'm fine, thank you."

"When—?" He motioned to her abdomen and swallowed.

"Don't worry," she assured him. "It's not time yet. This baby won't be here for another six weeks."

Relief relaxed his features before the V returned to his forehead. "You're well?" he asked. She suspected he wasn't just referring to this episode, but to her overall health.

"Yes, I believe so."

He watched her face then nodded and stood. He went to the scullery and brought her a cup of water. She took tiny sips, feeling the cool water trickle down her throat.

"Better?" he asked.

She smiled and relaxed against the back of the chair. The baby chose that moment to press on her. A tiny heel—or elbow, she wasn't sure which— traveled across her belly, the movement visible through the muslin of her gown. His eyes widened and flew to her face.

"What—?"

"My little mouse is active today." He went still, and she watched him watch her belly. He absently took her cup when she handed it to him. Then one of the miracles that she adored happened. A distinctive footprint appeared beneath the taut fabric of her dress, and she smiled as he pulled back.

"*Mon petit chou,*" he murmured.

"Little cabbage?" she asked.

"My mother used to call me that," he said. Confusion wrinkled his brow, and he lurched to his feet and left.

———

ALEX'S HANDS SHOOK AS HE closed the door to his room and leaned against it. The image of Regina's baby's foot reminded him again with sharp, tangible clarity of the little person she carried. The foot was tiny, the impression of five toes impossibly delicate. But it was more than that startling image that had driven him from the kitchen.

"Bonne nuit, mon petit chou." A hazy memory of a woman curled through his mind. He closed his eyes to try and capture it. He knew her instinctively as his mother, although he couldn't recall her face, or the precise quality of her voice. He had no memories of her, or his father.

Indeed, he recalled little from his life Before. Before two years ago. Before the monks of St. Augustine had pulled him from the heaving sea. He'd died, they said. They'd found him drowned beneath their monastery, a bullet through his chest and back. He didn't recall the preceding events, but an honorable man generally wasn't shot and dumped in the ocean.

His memory hadn't failed him entirely, though. He recalled his name, which he provided to the monks. He recalled his title, which he *did not* provide to the monks. He was reluctant to use it, despite the Bourbon king's restoration of the French nobility. What need did an unlanded Baron have for a title in a nation that despised nobility?

He recalled his profession—painter. He recalled his address—fashionable apartments off Rue de Richelieu. He recalled how to ride a horse and speak Italian and woo a lady. He recalled which brandy he preferred. He even recalled his works-in-progress and his upcoming submission to the Royal Academy's Salon. Other memories felt like puzzle pieces with rough edges; they almost fit, but not quite.

No matter how hard he tried, though, he couldn't recall how he came to be in the Channel below the cliffs of Le Havre.

It didn't take astounding mental acuity to piece together the fact that whatever had occurred at Le Havre was behind his nightmares. His headaches. His dreadful cliff paintings. All had begun at the same time, but even knowing that, he couldn't make his mind obey. He couldn't bring forth the memories of that night, much less memories of his life before Le Havre.

"Bonne nuit, mon petit chou." Like smoke, the memory of his mother vanished. He pressed his hands to the door to still them and opened his eyes. He stared into the middle distance, but the image wouldn't return no matter how hard he reached.

Tension coiled in the back of his neck, threatening a headache. He forced his muscles to relax and tried to clear his mind. Tried to convince himself it was better not knowing what he didn't know.

He turned his attention back to the larder's inventory. At least that was something he could control. Something he could fix.

The cottage's stock was poor indeed, although he'd spied a low bathing tub and a sliver of lavender soap in the scullery that were promising.

He'd need provisions from Brighton. With luck, the walk into town would clear his mind and relieve the edginess brought on by reminders of his failed memory. He'd need something with which to carry his day's purchases, so he emptied his bag onto the bed.

His now-empty flask. A case of cheroots. He opened the tin and studied the rolled cigars. He put one between his lips and tested it.

While he enjoyed the sweet scent of the tobacco, the taste between his lips didn't appeal. He'd found the case in his apartments two years ago when he'd returned from Le Havre and had assumed it was his.

He'd sampled one or two, trying to recapture pieces of his lost memory, but the taste hadn't jarred any recollections and he'd never found the experience enjoyable. Now he wondered if it was simply one more puzzle piece that didn't belong. He tossed the tin into the bag. Perhaps he could trade it for a chicken.

Next, he pulled his sketch pad, his paints and the rolled canvas. He opened the paint box and uncapped a small jar of vermilion pigment just to enjoy the familiar odor. The powder stained as he touched a fingertip to it. His brushes lined the box's central compartment, topped with a well-used wooden palette.

He set the box aside. He wasn't hungry enough to trade his sketch pad or his paints yet. *They're not serving any purpose*, a voice insisted. He insisted back that they would one day. He recalled his urge to paint Regina limned in white sunlight. He *would* paint again. Soon, he told himself.

He turned next to the canvas. The very notion of selling it still caused him to sweat with anxiety. Never mind that it was dreadful. Never mind that he hadn't been able to capture the easy flow of his art since Before. But he thought of Tilda, living on apples and weevil stew. Regina and her babe. Even Penny, who'd brought a midwife to set his shoulder. He put the canvas in the bag and tied the drawstring.

A tap on the door interrupted him. He crossed and opened it to find Regina on the other side. She clasped her hands before her and studied him with a concerned expression. At his continued silence, she spoke.

"If you give me your things, I'll wash them," she reminded him.

"That's not necessary," he said. While he'd often had a maid tend to his things, he'd thought nothing of it. It was a transactional arrangement and nothing more. It felt odd to have *Regina* laundering his clothes.

"Oh. If you'd rather clean them yourself . . ."

No, that didn't sound right, either. "Very well," he said. "Just a moment."

He closed the door and gathered his things together. He looked at the trousers he wore, stained with her stew, and set to removing them. He pulled on the pair he'd found in the attic, grimacing at the tight fit across his seat. He'd suspected they'd be too small, and they were.

He bent and squatted a few times to be sure the seam would hold. He rethought his decision, but it was only for the day, and his coat would disguise the tight fit somewhat. He'd have his own clothing back soon enough. Then he thought of Reggie's dubious skill in the kitchen and grimaced at the thought of trusting her with the wash .

He opened the door to find her waiting on the other side. She reached for the bundle in his arms, and he pulled it back.

"Have you done this before?" he asked.

"What? The washing?"

He nodded.

She narrowed her green eyes at him. "I think I can manage the operation of the washboard," she said.

He noticed she'd not answered his question. He pressed his lips together and handed her the bundle. Belatedly, he realized his smalls were on top. *Still warm.* Heat crept up the back of his neck as she took them, placing one hand on top of the pile to steady it.

Yes, Regina laundering his clothing was definitely odd.

––––

HIS SMALLCLOTHES WERE STILL WARM. Regina felt the heat beneath her hand as she took the pile of clothing from him. As a countess, this was a situation she had never encountered. Even as a married lady, there were countless servants to see to such domestic details. She didn't recall ever *seeing* Anthony's smallclothes, much less touching them. It just wasn't done.

Accordingly, there was no instruction for young ladies. No guidance on how to politely accept a stranger's warm smallclothes. Were they not strangers, were they just a common husband and wife living in this cottage, this was a situation that would have occurred regularly. How did others manage this degree of intimacy?

She realized she still stood at his door, her hand resting atop his clothing while he watched her.

She nodded and turned to leave with the heat of a blush staining her neck, then she caught sight of the pants he wore. Like the shirt, they were about two sizes too small. The blush bloomed to consume her entire face and she spun away, pressing her lips against a grin.

———

ALEX HAD FOUND A WOOLEN cap in the attic, along with the tight-fitting pants and shirt. It wasn't in much better shape than his own battered hat, but it would serve. He pulled it low on his head and stepped through the cottage door to find his nightshirt tucked in a corner of the porch. He distinctly remembered putting Robert in his pen last night, *sans* nightshirt.

He looked toward the pen and spied a small pile of dirt next to an equally sized hole. The blasted scamp had escaped, despite the lower rails he and Tilda had added. He scowled, resolving to address the pig later.

He adjusted the canvas bag on his shoulder. Regina and Penny were setting up the wash tub in the foreyard, and Tilda was teaching Robert to walk on a lead. To be fair, Robert was snuffling about the cabbages while Tilda followed, so perhaps *he* was teaching *her* to walk on a lead.

Not for the first time, he worried how she would handle the day when Robert would go to market. Or, with luck, the butcher. Judging by his size, though, that was still a few weeks away.

"I'm away," he said, closing the door to the cottage behind him. Regina saw him with his bag over his shoulder and her eyes widened. "You're . . . you're leaving?"

He'd told her he was going to Brighton, hadn't he? "I'm going to the market."

Her face cleared and she smiled. Had she thought he was leaving? For good? Her relief . . . pleased him.

Penny looked up and eyed his attire. "Oh, my," she said, fanning herself. He narrowed his eyes at her, and she turned back to the wash.

"Can I come?" Tilda asked, bouncing up to him, Robert's lead forgotten.

"No, you may not." He gentled his voice. "It's a long walk, and you're too heavy to carry." He knew a moment of panic as her grin deflated, and the urge to give in was strong. His natural inclination was to charm and please a lady, but he held firm.

She was a persistent thing, though. She crossed her arms and lifted an eyebrow, a caricature of Regina. He pressed his lips and shook his head. Her face transformed from mulish to gamine and she grinned at him.

"Please?" she asked, her hands pressed together.

He blinked. Now she was trying to *charm* him? He, who had charmed many a lady with an irresistible smile or a wink, now found himself on the receiving end. He didn't like it.

He shook his head again and stepped around her, nodding at the ladies. If he wasn't mistaken, Regina gave him a look of approval as he left. Yes, she was definitely charm-averse. The less he charmed, the more she seemed to like him.

The sun had burned off the morning's mist, and the brilliance of the blue sky was blinding. It was a fine day, but halfway to Brighton, Alex lamented the wisdom of wearing pants two sizes too small for the five-mile walk.

CHAPTER NINE

WALKING WAS DECIDEDLY UNCOMFORTABLE by the time Alex neared the outskirts of Brighton proper. And in his discomfort, he took a moment to reflect on his change in circumstance since Le Havre.

All indications suggested he'd once been a rising artist, with wealthy Parisians soliciting his work. Now he was hungry, penniless and chafed. His slide since Le Havre had been slow but consistently downward, his funds evaporating along with his muse. Although he couldn't recall his prior life, his crimes must have been vile indeed to warrant such a fall.

The crowd thronging the seaside promenade consisted of fashionable ladies and gentlemen as the town's fishermen had already sailed out for the day. An open carriage with two high-stepping horses rumbled past. He jumped back to avoid being struck and landed his foot in a puddle. It could only improve the state of his boots, he thought.

His first stop was Lafontaine's establishment, where he was greeted by the man's beribboned spaniel. Lafontaine was assisting another client, so Alex perused his shop. Despite the man's poor French accent, he had a good eye for art. Alex couldn't spot a forgery in the lot.

He approached the counter after the previous customer left.

"Monsieur!" Lafontaine said jovially. Then he noticed the bruise on Alex's forehead and the state of his attire and frowned. Alex supposed he appeared a regular ruffian. "You've hit a rough spot it would seem. Have you decided to sell the Marchand after all?"

"Perhaps," Alex said. "You mentioned a forgery when I was here last. Can you tell me more about the seller? A woman, I believe you said."

"Funny thing, that. Turns out it might not be a forgery after all."

"Why do you say that?"

"I could have sworn it wasn't legitimate, but I have a buyer now who was asking for that precise painting. Offered quite a bit, too." He eyed Alex speculatively then leaned on the counter and lowered his voice. "You haven't found the lady, have you?" he asked.

"Who's asking about it?" Alex forced the edge from his tone.

"A proper gent, about your height. Fair-haired, but slimmer, I think. Wouldn't leave his direction. If you have the painting," he confided, "I'm sure we can work out an arrangement. Something to benefit the both of us."

Alex tapped his fingers on the counter, and uneasiness slithered through him. What had Regina gotten herself into? "If I come across it, I'll let you know," he said. "But I suspect the lady's long gone by now. Are you still interested in this one?" He pulled the canvas from his bag.

The man's eyes narrowed as he studied it again. "I might be," he said.

"Fifty pounds." Alex forced a note of confidence into his voice and held his breath.

Lafontaine snorted. "It's not worth more than thirty."

"Forty-five."

"Thirty," Lafontaine insisted.

Alex prepared to replace the canvas in his bag. He might have scuffed boots, but he still had sense. Lafontaine knew the piece was worth more than thirty.

Lafontaine held up a hand to stop him. "Forty."

"That's acceptable." Alex's stomach turned as he handed the canvas over and accepted payment from the man. He was flush again, he reminded himself. He could buy a *horse* if he wished, or three. He could leave Brighton for London and not look back. In all honesty, it was what he *should* do, but the idea had less appeal than he would have thought as he recalled Regina's empty larder and the ladies waiting for him back at the cottage.

So instead of the livery, he made three more stops.

The seaside market, to order spices and smoked pork. Flour (minus the bugs), lard, eggs and other staples. A thick loaf of bread and fresh honey. Tallow candles (he'd exhausted his stub). A paper-wrapped cake of lavender soap. He sniffed it and smiled, closing his eyes on the memory of his lavender angel. He also ordered supplies with which to repair the roof, although they'd take some time to arrive from London.

Next, the bookseller's, where he acquired current issues of the financial papers.

And finally, the tailor's, for a blessed pair of ready-made trousers.

As he left Brighton, a farmer entered the market with a cart of pigs. One in particular, pink with dark-tipped ears, caught his eye as he gazed at Alex between the slats of the cart. Alex turned away before he pictured the fellow with a doll between his forelegs.

———

TWO MEN SAT IN THE dim light of The White Stag's taproom, hind quarters moulded to the polished seats of their chairs as they exercised their elbows with frothy tankards.

They'd enjoyed two (or three) pints too many, so their logic wasn't as firm as it usually was. Which was to say it wasn't firm at all. But both sat straighter on seeing the golden-haired man walk past the window again. They craned dirt-crusted necks to follow him from the bookseller's to the tailor's.

"I'm telling you, that's Nicky March," Cosgrove insisted, rubbing a finger along his crooked nose.

"Nah," his buddy said, smearing the window with his forehead. "That bloke's too common. Did you see the state of 'is boots?"

Round and round they went.

Cosgrove scratched his whiskered chin and flicked something from under his fingernails. He took another swallow of ale and reflected. "'Course it's been some time since we seen 'im, but I'd swear on me mother's grave that's Nicky March."

"You don't know where your mam's grave is," Perkins reminded him.

"That's neither 'ere nor there." Cosgrove swatted the comment away and paused to reflect. "Do you remember the Mayfair job? That was a right bam."

"Which one?"

"True. There were several." Cosgrove sighed, remembering.

"I 'eard Nicky March died a few years back."

"Then 'ow do you explain wot we just saw?" Cosgrove asked.

"I explain it 'cause that's not Nicky March," Perkins insisted, tracing a blunt finger along the twisted scar at his brow.

"There's only one way to be sure," Cosgrove said.

"We ask 'im?" Perkins said.

"We follow 'im."

Perkins twisted his lips. "I'm not sure. Betsy said as she might enjoy gettin' to know me tonight . . ." His eyes followed the comely serving maid as she crossed to serve another table.

"Betsy says that every night. And every night you go 'ome alone. Do you want to know if that's Nicky March, or not?"

And so, when the blond man exited the tailor's establishment, Cosgrove and Perkins paid their tab and left the warm comfort of The White Stag. It was only early afternoon, so they were forgoing hours of pub time, but both men agreed the sacrifice was necessary to settle the question of Nicky March once and for all.

They kept a discrete distance, accustomed as they were to surveilling men. Shortly past the tollgate, the crowds disappeared and the road narrowed. The chalk cliffs dropped to the sea on their right, and brown grass stretched to their left.

Hiding places were nonexistent on the open

plain. If he turned and spotted them, they'd have to think fast. Fortunately for them, he seemed absorbed in his own thoughts and didn't notice the men trailing him. Yet another reason this couldn't be March, Perkins thought. Nicky March would never have let anyone catch him unawares.

"Why's 'e walkin' like that?" Perkins asked.

"Looks like he's . . . chafed." Cosgrove said, shaking his head.

They followed the man for nearly five miles. "There's nothin' 'ere but wind and weeds," Perkins said. "'e's not goin' anywheres int'resting."

Cosgrove sighed. His ale was wearing off. "You may be right, my friend." They'd just decided to turn back and return to Betsy and The White Stag when they rounded a slight curve. Their quarry turned at a clump of scrub that marked the end of a lane. Cosgrove held up a hand, slowing them so as not to overtake March. There was no sense alerting the man until they knew what—or who—they were dealing with.

The man entered the foreyard of a small ramshackle cottage. He turned back once and looked to the end of the lane, but they remained still and hidden behind the thicket. When he resumed walking, they peered through the branches. Clean laundry hung on a line next to the small structure, waving in the breeze. A curl of smoke drifted from a vine-wrapped chimney, and windows sparkled in the sun. The roof looked like it could use some repair, and grass and scrub needed to be cut back from the porch, but it looked ... homey. Very domestic-like.

As they watched, brows wrinkled in confusion, a piglet trotted to the man trailing a lead, and a dark-haired sprite skipped to him. The man smiled when he saw her, and she wrapped an arm around his leg, hugging and chattering as he entered the house. A woman, clearly in the family way, appeared in the doorway and greeted them both. The smile on her face was soft and welcoming.

"You were right, Perkins," Cosgrove said, puffing his cheeks with a disappointed exhale. "That's not Nicky March."

––––––

ALEX WAS DISTRACTED ON THE long walk home, so it wasn't until he turned on the cottage lane that a prickle of awareness crawled along his neck. He turned and looked behind him, narrowing his eyes on the copse at the end of the lane, but he didn't see anyone.

His distraction had been complete. Not just because of the weight of the bag on his shoulder (which was considerable). Not just because of the chafing he felt (also considerable). But rather because of what he'd learned at the tailor's shop.

He'd exchanged his too-small trousers for a better fitting pair, and the tailor had suggested he limit his "overindulgences." Alex didn't think even Regina's cooking could reduce him sufficiently to fit the little pants. He was leaving the tailor's establishment when a bill tacked near the door caught his attention. "Missing Countess," it said. While the tailor assisted another customer, Alex pulled the posting from the wall and left.

It offered a sizable reward for information on the young countess. The Dowager Lady Foxwald, it explained, was in the family way and had gone to visit friends with her young daughter. They'd never returned home, and her family feared for their safety. The similarities were too obvious to ignore. He'd stuffed the bill in his coat pocket to read again later.

A countess. And he'd given her his smalls to launder.

He thought of asking her about the bill but discarded the idea as quickly as it occurred. If she confided in him, if she trusted him, he'd be obliged to assist. Things were bound to get messy. And one thing Alex Marchand *didn't* do was get involved in other people's problems.

She didn't seem to be in imminent danger. Whatever her reasons for leaving her family, they were not his concern. He might repair a pig pen, or fix a roof, but he did not *get involved.*

Plus, he knew instinctively if he questioned her, she would become defensive. Cross her arms and press her lips together. She might even ask him to leave again. So, he would remain silent about what he'd learned and focus on feeding them a proper meal. Nothing changed the fact that they needed supper.

He forced his musings behind him and focused on the cottage ahead. Warm relief filled him on reaching the little foreyard. Tilda spied him and dropped Robert's lead. She wrapped a small arm around his leg and hugged, beaming at him with her little teeth. And Regina . . . she stood at the entrance with her round belly and dark hair and smiled as if she'd been waiting for him.

He couldn't recall much from his time Before, but he was fairly certain he was *not* accustomed to homecomings like this one. He didn't deserve such an effusive greeting. He'd only gone to the market, but they acted as if he were Jason returned with the Golden Fleece.

He looked at Regina through new eyes, searching for the countess, wondering what had driven her to drag her child to this pitiful abode. What fears plagued her, and how did her forgery fit in? Why did she feel she had to—No. Not his problem.

He forced the conundrum of Regina Townsend, Missing Countess, from his mind. He smiled at them, loaded the larder with his bounty, then escaped to his room. He threw his bag on the bed and rubbed a hand over his face. Then he noticed the room.

The ceiling still leaked, but the cobwebs were gone. The little window shone behind a fresh lace curtain. The dust had been cleared. His flask and paint box, which he'd left in the center of the bed, were stacked on the little table. A small vase with more purple weeds had been added, and a cheerful quilt covered the bed, which didn't appear as lumpy as it had before. He lifted a corner to look underneath. If he wasn't mistaken, the mattress had been aired and re-stuffed.

They'd cleaned his room. Not just cleaned it. They'd made it a home. He exhaled a shaky breath. He didn't know what to say, what to do next. "Thank you" didn't come easily to one unaccustomed to accepting help from others. One unaccustomed to *getting involved*. And it seemed inadequate anyway.

Nevertheless, he plucked the thick stack of financial papers from his bag and left his room. Regina and Penny sat at the dining table, hands folded before them. Tilda watched the ladies and folded her own small hands in imitation. When they saw him, they smiled, waiting.

"The room's . . . nice," he said, rubbing the back of his neck. "You didn't have to go to the trouble, but thank you." He placed the stack of papers on the table next to Regina. "I picked these up for you."

She looked at him then at the papers, her brows raised. "Th-thank you," she whispered.

He nodded, went to the kitchen and began pulling items from the newly stocked larder. Carrots, onions, beans. *Not involved.* Smoked pork. Dried herbs from the cottage's small garden.

"What are you making?" Tilda asked.

Not involved. He pulled his head from the larder and looked at her. "Cassoulet."

"What's that?"

He thought how best to describe the flavorful stew of beans and herbs and meat. Rich and slow-cooked, best paired with a bright, fruity Marcillac . . . which he did not have. "Bean soup."

"Can I help?"

He sighed and looked at the ceiling. "Bring the chair."

She bounced and dragged the chair over the stone floor with a maximum of fuss and clatter. Standing on the seat, she braced her arms on the worktable and watched him. She picked up a sprig of dried rosemary and sniffed it. He took it from her and laid it back down.

"Do you know how to make Cassoul—castle soup?"

"No."

"Is it for princesses?"

He started to say *No*, but he didn't have the heart. "Yes."

"Oh. Mama says to make soup you have to—"

"We're not following your Mama's receipt."

She thought for a moment then said, "That's probably a good idea."

He chuckled.

"Can I chop the carrots?"

"No."

———

IT WAS A MISTAKE TO allow Alex to stay. *Mr. Marchand*, she reminded herself. She acknowledged the absurdity of standing on formality with his false name, but society's rules were there for a reason. She knew that all too well. Then she recalled laundering the man's smallclothes and scoffed. They'd gone far past the thin veneer of polite manners.

Regina observed him from the entrance to the kitchen. Tilda stood on a chair, pointing and asking questions. Alex's answers were short, but he tolerated her questions until she wore him down, and Regina heard him chuckle.

She wasn't sure what he was making, but if it

was an improvement over Penny's Chicken Feather Soup, or Regina's—well, anything—then it was bound to be good. Edible, at least. Her stomach rumbled in anticipation, but it was still a mistake to let him stay.

With each word, each expression, he dug a little deeper under her skin. And the financial papers he'd brought her . . . That had been unexpected.

She hadn't realized how unfit his room was until she and Penny began attacking it in earnest. There'd been an empty nest beneath his bed. An actual bird's nest. She didn't know many men of her acquaintance who would have suffered that room without complaint.

He was uncommon. Unlike anyone she'd ever met. Soft but prickly at the same time.

But no matter how intriguing she found him, she still wondered about him. There were too many unanswered questions. If he wasn't here for Foxwald, why was he here? Why was he content to remain at their drab little cottage, fixing pig pens and cooking for them? And perhaps more importantly, why did he feel the need to give her a false name? That couldn't be good, could it?

She acknowledged the annoying voice in her head that reminded her she'd given him her own false name. Well, not *false* so much as misleading. But her reasons for doing so were sound. What reasons could he have?

When no answers to that question were forthcoming, she speculated about where he'd gotten the funds for the market. His bag had been full when he'd returned, much more than she'd expected.

Ever suspicious, she'd checked the loose board in her room to be sure the canvas was still there. Relief at finding it rolled and untouched was swiftly followed by remorse. Regret that she'd allowed herself to become so distrustful.

She'd never set out to become bitter, and it angered her that she'd let the poet and his lies affect her so. But as much as she despised her cynicism, she dreaded the alternative. She feared Alex's effect on her. On Tilda. Where the poet's appeal had been transient—fleeting like fine mist—Alex's had substance. Where the poet had lured with empty words, Alex drew her with deeds. He was infinitely more dangerous than the poet had ever been.

CHAPTER TEN

1812, SIX YEARS BEFORE
LONDON

LADY REGINA TOWNSEND STOOD AT the edge of the ballroom and watched the dancers twirl. A sea of white satin and pastel silk rolled and spun beneath heavy gilt chandeliers. Everyone was in attendance, and the crush was stifling, but she sought one face in particular.

"He's here," her companion, Miss Elizabeth Milner, whispered behind a gloved hand.

Regina turned toward the entrance, controlling her movements. It wouldn't do to appear too eager. Albert Durand stood at the top of the stairs, an expression of artistic ennui arranged beneath his disheveled curls. He looked over the crowd, spotted her and slowly descended the stairs.

"He's coming this way," Miss Milner whispered

needlessly. Regina's hands grew damp in her gloves. "This is the third time he's sought you out," Miss Milner continued. "Certainly, you'll have an offer before the Season has ended."

Miss Milner's prediction was both cause for excitement as well as dread, since Regina's father was unlikely to approve such a match. But in the way of young ladies, the forbidden nature of the attraction only made it all the sweeter. It certainly didn't hurt that her chaperone, a distant cousin of her father's, had nodded off in her chair a few feet from where Regina and Miss Milner anxiously awaited Durand.

"Miss Milner. Lady Regina," Durand said, bowing over her hand.

Regina nodded, trying to appear sophisticated while her tongue remained fixed to the roof of her mouth.

"You truly are a vision," he said to Regina with a rakish tilt to his lips. "Dare I hope you've saved a dance for me?"

Regina consulted her dance card, but it was unnecessary. She had, in fact, saved a waltz, with a debutante's optimism that Albert would seek her out. "You are in luck, sir," she replied. "I have one dance left, and I've decided you may have it."

He winked and signed her card with a flourish, his blond curls glinting in the light of a hundred candles.

When he returned to claim his dance, she placed her hand on his sleeve and let him lead her out.

"Do you enjoy the evening, Mr. Durand?"

"Indeed, Lady Regina, it's much improved since I've acquired your company. Were it not for your beauty, I fear the Season would grow tedious indeed."

"You flatter me, sir. I'm certain there are many fine ladies whose company would please you."

"Ah, but there you are wrong," he said, and her heart fluttered. "I miss my beloved France, but your singular grace soothes my homesick heart and tempts me with thoughts of an idyllic life in the English countryside."

"And what would you do in the English countryside, Mr. Durand?"

"You must call me Albert," he insisted with a wink, and she blushed. "Why, I would write poetry, of course," he said. "But my true yearning, if you must know, is to settle myself to the task of creating a lovely home and family. I grew up in France with numerous cousins, you know, and it's always been my fondest wish to have a large family of my own. Tell me, do you long for the same?"

"Oh, sir, I do." She couldn't bring herself to call him by his given name; it would be much too forward. "My mother, as you know, passed when I was young, and my father has always been busy with estate matters. The days can be lonely with only oneself for company."

"And the nights as well," he said with another wink. She blushed again, a regular occurrence in his company.

"Lady Regina, it seems you and I are two souls cast from the same mould." He spun her in a dizzying turn, and she laughed, drawing the attention of the couples around them. "We shall escape together and set our sights on a peaceful manor in the English countryside then. Perhaps one with a folly, or a pond for our legions of children to fish."

"Perhaps both," she laughed, delighted with his teasing. Over the next weeks, his attentions grew more serious, and she began to crave the world he described. He grew bolder in his advances, encouraging her to step a toe over the bounds of what was proper, then another, until she stood with one foot wholly on the side of improper.

When the scandal broke—they'd been found in a darkened corner of the Loxleys' garden—she didn't lament too much. She was certain the furor would dissipate once they were married. But then her father informed her the poet couldn't be found. He'd left town without a by-your-leave. He'd not only taken Regina's reputation with him, but her confidence as well.

Six months into her marriage to Foxwald's heir,

she heard whispers that Durand had returned to London. That he courted another lady with a larger dowry. She imagined what she would say, what she would do should she encounter him. Pithy and cutting words filled her head with the perfect setdown. She would show him how little she thought of him, how superior her life was without him.

But when she spotted him across a crowded ballroom, her hands shook, damp in her gloves. The perfect setdown fled her mind, as pithy words were wont to do. So she determined to give him the cut direct instead. She'd never cut anyone before. *Make eye contact so there's no mistake*, she told herself, *then look away*. That's all there was to it.

She gripped her hands, straining to appear oblivious of his presence. He approached, his dowered debutante on his sleeve. *Eye contact, then look away*. But as he neared, disaster struck. She looked into his eyes, and ... he looked away first. *He'd* cut *her*, and her mortification was complete.

———

THE BABY KICKED, PULLING HER from her memories with a jolt. Tilda giggled at something Alex said, and Regina's heart fluttered in panic. She should put a stop to things before Tilda—or someone else—was hurt.

She moved to enter the kitchen, to remove her daughter from the danger of Alex's charm, but Tilda's giggle spread over her like warm honey, and she couldn't do it. She couldn't trade her daughter's current happiness to protect her from future pain, much as she might wish to.

She was suddenly very tired. While Penny assisted Alex and Tilda in the kitchen, she went to the parlor, their voices and soft murmurings following her. She settled in a chair and enjoyed—just for a moment—the tempting sounds and smells that flowed from the kitchen.

———

ALEX WATCHED REGINA OUT OF the corner of his eye. Watched her watching them. She'd almost entered the kitchen but had stopped. He knew a moment of disappointment when she left.

Tilda leaned too far on her chair, and he reached over to right her before she fell. The action brought a sudden memory fluttering through his mind.

Another kitchen, another teetering chair.

A rail-thin chef with a loud laugh.

Another gamine smile with little teeth.

"Don't lean too far or you'll fall."

"Look, Alex. The macarons *are finished."*

"Don't eat too many, Gabriel. You'll not be hungry for supper."

"You just want them all for yourself."

A soft voice on a softer whiff of floral perfume. "Come, boys, leave Etienne be."

"Mr. Marchand?" Penny asked. "Are you well?"

Alex nodded and clenched a fist to clear his head while Penny and Tilda watched him warily. He swallowed and forced his attention back to the pot before him. His spotty memory was proving to be a bloody nuisance. Steam curled from the pot while he tried to regain his wits. It was some moments before he could recall what he was cooking.

He tasted a small spoonful to test the bubbling stew. It needed longer on the fire, and the seasoning was a little off, but it was edible. Perhaps more thyme . . .

"I want to try it," Tilda said.

He put a little on his spoon and held it out to her.

"You have to blow on it," she said.

"Pardon?"

"Blow on it." She puckered her lips and demonstrated.

He rolled his eyes but did as she commanded. Once it was sufficiently cooled, he offered it to her, but she leaned in and ate from the spoon as he held it.

"Mmm!" she said, juice trickling down her chin as she grinned. He grabbed a linen and wiped her mouth. When had he become a nursemaid?

He let the stew simmer a bit more while he tidied the kitchen and answered Tilda's never-ending questions. Finally, he announced, "Princess Tilda, dinner is served."

He took the pot from the fire, watching his hands this time. Cautious of his shoulder, he carried the pot from the kitchen to the dining table but stopped when he saw Regina. She sat framed in the parlor's entry, her knitting resting atop her belly. Her head tilted forward as she dozed, and impossibly tiny socks dangled from her needles.

"Mama!" Tilda shouted. "Alex made Castle Soup!"

Regina jumped and the socks slipped. She recovered then smiled at her daughter. "That sounds delicious, poppet."

Setting the pot down, Alex entered the small parlor and bent to retrieve her knitting. He returned it to her, and she whispered, "What's Castle Soup?"

"You'll see."

Robert trotted by, and Regina said, "Tilda, why don't you take Robert to his pen? I think he'd enjoy being outside for a bit. But don't go past the privy," she reminded.

"I know," Tilda said on a long-suffering sigh as she led Robert to the door.

Alex held chairs for the ladies. "How is Tilda going to react when Robert goes to market?" he asked. They directed blank looks at him. "He'll be large enough in a few weeks, and you won't want to miss your opportunity."

"The farmer said he wouldn't be worth anything," Regina said.

Penny nodded. "He's a runt."

"He may be small, but he'll be worth something," Alex said. "Eventually. What else would you do with him?"

"I don't think . . ." Regina started, then stopped.

"He'll be expensive to feed if you keep him."

"We'll just continue to give him scraps like we've been doing."

He snorted. "Reggie, look around. You can't afford to give him scraps. You need to economize." Unless you have a fortune you haven't mentioned, he thought.

The door flew open and Tilda returned. All discussion of Robert's future ended, but Alex hoped he'd given Regina something to think about. Robert wasn't a pet spaniel. Like all creatures, he had a purpose, and that purpose was bacon.

Alex dished up bowls of cassoulet—*not* Castle Soup—and the fragrant steam made his mouth water. As he prepared to dip his spoon in, *finally*, Regina prompted, "Grace, please." He looked up and all three of their heads were bowed.

He drew a breath and bowed his own head. "Dear Lord. Thank you for this food. Amen."

"That was . . . brief," Regina said.

"Efficient," he replied, dipping his spoon. He tucked into his meal but kept one eye on the ladies. He smiled at their murmurs of pleasure, until he saw Regina's ecstatic expression. Her eyes were closed on a sigh, a smile tilting her lips, and his own smile slipped. He'd never seen anything so lovely.

"Wot's in it?" Penny asked, startling him from his thoughts.

"Carrots and beans and garlic and rosemary and thyme," Tilda recited.

"Onion and smoked pork," Alex added. Regina's and Penny's spoons hung suspended, and Penny's eyes darted to the window where future smoked pork dozed in his pen.

Alex mentally kicked himself. Regina looked at Tilda, who wore a blissful smile, oblivious of the undercurrents in the room, her cheeks full of Castle Soup. Cassoulet, he reminded himself, swallowing.

"It's quite good," Penny declared, taking another big spoonful.

———

REGINA'S STOMACH WAS UNCOMFORTABLY FULL. She'd eaten more of Alex's Castle Soup than she should have. She didn't realize how much she missed fine cooking, and Alex's was fine indeed. Not Briarly-fine, but fine, nonetheless.

Alex began taking their dishes into the scullery, and Penny went to check on Robert. Regina suspected Penny might be feeling a little guilty for enjoying the smoked pork.

"Penny and I will tidy the kitchen since you

prepared the meal," Regina offered. Alex looked at her, prepared to argue she was certain, but he didn't get the chance.

"My—Mrs. Townsend," Penny said, a strident tone to her voice. She stood at the open door, her jaw slack, and Regina and Alex joined her. Regina gasped and held a hand to her mouth while Tilda pushed between them to stand on the porch.

The days were still long and the sun hadn't fully set, so there was plenty of light to see by. Plenty of light to shine on Robert's perfidy, and the picture spread before them . . .

"Oh, my," Regina said.

Despite the additional rails Alex had added that afternoon, Robert had escaped his pen, *again*. And every item of laundry, save one, had been pulled from the line and dragged through the dirt. A swirling mass of muddied sheets and shifts and shirts decorated the foreyard.

The lone item, Alex's smallclothes, had been too high for the pig to reach. They waved on the line like a surrender flag, and Robert stood in the middle of the chaos, wiggling his hind end like a spaniel.

"Bloody hell," Tilda said.

Regina's eyes widened at her daughter's whispered exclamation. She rotated her head to look at Alex, who avoided her gaze and pressed his lips together. She turned to her daughter.

"Tilda, that language is not appropriate for a young lady, much less a princess."

"But Alex—"

"It's not appropriate."

Tilda crossed her arms and glared at Robert.

Regina turned back to Alex whose shoulders were shaking. "Are you *laughing*?" she hissed.

"You have to admit," he began, waving a hand at the linens. He saw the look on her face and clamped his jaw shut. "Right."

He went into the foreyard and stood in front of Robert. In a stern voice, he scolded the little pig. Robert stopped wiggling and tilted his head at Alex before settling his hind end into the dirt, forelegs splayed before him.

Regina felt her own lips twitch. It was too absurd. How had her life come to this?

Alex rubbed his forehead with his hand. If the man had any sense, any pride, he was likely questioning his own decisions that had led him to this point.

Regina started laughing and found she couldn't stop. She crossed her arms and clutched her elbows above her belly to hold the laughter in, but it couldn't be done. The sound was foreign to her ears, and tears ran down her face while Alex, Tilda and Penny watched.

"Reggie?" Alex asked.

She waved a hand at him, at the muddied linens, at his flapping smallclothes. "You—Robert—your—" she gasped.

He smiled then started to chuckle. Robert trotted over to him and nudged his leg in apology. Regina laughed harder and Tilda joined in.

"You're all mad," Penny said, probably recognizing the work ahead of them.

When Regina's tears had subsided, Alex said, "I suppose I should fix the pen. Again."

CHAPTER ELEVEN

FOUR DAYS LATER, ALEX REMOVED his cap and wiped his brow as he looked at the front of the cottage. He'd made progress removing brush from the foundation, and the vines choking the chimney were next. At least until the supplies he'd ordered to repair the roof arrived.

Dark clouds were building along the horizon, and the heavy scent of rain rolled in from the sea. He'd placed a ladder against the chimney and debated whether to begin work on the ivy as Tilda rushed at him from behind. "Where's Robert?" she asked, a thread of panic in her child's voice.

Taking his boot from the ladder, he turned to face her. "He's in his pen." He motioned behind him then noticed that no, Robert was not in his pen. He walked over to investigate as the first fat raindrops splashed his hand. A betraying pile of dirt next to a small hole told the all-too-familiar tale of Robert's escape.

"I told him not to go past the privy," Tilda said.

"I'm sure he's just investigating a nice shrub somewhere," Alex told her.

Her eyes were dark chocolate pools. "It's going to rain. He'll get wet," she whispered.

"Princess, he's a piglet. He'll get wet anyway. And besides, pigs like mud."

"Robert doesn't want to get wet," she insisted, wringing her hands. She was actually *wringing her hands*. He'd never seen anyone do that before. He slapped his cap back on his head.

"Go inside then. I'll look for Robert."

She grinned, a princess absurdly pleased with his fealty, then she raced for the door. He looked in all the obvious places—behind the privy, in the stable, beneath the apple tree—but no Robert. How did one track a pig? Then, through the copse at the end of the lane, he spied a pink blur.

He passed the thicket and crossed to the cliffs beyond the cottage. Ahead of him, Robert raced along the edge of the turf as the first whip of lightning snapped across the distant sky. Waves pounded the rocks below in a rhythmic cadence, and wind rolled up and over the cliff's edge, salty and chilled from the sea.

It raised the hairs on the back of his neck and the tendons there tightened, warning of the headache to come. He exhaled a steadying breath, wishing, hoping, but it wasn't enough to prevent the sudden, crippling pain from tearing through his head.

He squeezed his eyes shut, and a dark shape emerged through the blackness. Brown and winged, it billowed and rose in his mind's eye before sailing over the cliff's edge. Another flash of lightning streaked behind his eyelids. He pressed the heels of his hands to his eyes and let the pain crest over him like the waves thrashing the rocks below.

"Alex? What's wrong?" A muffled voice teased the edges of his mind, but he couldn't hear above the cacophony in his head. The roaring ocean whipping his coat about him. Rain needling his skin. Shouts. Chaos. The crack of a pistol. And then nothing.

His mind was black. Empty. Rain sluiced down his hands where he held them to his head.

Cool fingers wrapped his wrist and pulled one arm down. He peeled his eyes open. Regina's green eyes stared back at him. She stood before him, skirts clinging, rain dampening her hair. She didn't wear a cloak, only a thin shawl, soaked through.

"You'll become chilled," he said.

"What's happened? Are you all right?"

"Headache," he muttered, embarrassed and so very tired. His wool coat was sodden and heavy on his shoulders.

"Come inside where it's warm," she urged, pulling him by the hand.

———

WHEN ROBERT HAD ARRIVED AT the house, alone, Regina went to let Alex know. She'd found him at the edge of the cliff. At first, she feared he meant to jump—he stood that close to the crumbling rim. She called out to him, her words lost on the wind, then watched as he raised his hands to his head.

She went to him as quickly as she could, but he couldn't see her. Couldn't see anything, it would seem. It was clear he was in the grip of a terrible pain. He pressed both hands to his head, squeezing, as if to choke the pain out. She wasn't sure what to do, how to help him, but then, as suddenly as his tension started, he calmed. His hands had relaxed, though he still held them to his head.

Now she shivered as she urged him back to the cottage.

"Penny, please add another log to the fire," she said.

Alex stood inside the cottage door dripping and white. Regina had never seen anyone so pale. His skin stretched over his cheekbones like he'd been carved from the chalk cliffs.

She tugged first one sleeve, then the other from his stiff shoulders. His woolen coat was heavy with rain, and tight, but inch by inch she finally got it off. He seemed unaware of her efforts.

"Mama, what's wrong with Alex?"

"He's just a little chilled from the rain," Regina

tried to assure her. She forced her brow to smooth as she gave her daughter an encouraging smile.

Alex's eyes were bloodshot, but he finally turned them toward Tilda and offered his own weak smile.

"Where's Robert?" he asked.

"Safe and dry," Regina said, motioning to the corner where Robert snored with his doll. She tugged on Alex's hand again, leading him to the sofa. She pressed him down and tugged his boots off. It was no easy feat as her belly kept getting in the way.

"Here, my lady," Penny said, handing her a stack of clean linen towels. Regina unfolded one to dry his hair, rubbing and scrubbing as much to warm herself as to dry him. When she finished, his hair stuck out at all angles. Tilda giggled, leaning against his knee, and Alex gave her another smile.

Regina handed him the rest of the towels and sent him to his room to change. "Don't come out until you're dry," she commanded. Then she turned to Tilda and Penny. Alex wasn't in any condition to prepare one of his magical meals that night. She clapped her hands and forced enthusiasm into her voice.

"How does cheese toast sound?"

———

OVER THE NEXT WEEKS, ALEX didn't seem any worse for his headache at the cliffs. They settled into a routine that both comforted and unsettled with its domestic banality.

Regina and Penny did the wash and kept the cottage clean while Alex tended to the overgrowth about the cottage and began repairs on the roof. And he cooked.

After his first meal of Castle Soup, her conscience had reared its inconvenient head, and she'd expressed misgivings about the expense. She wished to retain as much of their meager funds as she could, but her principles wouldn't allow him to continue purchasing their food.

He'd insisted, however, assuring her that he was a growing man who did not wish to go hungry. He'd glanced at her belly and at Tilda when he'd spoken the words, though, and she wondered if perhaps he was thinking of other growing bodies as well. She wasn't sure where he'd gotten the funds, but she was not one to overlook good fortune, rare as it was.

Regina couldn't tell how much of her expanding girth was due to the baby, and how much was due to his cooking. He had a talent for sauces, that was for certain. She wondered if he'd worked in an inn or public house, but then she quickly discarded that notion. In her limited travels, she'd never visited an inn with such refined fare.

Robert began spending wash days indoors.

Regina acknowledged keeping a pig in the house wasn't ideal, but she certainly didn't want a repeat of his wash-day antics. Despite his own growing waistline and their continued efforts to contain him, he was still inclined to escape his pen, and one wash day a week was enough.

Regina also spent hours alternating between the financial papers and her baby's wardrobe, making notes about possible investments and knitting tiny caps and socks and blankets. Once the baby arrived, she would sell her painting to generate the funds needed to set her plan in motion.

With a twist of her lips, she thought of the Brighton proprietor who had turned it down. She'd have to try another shop, and another, until she found one willing to purchase it.

If she were honest, a good bit of her time was also spent watching Alex. Her fascination stemmed from more than his perfect lips and golden hair. More than the bright topaz of his eyes that watched and saw too much. He had a vitality about him that drew her. An energy that captivated her beyond her comprehension. It was growing tiresome.

She still didn't fully trust him—she didn't even know his true name—and the discord between her suspicious thoughts and her growing fascination unsettled her. She wondered again why he remained at the cottage.

In her experience, when a handsome man did something unexpected, there was a hidden motivation behind it. Alex was handsome, and he was a man. And yet he remained at their dilapidated little cottage with two women, a child and a pig, when he could have been anywhere else.

He struck her as the type of man who would be at ease on a fine estate with a jeweled heiress on his arm, not the type of man who mended fences or roofs. But he was here, against all reason, and that confounded her.

Twice, she'd almost confronted him. Asked him why he remained, what he hoped to gain, when he planned to leave. And twice, her courage had deserted her. For while she might question his motives, she couldn't deny she enjoyed his company. And as her baby's time grew near, she found his presence oddly, unexpectedly . . . comforting.

Oh, she knew he would be useless when the time came, as men were. It wasn't as if she didn't have Penny and Mrs. Simmons to care for her and the babe, but Alex was someone to talk to. Someone to laugh with. And she needed laughter, if only to forget about her uncertain future for just a bit.

Tilda rushed in from where she'd been helping Alex tidy the stable, and he followed at a more sedate pace. "Mama, Alex is going to teach me to paint," she said.

Regina lowered her knitting needles. She'd given up admonishing Tilda's use of Alex's given name since she couldn't help herself from using it in her own thoughts.

Her natural reaction to her daughter's announcement was to forbid it. She didn't need any reminders of Alex's artistic aspirations, but she couldn't deny Tilda's excitement, and she had to admit to a hesitant curiosity herself. For a man who claimed a painter's name, it was interesting that he hadn't spent any time actually painting. She was curious to see just what sort of talent he possessed.

"Perhaps you should change your frock first, poppet," she suggested, although she wasn't sure why. Tilda's dress sported streaks of something questionable from the stable. A little paint could hardly do further damage.

Tilda studied her dress with a child's convenient blindness. "I won't get it dirty, Mama."

Alex looked at Regina over Tilda's head and smiled. "Come, Princess, let's find you a magic cape." He went into the kitchen and returned with an old apron. He draped it over Tilda's front and began tying it in the back.

"A cape's supposed to go in the back," she told him, twisting to watch him tie.

He turned her to face forward and resumed tying. "Yes, but this is a magic cape, and it goes in the front."

Her brow wrinkled, then she shrugged. "What do we do first, Alex?"

Regina watched as Alex pushed Tilda's chair up to the dining table and began unpacking his paint box. Tilda's questions were endless, and Alex had an equally endless supply of patience to match. Regina grew sleepy listening to them.

When the sun made an infrequent appearance through the early winter gloom, she thought a visit to their little herb garden might perk her up. She wiggled to the end of her chair, preparing to lever herself up. Alex jumped to his feet and came to help her stand.

She started to thank him, then sucked a breath through her teeth as an uncomfortable tightening gripped her belly.

"What's wrong?" he asked. "Is it time? I thought you said the middle of December," he accused.

"No, it's not time," she chuckled. His brow creased as he watched her, and she hurried to put his mind at ease. "It's just practice. This happened with Tilda, and Mrs. Simmons assures me it's nothing to worry about."

"Should I send for her? What can I do?"

"There's nothing to do." She patted his arm. "I shall be fine. I'm just going to walk a bit in the garden."

As she left them, she passed the table where he'd set his sketch book. Bold lines depicted a seaside landscape that resembled the view from their lane. But what caught her attention was the figure he'd sketched in the foreground.

Even in its rough rendering, she could see skill in the lines and proportion. Could sense the light and shadow that evoked a sense of soft strength. Recognized the curve of a cheek that looked suspiciously like her own.

Her eyes widened, and he leaned over and quickly flipped the book closed. She spun from him, intent on the door, but she couldn't help the thoughts racing through her mind as she left the cottage. Was that how he saw her? Soft and strong? And more importantly, she couldn't deny his artistic talent. Had she been wrong about him?

———

ALEX WATCHED REGINA LEAVE AND rubbed his jaw.

"Is Mama all right?" Tilda asked, a brush dripping over her paper.

"Yes," he assured her, sinking onto his seat. Tilda watched him curiously so he asked, "Would you like some Prussian blue for your sky?"

"Yes, please."

He helped her mix the blue, his mind on Regina. How much of his sketch had she seen? Had she recognized herself in it? The thought made him uncomfortable. It was only a sketch—far from his best work. Certainly not something fit for others to see, much less Regina.

She was never far from his thoughts. Whether he was in the stable or on the roof or in the kitchen, she was there with him. His thumb still throbbed where he'd hit it with the hammer earlier that day. He blamed her. She appeared in his thoughts when he least expected (or wanted) her.

And that was the problem, wasn't it? He'd leave soon, for where he couldn't say, but she'd still be in his thoughts. He suspected it would take some time to reset his mind after he'd gone. To purge her from his system.

"That's enough," Tilda said, laughing. He looked down and saw he'd mixed enough blue for the sky *and* the Channel and the North Sea.

He put the lid back on the pigment, and his thoughts returned to Regina. He'd watched her over the last weeks, looking for signs of the countess beneath her simple exterior.

While she didn't hesitate to dirty herself with domestic chores—she'd washed his smalls for heaven's sake—she was regal, like her name. And more than once, Penny had slipped and called her "my lady."

So yes, the countess was there. And while Alex was determined *not* to involve himself in her troubles, he couldn't help his disappointment that she'd not confided in him.

They'd begun talking to one another in the evenings after supper. She'd knit while Penny readied Tilda for bed. He'd ask her thoughts on the financial papers, and she'd ask how repairs were coming on the roof. He teased, and she laughed.

But neither of them asked the other about their past, or their future. They lived only in the present. It was an arrangement that should have suited him fine. He couldn't explain why it didn't. As a man who would be leaving soon, past and future were irrelevant.

When Tilda jumped down from her chair to show her painting to Robert, he cleaned their brushes and packed his paints back into the box. Then, like a moon-eyed lad trailing his first dairy maid, he went to find Regina.

She sat on a small bench next to the little herb garden, eyes closed, one hand on her belly. For a moment, he panicked, thinking she'd misspoken earlier and this was more than "practice." But then she smiled to herself, and he realized she was merely enjoying the pleasant weather. He released his breath and approached her. She opened her eyes, and her smile broadened as he sat.

"Did Tilda finish her masterpiece?"

"I think it's a work in progress," he said. "She went to consult with Robert." He hesitated then asked, "You're well?"

"Yes. My little mouse is enjoying the sunshine. Or *little cabbage*, if you prefer."

He smiled, his eyes on her middle. She was perfectly rounded, like a little cabbage herself. He didn't think she'd appreciate the comparison, so he kept it to himself. Even without his charm, he knew no lady wished to be compared to a vegetable.

He couldn't forget the image of her baby's tiny foot with its five tiny toes. As he watched, a wave rolled across her abdomen. He'd grown used to the odd twitches and flutters of her belly, but the motion still unsettled him.

She looked down and laughed, then turned her gaze to him. "Would you—"

"Yes?"

"Would you like to . . . feel him? Or her?"

He went still for a moment before shaking his head, and her face fell. She looked down, a curl trailing in front of her ear to hide her face. He didn't want to disappoint her, but touching her unborn babe—feeling that rolling, twisting life inside her— would be the opposite of *not involved*.

"I should prepare supper," he said, placing his hands on his knees. She nodded but didn't look at him as he left. He felt like a cad. He *was* a cad.

When he entered the cottage, he found Tilda's painting drying on the dining table, and he paused to study it.

Five figures stood before a rough cottage. Robert was recognizable as the pink blob with muddy brown triangles for ears. Regina, with her cabbage-like belly. Tilda, with a princess dress. Or was that a cape? Penny in her apron.

And standing behind them all, larger than any of them, a man with yellow hair and a hammer. Regina's deceased husband perhaps? But no, he thought with a sigh. Although the facial features were off-center, Alex recognized himself.

Tilda had painted them as a family. Alex didn't have a family.

Not involved, he reminded himself. Bloody hell.

———

SUPPER WAS A QUIET AFFAIR. Alex watched Regina from the corner of his eye as his graceless handling of their conversation in the garden gnawed at him. His abrupt manner, his rapid exit, were the actions of a coward. He admitted it, but he didn't know how to fix it.

Even Tilda was subdued, clearly picking up on the others' restraint. After the dishes were cleared and the kitchen cleaned, the ladies retired for the evening. Alex, not knowing what else to do with himself, pulled the tub from the scullery. He'd been enjoying late night baths since discovering it a few weeks ago.

He filled the tub, warming it with several pots of

steaming water from the stove. By the time he stepped in, it was the right temperature. He folded himself into the small tub, bending until his knees rose above the tub's low sides.

Cool night air seeped in around the window frame, battling with the heat from the hearth. He huddled deeper into the shallow tub and recalled his large hip bath in Paris, and how it could be filled to sublime extravagance to cover a man's knees.

He lifted a linen cloth and the lavender soap. Over time, the cake he'd purchased in Brighton had melted to a thin slice. The intimacy of sharing that single slab with others *should* have made him uncomfortable. It was far more intimacy than he was accustomed to. Nothing said family more than shared soap, after all, but he smiled as he lathered his arms. He held the soap to his nose and inhaled the soft lavender scent, his eyes closed.

He'd need to make another trip into Brighton. They clearly needed more soap. Butter and eggs.

Wait. What was he thinking?

He scrubbed his hands over his face, clearing soap bubbles. He wouldn't be here long enough for more soap. He should have been long gone by now, in fact.

Right this moment, he should be courting a lovely heiress and settling his debts. Preparing to return to Paris and full-sized hip baths. Regina and her forgery—which he'd still yet to see—had distracted him from his course.

Then he sighed. The forgery. He'd nearly forgotten about it. In truth, he couldn't recall why he'd been so intent on tracking it down in the first place. Now that he knew Regina and Tilda, the forgery didn't seem to matter as much. Regina was hardly the scheming baggage he'd pictured when he'd first learned someone was selling a forgery of his work.

He gazed about the small kitchen, wondering where she kept it. The cottage was small. There weren't many places to hide anything. He'd been through every inch of the kitchen and its adjoining scullery and larder. The parlor was a simple space with few opportunities to hide a forged painting. Short of searching the ladies' rooms, he doubted he'd find it. And if he did, then what?

He thought of his faceless, nameless heiress, waiting to be courted. Then he thought of Regina, with her leaky roof and empty larder. The lumpy bed where he would sleep tonight. Put side by side like that, the decision should have been an easy one, so his reluctance to leave perplexed him.

He would be gone when the baby arrived, he assured himself. Regina had Penny and Mrs. Simmons to assist her, and he'd be useless anyway.

As long as he left before then, what did a few more days matter?

———

REGINA COULDN'T SLEEP. THE BABY had been kicking and twisting all evening, and she hoped walking a bit would help. She pulled a dressing gown around her night rail, eased her door open and listened. The cottage was still.

Alex had been quiet at supper. He'd probably been calculating how quickly he could leave. She hadn't been able to help the disappointment that stabbed her at his rejection of the baby. She shouldn't have been surprised—it had been an entirely improper suggestion, after all—but his refusal had stung. Still hurt, in fact.

But there was no mistaking it: the expression on his face had definitely been one of alarm. She could hardly fault him. Wasn't she the one who'd admonished him for being too familiar with Tilda? And what could be more familiar than asking him to touch her babe? What had she been thinking?

She stood at the top of the stairs. The entry below was quiet and dark. She padded down toward the parlor but stopped when she noticed soft light outlining the kitchen door. Alex. She hesitated and looked back toward the stairs. She should leave, but the light beckoned.

She pushed the kitchen door open and stopped at

what she saw. She fought the instinct to flee and stared instead. The fire, low in the hearth, cast its dim light on the room. Alex sat in the small wooden tub with his back to her, knees drawn up to fit his large frame. His skin was gilded from the firelight, and it rippled over the muscles in his shoulders and back. It was smooth, velvet over steel, marred only by a puckered round scar below his left shoulder.

She recalled a similar scar on his chest. To her knowledge, there was only one thing that made matching scars like that. He'd been shot. And quite close to his heart, if she was any judge.

Her stomach pitched in a queasy roll, and she pressed a hand to her mouth. What manner of person was he? What manner of people did he associate with? She realized again that she truly knew *nothing* about him.

His head came up, and water sloshed as he shifted in the tub. She pulled her hand back from the door and fled.

Back in her room, she closed the door and paced. She wasn't sure what disturbed her more: the fact that he'd been shot, or the perfection of his form.

What was she thinking? Of course, the fact that he'd been shot was more disturbing. For him, as well, she was certain.

She'd just gotten her heart to settle when a tap sounded on her door, unsettling it all over again.

She thought about ignoring the sound, feigning sleep. He would eventually go away. Then she realized her candle gave her away.

Sighing, she cracked the door open. Alex stood on the other side, shadowed in the darkness. The ends of his hair curled from his bath. His shirt was open at the throat, but thankfully, he'd donned it again. Perhaps he hadn't seen her. Maybe he just wished to request the salve again.

He leaned a hand on the door casing and looked at her through lashes that were damp and spiky. "The water's still warm," he said.

She choked at his implication, and blood rushed to her face. He'd seen her then. Knew *she'd* seen *him*. She swallowed. He wasn't the first man she'd ever seen in a state of undress. She was a wife. *Widow*, she reminded herself. A man's bare back shouldn't alarm her so. She steadied her breath and looked at him.

"I saw the scar." She waved a hand in the area of his heart. "What happened?" she asked.

He was silent for a moment as he stared at his hand on the door casing, and she thought he'd avoid the question. Then he said simply, "I was shot."

She waited for him to look at her. When he did, she asked, "When? How?" He was silent, so she added, "I need to know who you are."

He looked away again, fascinated by his hand.

"Two years ago, outside of Le Havre. I don't remember how."

"You don't remember? How ... how is that possible?"

He shrugged and looked back at her.

She chewed her lip. "I'm sorry," she whispered.

"For what?" He sounded surprised.

"That you were shot."

He pressed his lips together. "Don't be. I probably deserved it," he said. He pulled his hand down, turned and left.

He was right. She shouldn't be sorry. He probably *did* deserve it. Wasn't she herself just wondering about his character?

But something in his eyes as he said the words pulled at her. He'd always been kind to them, despite being thrown from his horse, dragged through the mud and bounced on a makeshift litter. And yet, he believed he deserved to be shot.

She would probably regret it, but she picked up her candle and followed him. She didn't trust him—she still wasn't sure which parts of him were true—but she recognized when a person was in pain. Whatever his sins, he was hurting.

She caught up to him in the parlor, slightly out of breath. He turned back to face her. "Did you change your mind about the bath?"

She blinked. "No, I—"

"I can assist you into the tub if you like."

"What? No, that's not—" She puffed a breath and looked at him. He was grinning at her, and he wiggled his eyebrows.

Was he *flirting* with her? She, who weighed as much as an elephant seal. And was shaped like one, too, now that she thought of it. No, she thought, he wasn't *flirting*. He was *avoiding*. She narrowed her eyes at him.

He sighed. "I wish I could tell you what happened, but I can't."

She nodded and took his hand in both of hers. "Regardless of what *you* think, I'm glad you didn't—that you're—"

"Alive?"

"Yes." She smiled.

He watched her for a long moment, his brown and gold eyes glittering in the candlelight. He seemed to be thinking, debating with himself, so she waited. Finally, he exhaled a decisive breath.

Stepping closer, he lifted his hand toward her belly. "May I?"

She held her breath then nodded. He pressed his palm to her. It was warm through the layers of her dressing gown. Solid. She hesitated then placed her hand atop his and positioned him where he could feel the baby. Held him there.

Tears burned the back of her throat.

She didn't know him—who he was, who he'd been, where he was going—but it was comforting to have another's touch.

She'd been alone for so long. Before Anthony. Before Albert Durand, even. Her loneliness had allowed her to fall for Albert and his false promises in the first place. But she'd been younger then, and naive. She wasn't the same girl now. She recognized Alex for the rogue he was, but that didn't mean she didn't enjoy the touch of another's hand. *His* hand.

The babe gave a swift kick then. Alex jumped and started to pull away, then stilled. He spread his fingers over her, feeling the small movements inside. His brow creased as he studied their hands pressed together. The baby settled, Alex backed away, and she felt the cool absence of his hand.

"Bonne nuit, mon petit chou," he whispered with a smile before turning toward his room. Goodnight, my little cabbage.

CHAPTER TWELVE

REGINA EYED THE PIG AND sighed. Alex was right. They couldn't keep Robert indefinitely. As much as Tilda—all of them—had grown attached to him, he was becoming too expensive to feed. Yesterday they'd given him the remains of Alex's delicious *boeuf à la Bourguignonne*—food that would have been better served on their own plates.

Keeping a pig as livestock was well and good, but she couldn't justify the expense of keeping a pig as a pet. She'd simply have to explain to Tilda that it was time for Robert to move on to his next job.

That evening as they were sitting before the fire, Regina brought it up to Alex. "As much as I hate to admit it," she said, "you were right about Robert."

He looked at her in surprise. "I was?"

She nodded. "He's becoming too costly. We—I— need to economize. Do you think—"

His brows lifted as he waited.

"Could you—" She stopped, unable to voice the words.

"Would you like me to take him?" he asked.

"Yes," she said on an exhale. "Could you?"

He nodded.

Early the next morning, Regina explained to a tearful Tilda that Robert had grown into a fine pig, but it was time for him to leave them, to go serve his life's purpose. Thankfully, Tilda didn't ask for details.

Regina choked as she said the words and nearly called them back in the face of her daughter's tears. Tilda sobbed at her side while they watched Alex lead the pig down the lane, and Regina couldn't help but think she'd made a mistake.

———

ALEX WATCHED THE PIG SHUFFLE beside him, snuffling in the grass and enjoying the weak winter sunshine. He refused to think of him as "Robert." For today, he just needed to be "the pig."

Did *the pig* have to be such a trusting thing? So ignorant of his fate? Were he wily and suspicious, this would have been so much easier, but he trotted beside Alex as if they were two friends out for a companionable stroll.

Regina was right. Of course she was; she'd only come to realize what he himself had been telling her.

Pigs were not pets, no matter how adorable they were. Tilda should have a kitten or a small princess-sized dog. Not livestock.

When they reached the outskirts of Brighton, Alex turned toward the busy market street. The salty scents from the sea competed with more earthy, pungent smells from the market: livestock, meats, a peddler's cart piled with apples.

Alex followed the sounds of shouting men to the end of the lane where buyers and sellers gathered. They volleyed loud offers for heads of cattle and sheep, grains and wool.

Alex entered the throng, and a buyer looked at him and the pig on the end of his lead. The man wore a rough woolen cap pulled low over his ears. His teeth were gapped in the front and blackened.

"How many?" he asked, spitting into the dirt.

"Pardon?" Alex said.

"How many head are you selling?" The man motioned to Robert. *The pig*, Alex reminded himself.

"Just . . . just this one."

"Just the one?" The man cackled and turned to another seller.

"Three shillings," a man next to him said. Alex turned. The man offered coins in one hand and reached for Robert's lead with the other. "He's on the smallish side, ain't he?"

———

ALEX'S SHOULDERS WERE ROUNDED WHEN he turned onto the cottage lane. Regina and Penny were in the foreyard hanging the wash to dry. He watched as Regina shook out a piece of damp linen and placed it on the line.

Her girth surprised him every time she turned. How much larger would she get? He was a man and therefore ignorant in the ways of these things—as he should be—but he thought he would keep that question to himself.

Tilda dragged a stick in the dirt, her shoulders hunched. Smoke trailed from the chimney, now cleared of vines. When had this pitiful cottage begun to feel like home?

Tilda heard him and looked up, tears staining her cheeks. She went still before shouting, "Robert!"

She ran toward them, took the lead from Alex's hand and skipped to Robert's pen, the pig trailing her with his distinctive totter.

"What happened?" Regina asked with surprise, watching her daughter.

Alex rubbed his jaw. "He's too old, apparently."

She turned back to face him. "Hmm," she said, but she was smiling.

"We'll just have to economize some other way." Did he say "we"? That's not what he meant at all. Her smile broadened, and she went back to the wash.

———

ALEX WENT TO GREET THE cart rattling down the path to the cottage. The remaining supplies he'd ordered for the roof had arrived at last. The sooner he could complete the repairs, the sooner he could make plans to be on his way. He didn't feel right leaving the ladies with the ceiling dripping. That couldn't be good for a new baby, either.

A little voice in his head told him he was stalling. He should have left long ago. He would have, too, if he thought they could have cooked a proper meal for themselves. As it was, they'd have starved without him.

The same voice that told him he was stalling also whispered that he "doth protest too much." Traitorously, it said if he truly wanted to be somewhere else, wouldn't he be? He shushed the voice and turned his attention back to the cart.

A tall man climbed down from the seat and rounded the back of the cart. He threw off a canvas tarp and began unloading crates of wooden shingles. He looked up and stared at Alex for a beat, a piece of straw clamped between his lips.

Alex was surprised to recognize one of the men he'd encountered on first arriving in Brighton. The one with the broken nose, who'd called him by another name. Alex narrowed his eyes, waiting, but the man only nodded once and went back to his task. Alex released the breath he'd been holding.

Regina and Penny stepped from the cottage, Tilda on their heels. "What's all this?" Regina asked. The cart driver looked at each of the ladies in turn. When he reached Regina, his eyes dropped to her belly before he turned back to Alex, measuring.

"Shingles. For the roof," Alex said, not taking his eyes from the man. He went to stand next to Regina, blocking her from the man's gaze.

"Can I help?" Tilda asked, bending to investigate the contents of the top crate. The man's intent regard was making Alex uncomfortable. He bent and lifted Tilda, and she was gratifyingly quick to wrap one arm about his neck. The man winked at Alex. Winked?

Alex nodded once then shepherded the ladies back into the cottage.

———

ALEX SPENT THE NEXT DAYS patching the roof and watching the lane for a return of the cart. The driver still believed he knew Alex, he was certain. And as much as he wanted to deny it, the man seemed familiar to him as well.

But the cart didn't return, and the holes in the roof slowly disappeared, so Alex pushed the man from his mind. Rain had fallen again that afternoon, and he was checking the ceiling for leaks he may have missed. He entered Regina's room and inhaled her lavender scent, smiling.

Her bed was pressed against an interior wall, away from the leaks that ran along the eaves. A stark white counterpane covered the thin mattress. The small table beside the bed held a single candle and one of her financial papers. Below the table, a large basket held knitted socks and blankets, linen caps and gowns.

Where would the baby sleep when it arrived? He looked about the room. Didn't a baby need a crib or a cradle? Or—what were they called? A bassinet? His eyes landed again on the basket and its impossibly tiny clothes. A blanket lined the bottom. For the baby, he realized.

What would drive a countess to forsake everything for a life that required her baby to sleep in a basket? What was she running from? More importantly, whom?

He bent to push the basket more firmly beneath the table, in case the ceiling continued to leak. As he slid it back, it bumped a loose plank on the wall. He straightened the plank, making a mental note to bring a hammer and repair it later.

"What are you doing?" Regina asked.

He bumped his head on the table as he stood. "Checking for leaks," he said.

"In the floor?" She wrinkled her brow.

"The basket," he clarified. "I didn't want it to be damaged if my repairs haven't done the trick."

She nodded, but she didn't seem convinced. Not for the first time, he wished she would confide in him. Tell him what she feared, why she was running. Then a voice in his head reminded him he didn't want to know. *Not involved.*

———

BRIARLY
SOUTHWEST OF LONDON

ROGER CHESTERTON, THE PRESUMPTIVE EARL of Foxwald, pressed back in his desk chair and admired the view. The earl's study at Briarly was sumptuous with its dark leather sofas and burgundy velvet window coverings. A lively fire popped in the hearth, and the scents of wealth and privilege enfolded him. He lifted his glass and admired the glints of candlelight on the amber liquid.

Leather-bound books filled the floor-to-ceiling mahogany shelves, and paintings of distant ancestors hung alongside Foxwald's newer acquisitions. Their stern gazes contemplated the room from gilded frames. Contemplated him. He imagined they were less than pleased with what they saw, but he didn't care.

He was just happy to be where he was—it was about bloody time—and he wasn't of a mind to give it up willingly.

Peterson stepped into the doorway and announced, "You've a guest, my lord. Mr. Arnold."

My lord. Foxwald would never tire of hearing himself addressed so. He'd spent his early years in a London orphanage, fighting and scraping for dry crusts and gruel. He paused to savor the rightful trajectory his life had taken then said, "Show him in, Peterson."

Peterson bowed and retreated. Foxwald sipped, savoring the smooth burn as the cognac slid down his throat. For all their flaws, the French did produce fine brandy.

"My lord," Arnold said as he entered.

Foxwald consulted his watch. "Arnold. I expected you earlier. What news have you? It had better be good."

Arnold bowed, his eyes fixed on a point beyond Foxwald's ear. The solicitor's false deference grated on him. He needed to teach the man a lesson, but it would have to wait. He needed him too much now.

"Apologies, my lord. We haven't located her yet, but—"

"How hard," Foxwald began, then lowered his voice to bite the words off one by one. "How hard can it be to find one woman and a child? A woman in her condition can't be missed. Assuming she still carries the babe."

"We haven't located her *yet*," Arnold repeated,

"but we've traced her to the coast."

"We live on a bloody island, Arnold. Be more specific."

"The southern coast. Near Brighton, I think."

"You *think*?"

"A shopkeeper recognized the description of the painting she took. He said a woman approached him to sell it, but he turned her away."

"And?"

"He doesn't know where she is, much less if she's still nearby. I offered a hefty sum for the painting on the chance she tries again. I've got men searching the area and checking other dealers, and we've papered the town with leaflets. If anyone's seen her, we'll know."

"That's good. I want her found."

Evelyn, Lady Foxwald sailed into the study on a cloud of gardenia perfume.

"Lady Foxwald," Arnold said, bowing.

She didn't acknowledge his greeting, but asked instead, "Have you found her?"

Arnold shook his head, and Lady Foxwald strode to the sofa. She arranged her skirts and looked pointedly at Foxwald, her nostrils flaring. "I told you, you should have handled this properly from the start."

"I am handling it now," Foxwald said.

She snorted and raised her chin. "What of the

other matter?" she asked Arnold. Arnold looked at Foxwald, awaiting his permission to continue. He nodded. He'd only have to endure Evelyn's questions later if she didn't hear the solicitor's report.

"I was just getting to that," Arnold said. "My men tracked Marchand as far as Kent. It appears he was courting a lady there some months back, but it ended. The staff are absurdly tight-lipped. It took some coin, but we finally found someone who reported Marchand planned to return to Paris. We've checked every ship that left Dover in the weeks after that, but he hasn't turned up."

Foxwald's hand tightened on his glass, and he ignored his wife's hard stare. The two problems threatened to dim the brilliance of his good mood. Two separate problems, each disturbing his peace in their own way. Of the two, Marchand was the priority. Foxwald's widow and her offspring could be dealt with easily enough, but Marchand had to be found. He knew too much.

"Find him," he ordered. "Talk to every petty criminal. Someone knows where he is. I want to know as soon as you've tracked him down," he said, dismissing Arnold.

Arnold nodded and left. Without looking, Foxwald sensed Evelyn opening her mouth. "You too, Evelyn. Out."

"I told you—"

"Out."

She stared at him for another moment before gathering her skirts. She turned to him at the threshold, determined to have the last word. "I told you he was no good for the job," she said, sweeping from the room.

Whether she referred to Marchand or Arnold he wasn't sure. He still couldn't believe Marchand was alive. He *saw* him go over the cliff in Le Havre. No one could have survived that, but there was no denying the evidence of his eyes.

He unrolled a canvas and spread it across the desk's smooth, polished wood. He recognized the seaside cliffs painted in somber shades of brown and amber. This was the fourteenth such painting he'd come across in as many months. He'd quickly bought up each one.

All depicted the same scene from different angles. The cliffs, stark and sharp against a stormy sky. A large bird flying—or falling—toward the churning sea. The colors were darker than was fashionable, darker than Marchand's typical palette. There was a vague hint of menace in the shadows and tones, but the artist's style was unmistakable. Recognizable enough to know the man still lived.

CHAPTER THIRTEEN

DECEMBER ARRIVED WITH ALL THE gray gloom Regina expected from winter on the coast. A damp wind sailed in from the sea, and the sky hung dull and heavy, promising more rain.

With the start of Advent some days past, she found she missed the festivities of the holiday at Briarly. Carolers and Yule logs. The making of the Christmas puddings. In normal circumstances, she would have been readying the household at Briarly to hang ribbons and evergreen, mistletoe and dried fruits. But these weren't normal circumstances.

She thought perhaps a nod to past traditions might help her spirits, so she rallied Penny and Tilda to help decorate the cottage. They'd torn an old linen cloth into strips to make ribbons and planned to gather holly and hawthorn from the copse at the end of the lane.

As she dressed that morning to go out, the ache in her lower back intensified. She thought nothing of it as she'd been feeling aches and a minor tightening in her belly for some weeks now. Mrs. Simmons didn't believe the babe would arrive for another two weeks. Ten days at least.

When a particularly strong cramp struck as Penny was assisting with her cloak, she breathed through it and pressed on. "My lady, are you well?" Penny asked.

"Yes, I'm fine, Penny." She smiled and took Tilda's hand.

"Is it time for the baby, Mama?"

"No, poppet."

"What's wrong? Is it time?" Alex entered from the kitchen, a stricken look on his face. Truly, the man looked as though he'd eaten a lemon. Or bad fish. Not for the first time, she suspected he'd leave when the baby arrived. The thought saddened her before she rallied herself. She'd been fine before he arrived, and she'd be fine when he left. But she'd miss him.

"No, it's not time," she assured him. She tied her bonnet and pulled her cloak about her. "Let us go, poppet, and find some lovely boughs for the cottage."

———

"IT'S TIME!" PENNY SHOUTED BREATHLESSLY as she entered the cottage on a gust of wind.

Alex, who'd been sketching at the little dining

table, jumped. The ladies had only been gone for half an hour. "What do you mean, *it's time*?" he asked.

"It's time!" Tilda exclaimed, following Penny. Regina wasn't with them.

"Bloody—would someone tell me what's happening?" Alex demanded.

"Mrs. Townsend—" Penny began, pressing a hand to her throat.

"Where is Mrs. Townsend?" he asked.

Penny looked behind her. "She was right—"

Alex didn't wait to hear the rest. He pushed past her to the door. Regina stood at the end of the lane, one hand on her belly, the other on her back. Alex raced to her.

"Reggie."

She looked up at him, breathing heavily through her nose, and cocked a sheepish smile at him. "I think it's time," she said.

He took her arm and placed a guiding hand at her back. "Mrs. Simmons said another two weeks. You should sack her."

Regina chuckled as he'd intended.

"What can I do?" he asked, forcing a calmness he didn't feel into his voice.

"I'm afraid this is all me now. There's nothing you can do."

As he led her to the cottage's entrance, Penny raced past them toward the end of the lane.

"Where are you going?" he asked.

"To fetch Mrs. Simmons."

"I'll go for Mrs. Simmons," he said.

"Do you know where to find her?" Penny asked.

"No, but—"

"I'll be quicker about it," she assured him. "You stay with my la—Mrs. Townsend."

Alex cursed himself for not acquiring a horse on one of his trips to Brighton. Not for the first time, he realized how woefully inadequate he was to the task of caring for another. How long would it take Penny to fetch the midwife?

Regina bent again, breathing heavily. He cursed himself again, this time for dragging his feet about leaving. Had he left when he should have, he wouldn't be here wondering what the *bloody hell* he was supposed to do. Wondering how he would let Regina down, for it wasn't a question of *if*, but *how*.

He felt a tug on the end of his coat and turned. Tilda had wrapped her small hand around his coattail and followed them back into the cottage. She looked at him, her brown eyes large in her face. Anxious. He smiled at her and took her small hand in his.

"All will be well, Princess. You'll have a little brother or sister soon."

"I'd like a sister, please."

Regina laughed, a soft sound that ended on a

small groan. "I don't think we get to choose, poppet," she said.

Tilda wrinkled her forehead, clearly not pleased with that answer.

"Why don't you get the paints from my room?" Alex said. "I'll help your Mama upstairs, then we can paint."

Tilda brightened at that and peeled off to his room. Regina looked at Alex incredulously. "You're going to *paint*?"

What? She'd been laughing a moment ago, but now she looked irritated. He hesitated before saying, "You yourself said there's nothing I can do. And it will give Tilda something else to think about."

She puffed her cheeks on a breath, and her eyes flashed before she nodded. "You're right, of course." During a lull in her pains, he guided her up the stairs and into her room. She settled on the edge of the bed and looked at him. She hadn't yet let go of his hand.

"Can I get you anything?" he asked. What did one offer in situations such as this? Tea? He knew he wouldn't mind something stronger.

She looked at her feet. "Can you ... can you remove my boots?" she asked, pressing her lips together, a vermilion blush lighting her cheeks.

He looked at her feet, then at her belly, and

smiled. Bending, he lifted one foot and untied the lace. He slid the boot off her stockinged foot. Her foot was swollen, but it still felt dainty in his large hand. His thumb brushed her arch and she inhaled sharply. He looked up. Her head was bowed, her eyes closed, and he pressed harder with his thumb, circling it on the sole of her foot.

"I haven't been able to reach my feet for weeks," she said. "At least not comfortably."

He chuckled and removed her other boot. He ran a palm around her ankle and over the fine bones before pressing his fingers along the sole.

She clutched her belly again and inhaled a sharp breath. He dropped her foot and stood, running a hand through his hair. "I'll go," he said.

"Yes," she panted. "No." Clearly, she was torn. Finally, she said, "Please, care for Tilda."

He nodded and left before she could call him back.

Tilda had found his paints and attempted to mix Prussian blue herself. She looked like a fairy, with more blue pigment on her than on the palette. He grinned and tried to scrub some of it off her nose, but there was no help for it. She would be blue for quite some time.

Over the next hour, he divided his attention between Tilda and Regina. With Tilda, he was cheerful, encouraging her as she painted a portrait of Robert beneath the apple tree. At least he thought it was Robert. He appeared to have grown a fifth leg . . . Or no, that was his tail.

With Regina, he vacillated between wonder at her resilience and fear of his own mistakes. He didn't know what to do to ease her pain, much less see a new life into the world. What if Penny didn't return with Mrs. Simmons in time? What if Regina had to depend on him? Heaven help them all.

He'd just returned to her room to find her pacing next to the bed. He offered her water in a chipped cup he'd brought from the scullery. She shook her head, and a grimace crossed her face. She stopped pacing and placed one hand on the wall. He was acquainted with pain and wished he could relieve hers. Then he thought of the monks of St. Augustine.

He waited until she relaxed, then he spoke. "When I was shot . . ."

She angled a sharp look at him, and he took a deep breath. He'd not shared his story with anyone before.

"When I was shot, I recovered at a monastery. The monks taught me some techniques to get through the pain. I could teach you. If you'd like, that is."

She hesitated then nodded jerkily, and he explained his tricks with the ribbon and the box of pain. She eyed him skeptically, and he realized this was information he probably should have shared before now.

"I can't explain it," he said, "but it often works. For me at least. I don't know if it will work for . . . this." He waved his hand in the general direction of her belly.

During the next lull in her birthing pains, he turned to leave. He should check on Tilda again. Make sure she hadn't found the vermilion. Regina gripped his hand, though, and didn't let go. He looked at her, surprised at the earnestness in her face and the bone-crushing strength in her hand as she squeezed his.

"Thank you," she said, loosening her grip.

"For what?" He truly hadn't done anything to assist her. For all he knew, the pain tricks were figments of his imagination and would be useless to help her.

"For being here."

He wanted to laugh. He couldn't wait to leave, and she was thanking him for being there.

"You've been a true friend to us. You could have left weeks ago, but you didn't. Why have you stayed?"

What could he say? That he had nowhere else to be? He'd told her that before, but it seemed inadequate. That he was compelled by her, drawn to her in a way he couldn't explain, a way that made him uncomfortable and hopeful at the same time? That he'd grown fond of Tilda and Penny. Robert, even? That they'd begun to feel like a . . . family?

He opened his mouth, but she squeezed his hand again, hard, and scowled.

———

PENNY EVENTUALLY, THANKFULLY, RETURNED WITH Mrs. Simmons. Alex was relieved to turn the situation over to the midwife, but somewhat unsettled to feel so . . . unnecessary again. *You wished to be uninvolved,* the voice in his head whispered. *You can't have it both ways.* He ruthlessly ignored it and assisted Tilda with her trees. They'd always been a sticking point for him as well.

"Do you think I'll have a brother or a sister?" she asked.

"I suppose only God and the angels know the truth of that."

She studied him for a moment, considering. "My Papa's in heaven," she said. "Do you think he knows?"

Alex had never been one for church, so he hedged. "Maybe."

He debated asking questions about her Papa but decided that prying information from a child would be dishonorable, even for him. He wracked his brain for what he knew of the Earl of Foxwald and came up empty. The title sounded familiar, but he didn't think he'd ever met the man. Would never have had any cause to.

Finally, he gave in to his curiosity. Just one question. If she wanted to talk, he'd let her, but he wouldn't force her. "What was your home like before you came here?"

She shrugged, dabbing blobs of green that he assumed were leaves onto a swipe of brown that he assumed was a branch. He thought a shrug was to be her only response, but then she whispered, "I'm not s'posed to talk about it."

She was clearly torn, indecision pulling the corners of her mouth down, so he smiled and ended her misery. "That's all right. We don't have to talk about it."

He crossed his legs and turned back to his sketch pad, but she continued to watch him, her brush dripping onto the page. A minute, then two, passed, the pool of green paint growing on her paper. It seemed she had something on her mind. He sighed and looked up. "What?"

"Are you my new Papa?"

A flutter quickened in his chest, and he lowered his pencil and studied her. Looked past the blue staining her nose and chin. Her eyes were wide chocolate pools, awaiting his answer. "No, Princess. I'm not your Papa, but I can be your friend, and friends are better, don't you think?"

She looked at the page before her and bit her lip, nodding.

He watched her fill in the trunk of her tree, her grip on the brush all wrong, and a vision rose in his mind. Of him, and Regina and Tilda. A tiny baby. Happy in this cottage. His hand shook, and he flattened it on his sketch pad to still the motion. Then he allowed the image to return and fill his mind, and he examined it. Poked and turned it.

No, it was all wrong. There were so many reasons why it was wrong that he couldn't list them all, though he tried.

Regina was a countess.

Regina was a countess running from something. Or someone.

He was . . . well, himself.

A painter with no paintings.

A man with debts and gaping holes in his past.

A man who didn't get involved.

Certainly not a man ladies and children should depend upon.

———

AT THE NEXT PAIN, REGINA tried breathing like Alex had taught her, slow and rhythmic. She pictured a ribbon of pain leaving her body and exhaled. She forced herself to relax and inhaled again. The pain was still there, but . . . more bearable. Until it wasn't.

"Bloody hell," she cursed. Then her muscles relaxed and the pain subsided, only to repeat the cycle all over again.

She'd been relieved when Mrs. Simmons had arrived, but sorry to see Alex go, despite his dubious pain-relieving techniques. She shouldn't want him there—she was humiliated enough with what little he'd witnessed so far, and it would only get worse. But his presence had been . . . comforting. She wasn't sure why, when he was clearly so uncomfortable to sit with her, but she'd felt more peaceful with him there.

This birth was singularly different from Tilda's. Her anxiety about the future aside, she felt less alone. When Tilda was born, she'd lived on an estate the size of a small village, surrounded by every luxury. She'd had a household teeming with staff. No fewer than four women had been with her at every moment of the birth—from servants to the midwife to women from the neighboring estate. Her husband and father-in-law waited in the study, but still she'd been terrified and alone.

Now, with just the four of them in this tiny cottage, with the specter of an uncertain future looming, she didn't feel alone. She felt strangely . . . optimistic.

———

TWELVE HOURS LATER, REGINA WAS ready to take her optimism and fling it from the nearest window. The baby's progress was slow. Alex's mind tricks were long forgotten, and she wanted to rail at him, but he was conveniently absent from her side.

Mrs. Simmons assured her the babe was nearly here, but Regina was convinced he or she would never arrive. She would be huge and swollen for the rest of her life, doomed to wobble about forever.

But then, he did arrive. She had a son. She laughed and cried when Mrs. Simmons lowered him into her arms swaddled in soft wool. Foxwald and his threats were meaningless while she held her son.

She counted ten toes and ten fingers, although he could have had a few more or less, and he still would have been perfect. He had a dark thatch of hair and ruddy cheeks. His head was beautifully misshapen, but she knew that would right itself. She stroked a finger down his cheek, and he turned toward her.

She smiled and closed her eyes, pleased with the world as Mrs. Simmons tucked a soft wool blanket more firmly about them.

——

ALEX GREW MORE CONCERNED AS each hour passed. He knew these things took time, but shouldn't he have heard something by now? What if something went wrong? If, heaven forbid, something happened to Regina, what would become of Tilda? She slept in a chair in the parlor, dark curls hiding her blue face. He covered her with a blanket and stoked the fire before taking the chair next to hers.

Care for Tilda. Regina's whispered words from

hours before came back to him.

He thought of all the weeks he'd ignored Regina's secret. *Missing Countess.* All the time when he should have pressed for her story. For details about her family.

If something happened to her, he'd need to understand why they were running. Like it or not, no matter how much he protested to himself, he was *involved.* He'd not hand Tilda over to just anyone, and certainly not to someone who would endanger her. He sighed, knowing if it came to it, it would be up to him to see that she was safe.

He wasn't anyone's protector. He was far from a hero.

Care for Tilda. The words replayed in his mind. They ricocheted, echoes of similar words from more than twenty years ago, until a memory jolted his mind with lightning swiftness.

The force caused him to jump up and pace the parlor. He ran a hand through his hair, heedless of the disarray he caused. Nausea swam in his gut as the memory emerged. Like a painting, the memory began rough, lightly sketched, until painterly details filled the empty spaces, and a full picture appeared.

CHAPTER FOURTEEN

1796

LONDON

CARE FOR GABRIEL.

Eight-year-old Alexandre Marchand bent and watched his younger brother's chest, waiting. *There.* Gabriel still breathed. His face was pale and glistened with sweat, his lips bloodless. A rattle shook him, and Alex squeezed his brother's hand.

Gabriel opened stiff eyes and looked at him. "Alex," he whispered, smiling. Gabriel always smiled, even with the dark gap where he'd recently lost a tooth. Alex looked beyond Gabriel to see the orphanage's administrator falsely haloed in the dim light beyond the sick ward.

He tried to duck into the shadows next to Gabriel's bed, but Mrs. Powell spotted him and strode forward with gleeful malice. *"King Loo-ee*, I warned you what would happen if I found you in this ward again." She grabbed him by his rough linen shirt and began dragging him. His feet kicked as he tried to gain purchase on the cold stones.

"Mrs. Powell," he protested. "Gabriel is ill. Please, can't you help him?"

"Your brother is only ill because he disobeyed. You'll likely suffer the same fate. Now off with you," she shoved him, and his knees hit the stone floor hard. He turned and scuttled backwards, his hands sliding in filth.

"Please," he said. "I'm supposed to care for him. He needs a doctor."

"Do you see a doctor here?" She looked about as if she might discover a physician in the ward's shadowy corners. The physician's appearances in this particular ward were few and far between, and even more so for French orphans. Mrs. Powell advanced and lifted him by his collar again. His toes scraped the floor as she dragged him from the room.

"Gabriel," he cried, before she cuffed him on the ear.

"Stop crying, *Loo-ee*" she ordered. Not for the first time, he regretted telling her his full name. His parents' names. He was Alexandre Louis Nicolas Marchand. Heir to Louis, Monsieur le Baron Marchand. Eldest son of Heloise Marchand.

He'd once been proud to say his name, but the very English Mrs. Powell insisted on calling him *King Louis—Loo-ee—*at every turn, to the point that the other children mocked him. He'd taken to calling himself Nicky March, which the others accepted more readily. He'd even begun hiding his French accent, and he hated himself for it.

Later that night, after the lanterns had been turned down, Alex huddled under his thin blanket and tried to ignore the older boys. They whispered gruesome tales in the dark. Stories of monsters that lurked the halls and the crooked specter of death that stole sick children. Dressed in black like a vicar, he crept in from the sewers, so quiet that no one heard him coming.

Alex squeezed his eyes shut and covered his ears to shut out their ridiculous games, but he couldn't forget about Gabriel, sick and alone. When the whispers stopped, he crept from his thin cot and returned to the sick ward.

The beds leading to Gabriel were full of children no one wanted. Nothing was worse than an orphan, except perhaps an ailing orphan. The stench of sickness was overwhelming, and Alex gagged. Tears of failure and desperation stung the backs of his eyes.

His mother had begged him to watch over Gabriel as she'd tearfully pushed both boys toward their English grandfather, who'd smuggled them to England and away from the Terror. They'd left France the same day his mother and father had been guillotined, and Alex had watched over Gabriel ever since. First during the months with their grandfather, and then in the orphanage after he too had passed.

He stepped lightly across the orphanage's damp stone floor, his bare feet numb to the cold and filth. Tiny feet skittered in the dark, and Alex swiveled his head, watching and listening for the specter of death. He felt his way along the beds, bumping a foot here, a head there, a cold hand, until he finally reached the eighth cot, two rows in.

He listened intently for Gabriel's rattled breath, but he couldn't hear him. He reached for his brother's hand but found only threadbare linen and moldy straw. He patted the length of the short bed, feeling, confirming the emptiness. He was too late.

Alex huddled beside the bed and wept silently until his tears dried. He dared not make a sound and incur the wrath of Mrs. Powell or the specter of death. Footsteps echoed in the long hall outside the sick ward. He waited until they passed, then, alone and purposeless, he left the orphanage.

———

ALEX STRUGGLED TO BRING HIS mind back to the cliffside cottage. Tears burned the backs of his eyes and he sat again, hard. He struggled to catch his breath. Indeed, his ribs seemed to be squeezing his lungs. His body was too small to contain the emotion roiling inside. His fingertips tingled, numb from shock.

Gabriel. His only brother, lost to him when he'd been six and Alex eight. How could he have forgotten Gabriel?

One after another, images tumbled through his mind. Gabriel and Alex watching their French chef, Etienne, preparing pastries. Gabriel, sneaking a *macaron* and packing his cheeks with it. Gabriel, watching Alex teach him to tie a knot. Gabriel, with his persistent smile, beaming even in the months after they'd been taken from their parents and France.

Guilt washed over Alex in a hot flood. He'd let Gabriel down horribly. He knew in his mind that, at eight, he couldn't have saved his brother, but his heart refused to listen. His hand shook as he pulled it through his hair, and nausea rocked through him.

Other bits of his life from before Le Havre flashed. Pieces of himself he'd lost the night he'd been shot. Memories of his mother, soft and bright, flowed like warm water over his mind. She'd been half-English, but her words always carried the soothing cadence of her beloved French heritage. His father, stern and larger than life, but always with a ready smile for his mother.

He also recalled his years on the streets of

London after leaving the orphanage. First, as a petty thief, taking what he could to survive. Then, as his skill and cleverness grew, he'd swindled, running jobs on men with more money than sense. It was no wonder his mind had decided to forget.

He closed his eyes and stretched his mind, grasping for the events leading up to Le Havre, but they remained just out of reach. The why and how of his shooting still escaped him. Knowing what he knew now, though, perhaps the black hole in his memory was for the better.

Alex rubbed the back of his neck, blowing out a breath. Despite his grief for Gabriel, for his parents, his relief was profound. He had history, a heritage. He'd not realized how disconnected he'd been since waking up with the monks at St. Augustine. Adrift and unknown, without identity. Now he felt anchored, grounded in a way he hadn't been for the past two years.

He'd idled at Regina's little cottage because he had nowhere else to go. That hadn't changed, but at least he was gaining a sense of himself, of purpose. He could choose to return to Brighton and resume his original plan to find an heiress. He could choose to return to Paris. He could choose to travel to London. He was not adrift.

A log cracked in the fireplace and released a shower of sparks before settling in the grate. Tilda murmured and snuggled deeper beneath the blanket, one stockinged foot hanging off the chair. Her toes felt chilled, so he tucked her foot beneath the wool and wrapped the blanket more firmly about her. She slept peacefully. Trusting the adults in her life to care for her.

Are you my new Papa? Tilda's question echoed in his mind.

He'd let Gabriel down. That truth was absolute. It would not go away, whether he remembered it or not. But could he live with it? He'd stumbled on Regina and Tilda quite by accident. Yes, he could choose Brighton or Paris or London, but did he wish to? Could he choose, instead, to stay?

Upstairs, a baby was coming into the world. Somewhere—heaven or hell, he knew not where—a man was missing the birth of his child.

Alex wondered how he would feel were his own child arriving in the world. Fear, pity, remorse . . . all were emotions he knew he *should* feel for any child with himself for a father. But, curiously, *wonder* and *hope* warmed his chest.

He should have heard something by now. He vacillated between going up to Regina and remaining below with Tilda. He'd just placed a foot on the bottom stair when Mrs. Simmons appeared at the top. She wore a broad smile, and he took the steps two at a time.

——

Regina's eyes were closed when he entered. She lay propped against a pillow, her face pale and her hair mussed. He thought she'd never looked lovelier. Penny dozed in a chair in the corner, clearly exhausted from the last hours, while Mrs. Simmons bustled about the room. Regina's eyes lifted, and she smiled when she saw him.

"I have a son," she whispered, and he noticed the bundle in her arms for the first time.

He moved closer, and she pulled the edge of the blanket down so he could see. The infant was . . . red and wrinkly. Not attractive at all. But Regina seemed pleased, so he nodded and said, "He's a handsome lad."

She smiled at him, her eyes laughing. "Give him a few weeks and you won't be able to resist him." She sobered, as if realizing the implication of her words. Did she expect him to still be there in a few weeks?

His heart grew lighter and he smiled. "I'm sure you must be right. What will you name him?"

She lifted one of the baby's tiny hands, and his fingers wrapped around hers. Alex marveled at the new life where there had been none before. "I haven't decided yet, but I suppose there's no rush." Her forehead wrinkled in thought, and she continued. "How's Tilda?"

Blue, he thought, but he kept that detail to

himself. There was still time to clean her up.

"She's sleeping. Did you know your daughter snores? Loudly." His eyes widened with surprise.

Regina laughed softly then kissed the top of the bundle in her arms. Alex's stomach flipped at the sight, and he stood straighter.

"She must get that from her father, because I assure you, I don't snore," she said.

It was the first time she'd mentioned Tilda's father, and she seemed oblivious of the slip. Her eyes drooped, and she yawned behind one hand.

"Congratulations, Reggie," he whispered, but her eyes were closed.

———

WHEN REGINA VENTURED DOWN THE stairs two days later, her son in her arms, she was amazed at the sight that greeted her. The cottage was a veritable forest of greenery. Hawthorn and holly boughs were tucked into every crevice and draped every lintel.

"Mama, we decorated for Christmastide," Tilda said, bouncing up to her.

"I see that." Regina turned in a circle, taking it all in.

"Alex told me not to tell you so it could be a secret."

"What a wonderful surprise!" She ruffled her daughter's hair with one hand.

Alex approached from the kitchen, a grin on his

face. He looked ... different. He'd always had a tense, pinched look about him, but now he seemed ... at ease. She supposed everything and everyone seemed rosy to her now.

Wonderful smells followed Alex from the kitchen and her stomach rumbled. He smiled and looked at the bundle in her arms as a tiny fist waved and punched the air. "How's the little gent?"

"Fussy, I'm afraid. You've all been very busy," she said, motioning to a clump of greenery on the mantle.

"Aye, that we have, Mrs. Townsend," Penny said, taking the baby from her arms. "And mind you take notice of *all* the decor," she whispered. She looked up, directing Regina's gaze to a bough hanging from a length of linen ribbon before the kitchen door. A kissing bough, if Regina wasn't mistaken. She felt warm color creep up her throat into her cheeks. She looked at Alex, but he studiously avoided her gaze.

He cleared his throat. "Are you hungry? I started a *pot-au-feu*, but I can get you some bread and honey, if you'd like. Or some ham. Or tea. Would you like some tea?"

She'd never had a suitor ply her with food. Not that Alex was a suitor, she reminded herself, looking at the kissing bough from the corner of her eye.

"That all sounds wonderful, but what I'd really

like first is some fresh air. I think I'll take a short walk outside." She reached for her cloak on a peg by the door.

"Would you like company?" he asked. He took the cloak and draped it about her. His long fingers grazed her shoulder, and she suppressed a shiver.

"Yes, that would be nice."

———

THIS WAS RIDICULOUS, ALEX THOUGHT. He wasn't a man accustomed to nerves, but his hand shook as he placed Regina's cloak about her shoulders. Penny's not-so-subtle mention of the bough dangling before the kitchen door had brought a blush to Regina's face, and his own cheeks had grown warm.

After completing the decorations in the parlor, Penny and Tilda had crafted the kissing bough from leftover sprigs. It was misshapen and bare on one side, with dried bits of leaves that cracked and crumpled at the touch.

It was quite pitiful, but Penny had insisted on hanging it in the most likely spot to catch him: in front of his kitchen. She'd also placed a bough *in* the kitchen, lest he miss the first. He'd shaken his head and tried to ignore her obvious matchmaking attempts.

He'd never needed assistance before in wooing a lady. Not that there was any wooing occurring, he reminded himself. Regina had just had a baby. She had other things on her mind, and Alex wasn't sure how he felt about his newly recovered memories just yet. Yes, they were a long way from wooing.

But Penny had been insistent on the kissing bough, and now he ducked beneath the infernal clump every time he entered the kitchen. In fact, it seemed to be all he could think about. That, and what would happen were he to catch Regina beneath it.

He followed her outside and they sat beside the little herb garden. It lay fallow, save for some bits of parsley and thyme that persisted in the wintry air.

He flexed the fingers of one hand, thinking through what he wanted to say. He wanted to tell her about Gabriel and his parents. His past as a petty thief. The need to tell her, to open his heart and bare himself to her, was overwhelming. He couldn't continue in this manner, with her oblivious of his past.

He didn't expect her to understand. He expected her to turn away from him, in fact, and he couldn't blame her if she did. He opened and closed his mouth, torn. In the end, he simply said, "It's a lovely day."

She looked at him oddly, then up to the gray sky and nodded. They sat together in awkward silence.

Penny and Tilda brought the baby outside, bundled in layers of wool, and they visited with

Robert at his pen. Some moments later, Alex asked, "Have you decided on a name? For the baby," he added unnecessarily.

She seized on the question. "I thought to name him after his father. Anthony. A boy should have a sense of history."

"History's important," Alex acknowledged. He knew now just how important. "Anthony ... Townsend?"

After a brief hesitation, she nodded, and he realized he didn't even know if Townsend was the Foxwald family name, or an assumed name she'd adopted. He wished he knew more of the English peerage.

If what he suspected was true, her tiny son was the new Earl of Foxwald. That was assuming the previous earl didn't have older sons. And if her son was the next earl, then she was running from powerful forces indeed.

Alex had no money, no power, no means to protect her, but he found he wanted to do just that. Protect her and keep her safe. Keep *them* safe. The feeling was foreign to him.

They looked to where Tilda cooed over Anthony in Penny's arms. "Tilda will be a fine sister," he said. He paused on an inhale, then forged ahead. "I had a brother," he told her.

She looked at him in surprise.

"I—I didn't know. What happened?"

In slow, halting sentences, he explained what he recalled of Gabriel. Of their flight from France during the Terror, the loss of their grandfather shortly after arriving in England, and their months at the orphanage.

"I'm sorry," she said. "For you, for Gabriel. He was lucky to have you."

"He was alone when he died. I wasn't with him when it mattered."

She looked at him in surprise. "You mustn't torture yourself with that. You were a child yourself. It couldn't be helped. You were betrayed in the worst possible way, by adults who should have protected you."

He appreciated her words, but he couldn't believe them.

CHAPTER FIFTEEN

LEX'S STORY PULLED AT REGINA'S heart, and a tiny bit of guilt settled in for ever doubting his French-ness. It was buoyed by her relief at realizing he'd not lied about that.

He shifted on the bench, and she sensed there was more to his story. She waited for him to continue.

"Do you remember when I said I couldn't recall being shot?"

That was not something one forgot. She nodded warily.

"I still don't recall those events, but other memories have started to return. Memories from my life after I left the orphanage. "

"What do you mean?"

His subtle French accent rolled over her as he described his life before he'd been shot at Le Havre.

He'd lost so much, she realized. Again and again. First his parents, then his grandfather, then his brother. She ached for the boy who'd grieved alone. For the boy who'd left a cruel orphanage to join the crueler streets of London. She recoiled at the schemes he'd done while marveling at his resilience.

He'd adapted to his surroundings, whether they were dark alleyways or French salons. Or pig pens. His manners, his cultured voice, his . . . food. All were the trappings of a well-to-do gentleman, but the street boy he described was anything but genteel. He was contradiction layered atop paradox, and her confusion mounted.

She sorted through what she knew of him.

He was an artist. As reluctant as she'd been to believe it, she could no longer deny the skill she'd glimpsed.

It seemed that he was also French, as he'd told her from the beginning.

She'd assumed from the first that he was deceitful, but he'd only shown them kindness. Was it possible she'd been mistaken?

Picturing him as he'd been these last weeks, cooking for them, painting with Tilda . . . comforting her during her confinement. She couldn't reconcile that man with the dark deceiver of her imagination. With the London swindler he confessed to be.

And there was still the matter of his scars. He'd been shot. He didn't recall the circumstances surrounding that event, but certainly there was a tale waiting to be told there. Memories waiting to be recalled. His past, by his own admission, was built on lies and deceit on the streets of London. Would she be foolish to disregard that? More importantly, *could* she?

He watched her with apprehension, like a felon awaiting his sentence. She looked from him to Tilda and Penny and back again. The golden flecks in his topaz eyes glinted in the wintry sunlight. She was so tired of not trusting anyone. Of being alone.

What if she just . . . let go? What if she shared her troubles with him? Trusted him with her story? She knew he couldn't solve her problem—only distance and money could do that, but the thought of talking with another person . . . She rolled the idea around in her head. For the first time, her mind didn't shout *No!* It whispered a hesitant *Maybe.* Not now, not today, but maybe . . . soon.

———

SEVERAL NIGHTS LATER, REGINA WAS no closer to unburdening herself to Alex, despite her desire to the contrary. She'd tried to speak the words, but they wouldn't come. She'd been mistrustful for so long, and old habits were hard to break. Thoughts of Alex and her little family's future kept her from her bed well into the night.

She needed to decide her next steps, and soon. She couldn't return to Briarly, not while Foxwald was intent on controlling her son's future. Not when there was a chance he would separate her from him. But it was Christmastide, and the cottage was adorned with greenery. She convinced herself there was time enough to worry about the future in the new year.

She'd just settled Anthony back in his basket when she heard noises coming from downstairs. She seized on the distraction—anything to stop the circular motion of her thoughts. Alex must still be awake.

Before entering the kitchen, she listened at the door for sounds of splashing water. Whether she hoped to hear such sounds or not, she refused to contemplate. Her cheeks burned as images from the night she'd found him in his bath rolled through her mind, but no sounds of water filtered through the wooden door.

Instead, she heard the dull metallic thud of a pan on the wooden table. Was he ... cooking? At this hour?

Soft light outlined the edges of the door, and she eased it open. Alex stood at the kitchen's worktable, bathed in the glow from the low fire and a lone candle. Forehead creased, he lifted a biscuit from the plate before him and took a bite. He looked up, saw her in the doorway and smiled around his full mouth.

"What are you doing?" It looked as if he'd used

every pot and pan in the kitchen. Sugar dusted the table's surface, as well as bits of eggshell and . . . almonds? She entered the kitchen, dazed by the mess.

He chewed slowly, shaking his head. "*Macarons*," he said flatly. "I can't get them quite right." His subtle accent, once a source of irritation and suspicion, flowed over her like warm chocolate. She'd always adored chocolate.

"I've never had one," she said.

He pushed the plate closer to her. "My mother used to enjoy them with her coffee," he said.

Regina lifted one from the plate and nibbled the edge. Her eyebrows lifted. It was crisp and light, with an earthy almond flavor. Soft and creamy on the inside. She'd forgotten how much she missed the confections and pastries from Briarly's kitchens. "This is delicious," she murmured, taking a larger bite.

"It's too dry," he said, popping the last bit in his mouth. "I need to adjust the combination of egg whites and sugar." He dusted a crumb off his lower lip, and her eyes followed the movement. "Why are you awake?" he asked, pulling her eyes back to his.

It was the perfect opportunity to tell him what kept her awake, the problems that plagued her, but she just shrugged and heard herself blame her infant son. "Anthony keeps me up."

"Since you're here," he said, "You can be my assistant." He stepped around her and pulled an apron from a peg by the door.

"What? No," she said. "You know that's not a good idea."

"It'll be fine," he assured her. "I'll tell you what to do." He dropped the apron over her head, turned her and began tying. She felt like Tilda in her magic cape. Alex's fingers fluttered at the tie, cinching it around her and setting it with a quick tug. Her lower back tingled and warmed where his hands grazed her through the fabric of her gown. *Stop,* she ordered herself. *He's just a normal man, with normal hands.*

And of course, such a thought was guaranteed to drag her gaze to his normal hands as he wiped the table.

"How do you know how to cook?" she asked.

He stopped wiping for a moment. "We had a kind—and patient—chef when I was young. Etienne. He let Gabriel and I help in the kitchens, and the rest I improvise. It's mostly trial and error, which explains the mess, I suppose." He looked at the pots and pans and broken eggshells around them and grimaced.

"How is it you *don't* know how to cook?" he asked, one eyebrow raised. "Isn't cooking one of the first lessons in wife school?"

She laughed. *"Wife school?"* He smiled in reply. It felt good to laugh. "You'll be surprised to know I haven't spent much time in a kitchen." Belatedly, she realized her slip. A countess might not spend much time in the kitchen, but a common widow would. She bit her lip and took another biscuit.

"No, I'm not surprised to hear that," he said. "I've tasted your stew, after all."

She pressed her lips together, then relented and smiled.

"You have a lovely smile, Reggie," he said softly, and her smile slipped of its own accord, as it always did when faced with charming words from a charming man.

He cracked eggs into two bowls, separating the yolks from the whites. He handed her the bowl with the whites and two wooden spoons tied together.

"What do I do with this?" she asked.

"That," he said, pointing at the spoon bundle, "is a whisk. You whisk with it. Whip the whites until they form stiff peaks."

She looked at the egg whites. They were a long way from stiff peaks, but she began stirring with her bundled spoons.

He watched her for a moment, one hand on his lips. "Stir like this" — he made a looping motion with his hand — "to incorporate air into the eggs."

She tried to imitate him, but only succeeded in

sloshing egg white over the edge of the bowl. She couldn't help but smile at his look of disgust. "I told you this wasn't a good idea," she reminded him.

He inhaled, pressing his lips, then moved to stand behind her. He reached around and placed his hand over hers on the spoons.

"What are you doing?" she squeaked. Had that sound truly come from her?

He was silent for a moment, and she thought he wouldn't answer. Then his voice vibrated near her ear. "I'm showing you how to whisk."

She pressed down a shiver at the nearness of his lips, the heat of his hand on hers. His warm citrusy scent wrapped around her as he moved their hands together, bending at the wrist, until the motion became more fluid. He slowly picked up more tempo as they whisked the eggs.

Heat rolled from his chest at her back, and her hand burned where he held it. Sensation flooded her, made her breathless. She'd never felt like this with Anthony. Or the poet, for that matter. Alex nuzzled her neck as he inhaled, and his hand on hers slowed.

"Who led you astray, Reggie?" he whispered.

She jumped and their hands came apart. "I think I have it now," she said.

He moved away from her, a smile on his face.

"What will you be doing while I whisk?" she

asked, more as a distraction for herself than out of any real desire to know.

"I'll grind the almonds." He placed a handful of nuts into a mortar and began grinding with a deft twist of his wrist. Regina forced her breathing to calm as she whisked.

His words from their afternoon in the garden rose in her mind. He'd shared his pain, made himself vulnerable to her, and she'd not given him anything in return.

Her eyes on her bowl, she forced a calmness to her voice that she didn't feel. "He was a poet."

She felt Alex's eyes on her as his wrist worked the pestle in a steady twist.

"I was eighteen and . . . foolish."

"I think he must have been the foolish one." She nodded, not looking up.

———

ALEX WAS SURPRISED TO SEE he'd ground the almonds to flour. Regina's nearness, and her small disclosure, had distracted him. Her brief admission wasn't much, but it was a start. A poet—he must have been a right scoundrel. Anger and jealousy slithered through him. Anger on Reggie's behalf, jealousy that she'd cared enough about the man for his actions to matter.

Regina tilted her bowl toward him. "Are they finished?" she asked.

He looked at the egg whites and shook his head. "No, they need more whisking."

She turned back to the bowl, rotating her wrist in the manner he'd shown her. Sort of.

Perhaps he should show her again, he thought, fighting a smile. He recalled her heat against him as he'd held her hand. The lavender scent behind her ear. What would she do if he turned her and kissed her senseless? Would she squeak as she'd done earlier? He hid his grin.

"Now?" she asked.

His fantasy evaporated like steam, and he inspected the egg whites, nodding. She watched while he folded in sugar and the ground almonds, then dropped fluffy mounds on a pan to bake.

While they waited, he put on a kettle for tea and gathered two cups. "*Macarons* should be enjoyed with coffee or chocolate." He sighed. "Tea will have to do."

When he pulled the pan from the fire, he smiled. He could see they were perfect.

———

REGINA SMILED AROUND A MOUTHFUL of biscuit. Crisp on the outside and smooth on the inside, the *macaron* had a deliciously nutty almond flavor without being too sweet. Even as good as the first one had been, she could see why he'd insisted on perfection. *This* confection melted on her tongue.

"You're quite talented," she told him, licking a crumb from her lip.

He swallowed and watched her lips. Interesting. She licked the corner of her mouth again, and his intent regard warmed her insides. His topaz eyes moved to hers, and what she saw there took her breath. Heat and yearning and something more that she couldn't name.

She pressed her lips together and prepared to step away, but he lifted a hand to her chin. His thumb brushed her bottom lip, tracing the path where her tongue had been. She stilled, watching him, afraid to move. His perfect lips tilted in a smile, and he looked up. She followed his gaze and realized they stood under one of Penny's kissing boughs.

Her good sense should have told her to leave. She listened, waiting for it to speak up, to remind her of poets and the rippling effect of poor choices. But when her good sense did raise its head, it just said, *Finally*.

Apparently, some part of her had been waiting, wanting his kiss.

Alex narrowed the already-short distance between them and hesitated, giving her a chance to retreat. She stood her ground, and he pressed his mouth to hers. He lifted his hands and held her, his thumbs stroking the sides of her face, while his lips angled and kissed the corners of hers.

All thought disintegrated, all notion of ripples and choices, and she returned his kiss. He tasted of almonds and warm sugar, and his lips were as perfect on hers as she'd imagined.

When he pulled away, she was dizzy and her lips tingled. He held her face between his broad palms, pressed his forehead to hers and smiled.

"You were wrong," he said.

"What"—she cleared her throat and tried again—"what do you mean?"

"You said assisting me with the *macarons* wasn't a good idea. I happen to believe it was the very best of ideas."

CHAPTER SIXTEEN

TO HER SURPRISE, REGINA SAW little of Alex in the following days. He took to spending his afternoons and evenings in the stable, of all places. She wasn't sure how to take that, so close on the heels of the kiss they'd shared.

It was entirely possible she was out of practice. Her husband had been gone for nearly a year now, and even before he passed, they'd rarely shared a kiss. It wasn't inconceivable that she'd forgotten how to do it properly. Perhaps she'd never known how to do it at all.

It had certainly felt like a proper kiss to her, but perhaps he had higher kissing standards. She frowned, and rubbed a finger over her bottom lip, recalling the tingle she'd felt when he'd pressed his lips to hers.

There hadn't been any more midnight *macaron* lessons. Not that she was wishing for one. Not that she listened from her room for kitchen sounds each night. As if to punctuate her thoughts, noises came from the kitchen where Alex was preparing supper.

He emerged and placed a steaming dish on the dining table as Penny approached with Anthony.

"Is he asleep?" Regina asked Penny.

"Yes, just now. I'll fetch his basket from upstairs, and he can sleep while we have our supper."

"I'll get it," Alex offered.

———

ALEX CLIMBED THE STAIRS AND entered Regina's room. Traces of her lavender scent lingered, reminding him of their *macaron* kiss. He smiled, recalling the tender softness of her lips beneath his. When was the last time he'd been so enamored of a lady? Perhaps as a lad of fifteen, when he'd had his first kiss with a pretty barmaid. But no, that had merely been youthful infatuation.

This was ... different. Much more than infatuation. He had, in fact, been thinking he ought to attempt eclairs, if only to have another excuse to bake with her. He wouldn't mind another kiss, or ten. A lifetime of kisses. He imagined her with a dusting of flour on her cheek, eclair cream on her lips, before he pulled his mind back to the present.

Before he could even consider eclairs, he needed to finish the project he'd begun in the stable. Christmas would be here in two days.

Anthony's basket was where he'd seen it last,

tucked in a corner near the bed, beneath Reggie's small table. He bent to retrieve it, and as he did, he bumped the loose board in the wall again. He pulled the basket aside and investigated to see what he'd need to fix the board, and the slat came loose in his hand.

He lifted the corner and slid it to the side. A small dark recess lay behind the panel, and there, tucked in Regina's wall, was a single rolled canvas. Alex held his breath and stared, then sat back on his heels. This felt like one of those essential, deciding moments in a classical drama. The suspended minute when the audience was divided in their guidance for the hero. Do versus Don't. A decision severing Before from After.

He scrubbed a hand over his jaw, thinking. He no longer cared if Regina had a forgery of his work. If she thought it would help fund her investment plans, then so be it. He didn't begrudge her attempts to secure her family. He could leave the canvas and replace the wood slat. Never mention or think of it again.

Then he recalled Lafontaine and his buyer. Someone was looking for this particular piece. What had the dealer said? *A proper gent.* What was so important about this piece? He could take a quick look and know for certain if it was authentic or a forgery. Then perhaps he'd know why someone was seeking it.

He listened for sounds from downstairs and heard Regina and Penny talking. They'd wonder where he was if he didn't return with the basket soon. He'd have to be quick.

Reaching a hand into the wall, he pulled the canvas free. The bed creaked beneath his weight as he sat on the end, and he winced at the sound. He listened again, but no footsteps approached. The rough texture of the canvas was familiar beneath his fingers as he tapped it against his thigh. Just a quick look, then he would put it back. He inhaled and unrolled the painting against the bed's counterpane.

It was a rural landscape. He studied it, noting the light and shadow playing in the brown and amber tones. He instantly recognized his own hand in the long brushstrokes of the trees and clouds, but a woman had been added to the foreground by another artist. A breeze tossed the loose strands of her hair, but the direction of the movement was all wrong.

To an untrained eye, he supposed it was a decent enough addition, but to him, it was painfully crude, obviously the work of a novice. The signature at the bottom lacked his typical flourish where he curled the stem of the final "d" above the rest of his name. He'd expected a forgery, but this odd piece combining his painting with another's confused him. Who had added the woman and the signature, and why?

A memory tickled the edge of his mind. He reached for it only to have it dance and shift and dissolve. The familiar tightness gripped the back of his neck, and he braced for one of his headaches. But instead of the crippling pain, new memories assaulted him, pulling him under. It was as if he'd fallen into the sea all over again.

———

1816
ALEX'S APARTMENTS
RUE DE RICHELIEU, PARIS

ALEX ADJUSTED A CURL AGAINST Madame Lavigne's neck and repositioned her arm. Satisfied, he stepped back to his easel. Afternoon sunlight flooded his studio through a large bow window, creating sharp planes of light and shadow on her profile. Picking up a piece of charcoal, he sketched where he wanted to place her in the scene.

She stood motionless, patient while he worked. She was one of the better models he'd engaged lately. Many of them presumed an intimacy with the artist he wasn't always willing to share. They flirted and talked when he just needed them to remain silent and still.

He was adding a contour to her silhouette when the door opened, and Roger Chesterton entered without knocking. Alex looked at him out of the corner of his eye as he worked, noting the man's agitation seemed especially high today.

"When will it be finished?" Roger asked, pulling a slim metal case from his waistcoat pocket. No greeting, no preamble. Roger didn't waste words on those he deemed beneath him. Alex, with a past carved from the streets of London, was far, far beneath Roger's notice.

Roger conveniently forgot that his own past wasn't as far removed from Alex's as he'd like to pretend. They'd both survived and escaped the same orphanage. The difference was Roger had gone to live with wealthy relations, while Alex went to live on the streets of London. That they'd "found" one another again—on competing sides of a London swindle—was a fact Alex often regretted.

He straightened from the easel and glanced at the other man. Roger awaited his answer, but Alex refused to be rushed. "Soon enough," he responded, wiping charcoal from his hand with a rag. Roger's eyes were hard and blue, empty. Not for the first time, Alex rethought their acquaintance. Roger exuded arrogance, and with arrogance came recklessness. Alex determined this would be the last time he worked with the man.

Roger removed a thin cheroot from his case and lit it on a candle. He drew on the cigar and moved to view Alex's easel, puffing a cloud of blue smoke. Alex waved it from his canvas irritably. Casting a leering glance at Madame Lavigne, Roger continued. "I've found a new buyer, and we're moving the date up. Gaston, in Le Havre."

Alex had lived in Le Havre before removing to Paris and was familiar with many of the art dealers there. He mentally reviewed the names he knew. "Gaston?" he said with surprise. He'd not met the man, but he knew him to be a minor dealer with more flash than substance. "He can't afford this. And I heard he has a young wife and child."

"He can afford it," Roger insisted. When Roger set his mind on something, he was immovable.

Alex had gone along with Chesterton's schemes in the past, but he had his limits. He only targeted marks who could afford to lose a little, and never men with families. Alex could be immovable as well; he remained firm.

"We're not selling to Gaston," he said. He dismissed Madame Lavigne with a nod of his head. She collected her things and moved to leave. Roger smirked at her rudely as she skirted him.

"I'll thank you not to harass my models," Alex snapped at him when she'd gone.

"Apologies, chap. I assumed her charms were for the taking, but if you've a singular interest . . ."

Alex ignored the man's crudeness and returned

to the subject at hand. "We agreed to sell to Allard. Gaston was not our target. And why Le Havre? It's a three-day ride from here."

Allard was a dealer on Rue St. Augustin. The man had questionable morals and even more questionable sources of income. Alex suspected much of his early wealth had originated during the Terror, from the spoils of murdered aristocrats. Alex had no qualms fleecing him. The irony of his particular code of honor was not lost on Alex, given much of his own income was somewhat questionable.

Their swindle was a simple one, ageless and remarkably effective. Chesterton would approach the mark, a dealer they'd selected ahead of time, with a painting to sell, then a prearranged distraction would pull Chesterton from the dealer's side.

Meanwhile, Chesterton's wife, dressed in silks and fine paste jewels, would enter the establishment and spot the painting. She'd claim her devoted—and very wealthy—husband would pay dearly for it if the dealer could secure it for her.

The dealer would be only too happy to pay an exorbitant amount on the promise of greater gains when he sold the piece to the lady's husband. Of course, the lady and her husband would never return to make the purchase. *Caveat emptor* was the rule they lived by. Buyer beware.

Alex's role was to provide the paintings. As an

unknown artist, it had been a way to support his studies at *L'Academie*. But now, as his work was gaining recognition, he grew more reluctant to put his name to such pieces. And he'd never condoned running the swindle on men who couldn't afford their price. Not that his tenuous scruples made their game acceptable, but it helped assuage his guilt a tiny bit.

"The plan has changed," Roger said, watching the street from the bow window. He consulted his watch, impatience lacing his words. "There's a lot at stake with this one. I'll need the finished piece in two days. See that it's ready." He slapped his gloves on his palm and turned to face Alex.

"If we're not selling to Allard, then I'm out of it," Alex said, turning toward the door. He felt Roger's empty blue eyes boring into his back.

"When I'm an earl, I won't have a need for these games. We can end this, and you and I need never see one another again. But until then, you're not out, *Nicky*." He stressed Alex's childhood name. A reminder that he knew Alex's past, and the crimes he'd committed on the streets of London.

The threat wasn't a new one, but lately, Alex had grown tired of hearing it. He'd grown tired of the swindle. Tired of Roger. Tired of his own role in the scheme. Heart racing in anger, he narrowed his eyes on Roger. "Show yourself out," he said as he left the room.

When he returned to the studio hours later, he noticed two things. One, Roger had forgotten his cheroot case, and it rested on the mantel. And two, the easel was empty, his canvas gone. It looked as if Roger meant to proceed without him.

After three days of arguing with his conscience, he decided to ride out to Le Havre. If he wasn't too late, he'd warn Gaston and give the man a chance to avoid Roger's scheme. Then he'd be well and truly out of it.

He went to Gaston's place of business, but the man was not there. He made discrete inquiries, but no one had seen him. Finally, an associate told him what he'd dreaded to hear. Gaston had scraped his life's savings together to meet Roger's price, and the swindle had gone as planned. For all intents, Gaston was ruined.

Alex stood in the shadows outside the man's home, trying to determine his next steps. He was afraid there was little he could do now that Gaston had fallen for Roger's scheme. He was about to leave when a noise to his left caught his attention. He turned to see Roger approaching.

"I suspected you were the one inquiring about Gaston," he said. "You're too late. It's done."

Alex narrowed his eyes on his associate—former associate, he reminded himself. "I told you he couldn't afford it."

"It would seem you were correct," Roger said,

grinding a cheroot beneath his boot. "I heard the fool has already taken himself to the cliffs off the Étretat road."

Alex knew the point. It was a well-known spot that had seen centuries of anguish and despair drowned in the sea below.

————

ALEX DUG HIS HEELS INTO his tired horse's flanks. Sweat dried on his face as he raced over darkening fields. Lightning flashed and thunder echoed in the distance, warning of an oncoming storm. He hadn't passed another soul for three miles. It was no accident despairing souls had long chosen the lonely place to end their misery.

When Alex reached the turnoff, he pulled up and dismounted. His heart was racing, thumping in his chest, but he'd have to go the rest on foot or risk being decapitated by a low hanging limb. He held an arm in front of him, pushing branches aside as he went. A spider's web caught him in the face, and he pulled at the sticky filament while he hurried through the darkening trees.

He made no attempts to be silent. Haste was more important. He needed to reach Gaston before it was too late.

The branches finally thinned, and a flash of lightning lit a clearing beyond. A promontory atop the steep cliffs, overlooking an ebony sea. Wind whistled across the flat outcropping, disturbing the trees behind him. The sea, not wanting to be outdone, crashed and frothed at the cliff base below. Lightning sparked once more, illuminating pregnant clouds, and the scent of rain was heavy.

Pierre Gaston stood at the edge of the cliff facing the sea. His shoulders hunched in a brown greatcoat that flapped about him like wings. He held a leather bag in one hand, and he was alive. Alive was good.

"Gaston," Alex said softly, not wanting to alarm the man so close to the cliff's edge.

Gaston's head came up and he turned. He narrowed his eyes at Alex. "Who are you?"

"That's not important. Come away from the edge."

Gaston ran a hand over his face. "I don't have any alternative now." He looked at the sea behind him.

"Here, step away from the edge," Alex encouraged again, trying to keep desperation from his own voice as he held out a hand.

"I've lost it all," Gaston said on a plaintive exhale. Even in the shadows, his anguish was clear. Alex imagined he could smell the man's fear.

Alex held both hands up, palms out. "Let's talk about this. Nothing is as bad as that. I know Chesterton. I know what he's done. We can make it right."

The rain began then, splashing Gaston's coat and hat, his leather bag. It fell in big drops, leaving dimples in the dust.

"I gave him everything I had." Gaston's voice rose above the churning waves below. "Now all I have is a worthless painting." The bag dropped from his limp fingers, and he took a step closer to the cliff's edge.

Alex swallowed. Rain was falling in earnest now. It ran into his eyes, and he wiped it away. "Don't do anything rash. Think of your wife and family. Let me help."

"I think of *nothing* but them. I've ruined them. What can *you* do?" he asked with a sneer. "Can you get my ten thousand back?"

Ten thousand? Bloody hell. Roger had grown bolder than he'd suspected.

"Yes," he promised. It would take Alex two lifetimes to accumulate that much, but he seized the chance to convince Gaston. They'd worry about the money later. Gaston looked up, and hope spread across his features. "Yes," Alex said again, more firmly.

Gaston took a step forward, away from the cliff's edge, but his back foot caught, and the chalky ground beneath him crumbled. Horror distorted his face in the suspended moment before he tumbled from the cliff's edge, flailing and scrabbling for purchase. His cry echoed off the stone as he dropped.

"No!" Alex ran to the cliff's edge, but it was too late. He peered into the dark froth, listening for a sound other than the waves and the rain and the wind. He couldn't see the water below, but it was unlikely the man had survived the fall into the sea. Still, Alex stared into the darkness, watching and listening, until he heard a click behind him.

He turned to find Roger pointing a flintlock pistol at him. His cold blue eyes shimmered as lightning flashed.

Alex sighed. He'd never expected to live a long life. He thought of the ones who'd gone before him—Gabriel, his parents—all more deserving of life than him. It confounded him, how he'd outlived them.

"If you're going to shoot me, just do it and be done with it. Otherwise, I'm leaving." The words, so similar to what he'd spoken in his studio just three short days before, seemed inadequate to the situation. But with the flintlock in front and the sea behind, defiance was his only option.

He moved to leave, and the flintlock went off. The report was deafening, the flash of the muzzle blinding. Alex was surprised to find he was flying, until he wasn't.

———

LIKE PIECES OF A CHILD'S puzzle, the rest of Alex's memories snapped into place. He rubbed his chest where the scar from Roger's bullet puckered.

"Alex?" Regina's voice floated up the stairs, followed by the soft sound of footfalls on the treads. How long had he been in her room? Too long. He replaced the wooden slat and tucked the canvas in his waistcoat as Regina appeared in the doorway.

"Are you all right?" she asked, approaching him.

"Headache," he murmured. He rubbed his head, hating himself for the deception. She hesitated then rubbed cool fingers along his temples, smoothing her thumbs over his brows. He leaned into her touch, his stomach turning because he enjoyed it so much. Would she touch him so if she knew what was in his waistcoat? Probably not. Most certainly not.

She bent, and her eyes gazed into his as her lips tilted in a smile. He watched them curve and imagined their softness beneath his own. His desire must have shown in his eyes, for she stilled.

He leaned forward and touched his lips to hers. Her mouth relaxed beneath his, then she pressed forward with soft kisses, teasing the corners of his mouth. "Your head," she murmured.

Damn his head. Damn the stupid painting in his waistcoat. He pulled back and smiled at her. Her hands were cool and soft where they rested on the sides of his face. "It's better," he said.

———

LATER THAT NIGHT, ALEX TOOK the painting out and examined it again. He didn't know what to do. The way he saw it, his options were limited.

He could replace the canvas and pretend he'd never seen it. But someone was looking for it—probably Roger. That someone would eventually find it if Regina went to sell it again. If the buyer was Roger—and he had no reason to assume otherwise—he knew him to be dangerous. He had the scars to prove it.

Why Roger was intent on the painting was anyone's guess. Did he fear it incriminated him in Gaston's death somehow? Or did he think it would lead him to Alex? That didn't make any sense. Roger was the last one to have the painting after Le Havre. Why would he assume Alex had it now?

Regardless of the *why*, Alex knew he needed to get rid of the painting. Throw Roger off the trail. He couldn't let him find Regina. Tilda. The baby. A cold sweat covered his skin at the thought.

They were *his* family. Perhaps not by blood, but they were his. He couldn't lead Roger to them, so leaving the canvas for her to sell was not an option.

He thought of Lafontaine and his offer. He needed to return to Brighton. Soon.

CHAPTER SEVENTEEN

CHRISTMAS EVE DAWNED CLEAR AND bright with a sapphire sky. It was the kind of morning that caused hope and optimism to swell in one's chest.

Regina checked on Anthony in his basket, careful not to wake him. Her son's fingers curled into a fist, and his lips puckered in his sleep. She brushed the dark, downy fluff from his forehead, amazed as always at the little life she'd borne.

She thought of Alex's mother and what she must have endured as she sent her sons away. The pain she must have suffered knowing they would be robbed of their mother, their father. She rubbed a fist on her chest, feeling the ache behind her breastbone.

She tried to imagine Anthony at eight, forced to endure the trials that Alex had experienced. She couldn't do it. The thought of any child enduring what Alex had—the pain, the loss, the loneliness—

was inconceivable. No one should be alone like that. The urge to confide in Alex, to let go of her fears, grew stronger. She chewed her lip, thinking. Deciding.

She would do it. She would tell him who she was, why she was running. Why she had to keep running. She'd tell him tonight. She didn't know what the future held for her and her children, much less for her and Alex. But perhaps in opening up to him, both of them would feel a little less alone in the world.

She left Anthony to sleep and went downstairs, where she was surprised to see Alex in his cap, his bag on his shoulder and one hand on the doorknob. He looked up as she approached, and the intensity in his eyes startled her. She stopped on the last stair, her brow furrowed.

"I need to go to Brighton. I won't be long," he said.

"Oh. All right." Something was off about his demeanor, and she looked into his eyes, trying to read his thoughts. She opened her mouth but couldn't think of anything to say, so she clamped it shut again.

He gave her a soft smile and touched her cheek with a finger before opening the door. She watched him walk down the lane and through the little copse at the end before he disappeared.

She swallowed and stopped herself from

following him. He would be back soon, she assured herself. But why did she feel like he had just said goodbye?

———

ALEX HAD RISEN EARLY, HOPING to leave for Brighton before the others woke. Then Regina descended the stairs and he'd almost decided against going before reason reasserted itself. Ignoring her painting, and the threat it represented, was not an option.

As he walked the empty road to Brighton, guilt ate at him. He had a long list of things for which to feel guilty, but the most pressing ones circled round and round in his head until he thought he would go mad.

One: He'd taken Regina's painting. The one thing she'd been saving to finance her future for her family. He consoled himself with the fact that he could secure a better deal with Lafontaine than she could. Hopefully, any profit he made on the sale today would soothe her pain. She could thank him later, although he doubted she would.

Two: He felt oh so guilty for enjoying Regina's kiss last night while her painting rested in his waistcoat. She would not appreciate that he'd enjoyed her lips while deceiving her, but if he had it to do over again, he would still kiss her, and he would still enjoy it. He was the worst sort of reprobate.

Three (because two reasons for his guilt weren't enough): He'd recalled a big piece of his past—a significant piece—and disgust curdled his stomach for the role he'd played in Gaston's death.

He'd told Regina about his life on the streets of London, about his days as a petty thief. But this . . . this was so much more. A man had died. It didn't matter that he'd tried to stop it. It was too little, too late. He'd always suspected he was bound for hell, but that was before he had all his memories. Now he knew for certain.

All of his guilt added up to one thing: In all likelihood, he'd need to leave soon. Once Regina realized he'd taken her painting, once he told her about Gaston and the swindling schemes, he couldn't imagine she would wish anything more to do with him.

Lafontaine's establishment appeared much as he remembered it. The signboard creaked in the sea breeze, but the windows were dark. He'd miscalculated, and the shop was still closed. He checked his pocket watch. From the sign on the door, Lafontaine wouldn't open for another hour.

He still had some funds left from the sale of his own painting; now was probably a good time to purchase a horse, especially if he'd be leaving soon. Preferably, one that wouldn't bolt at the first sign of a pig. He made his way toward the market at Black Lion Street and acquired a nice chestnut mare with an ebony mane.

Later, he watched Lafontaine unlock the door to his shop and turn the sign. He paid a boy to watch his new horse, then he counted to one hundred before venturing across the street. He didn't want to appear too eager.

Lafontaine smiled upon seeing him. "Are you here to sell another Marchand?" he asked. Alex looked at the shop's walls, but he didn't see his painting. The man chortled. "The last one sold in a day. A tourist from London, I believe. There's no accounting for taste, is there?"

Alex checked his irritation and asked, "Your buyer for the Marchand forgery. Has he returned?"

"Oh my, yes. The man's most insistent on that particular piece. Heaven knows why."

"Can you describe him again?" Lafontaine had described the man to him before, the first time Alex had entered his shop, but that was before he had his memories.

"Let me think." Lafontaine pulled on his ear and gazed into a corner of the shop. "He was tall. Not quite middle-aged."

"Thin? Fat? Fair? Dark?" Alex asked, then reminded himself to temper his tone. It wouldn't do to show too much interest and drive the offer down.

"Thin and fair, I'd say. Are you acquainted with the man?"

That didn't sound like Roger, Alex thought. Roger

was tall and dark. Broad in the shoulder. "No, I don't think I know him," he said truthfully, although the man had a large network of associates. "But if he's still interested . . ." He let his voice trail off.

Lafontaine looked at him shrewdly. "I believe we can reach an arrangement," he said.

Alex pulled the canvas from his bag and spread it on Lafontaine's table. The man leaned forward to inspect it, his lace cuff dragging across the trees as he trained his loupe on the brushstrokes.

"Yes, this is the one he's seeking. You can tell it's a forgery by the signature. It's lacking the curly little swoop here."

Curly little swoop? Alex didn't do "curly little swoops." He pressed his lips together and allowed Lafontaine to continue.

"And the female figure is clearly not in the artist's typical style. So, you tracked our lady forger down, did you?"

Alex looked up at Lafontaine through his lashes. "Indeed," he said casually. "She was halfway to Manchester, but I was able to convince her to sell. What's your offer?"

Lafontaine named a sum and Alex nearly choked. He wondered briefly if Roger wasn't running a new swindle. Would Lafontaine pay an exorbitant amount for the painting, only for Roger to turn up at Alex's door for his cut?

He hesitated, not sure he wanted to entangle himself in such a scheme if that indeed was what Roger was up to. But did he have any choice? He couldn't take a chance that the painting would be traced back to Regina. He needed to get rid of it quickly. He agreed to Lafontaine's offer and exchanged the painting for a hefty stack of banknotes.

Alex asked idly, "If I bring another Marchand or two, will you buy them?"

Lafontaine nodded. "There's been a lot of interest in Marchands lately—both authentic and forged. Bring them to me and we'll talk."

Alex nodded. Lafontaine's spaniel thumped her tail as he was leaving. "Lafontaine," he said, holding the door. "You ought to be mindful of swindlers. I hear they've been active in the area." A flash of panic crossed the man's face as Alex closed the door.

———

As Alex left Lafontaine's, he was waylaid. The man who'd delivered his supplies from Brighton—the man from The White Stag—stepped in his path, blocking the sun. He now remembered him as a petty thief he'd known in London's rookeries.

"Cosgrove," he said, nodding.

"I knew it was you," the man said, grinning. "I told Perkins as much." He fell into step beside Alex. "I figured you must be working a job. What's the angle?"

"There's no job, Cosgrove," Alex said, keeping

his eyes straight ahead. He had no wish to prolong this conversation.

"We saw you with the woman. I want in on it," Cosgrove said.

"We? Who's we?" Alex knew a moment of panic. Who was Cosgrove working with?

"Me 'n Perkins," Cosgrove said. "C'mon guv, give over. She's not your usual mark. An' judgin' by the shape of that cottage, she ain't got anythin' worth havin'."

"That's not my life anymore," Alex said. They'd reached his horse, and Alex tossed the boy a coin. He sighed and turned to face Cosgrove. "And you'd do well to leave the woman out of it," he added.

Cosgrove looked at him in surprise, then he laughed. "The woman, the youngin' ... the babe. You think they're your family, dontcha? Guv, sharps like us ... we don't 'ave families." He slapped Alex on the shoulder and cackled. "Wait 'til I tell Perkins."

CHAPTER EIGHTEEN

ORNING WAS FADING INTO AFTERNOON, and Alex still hadn't returned. Regina tried to distract herself with her financial papers, but weeks of sleepless nights with Anthony were catching up. She yawned as she stared at the page in front of her. The numbers blurred and she rubbed her eyes.

She tried to remember how long it had taken for Tilda to sleep through the night, but she'd been at Briarly then. Surrounded by staff. Even with Penny here to help with baby Anthony, she was exhausted.

She closed her eyes for a minute, and when she opened them, Tilda sat across from her at the table. She smiled at her daughter, and Tilda gave her a broad grin then turned back to the page before her.

Regina leaned forward, then asked, "Is that Alex's sketch pad?"

Tilda nodded, her eyes focused on her drawing.

"And his charcoal?"

Tilda nodded again.

"Poppet, you can't go into Alex's room and take his things."

"He said he'd paint with me today."

"I'm sure he'll be back soon, and then you can paint. But for now, why don't you show me your drawing, then return his things to his room?"

Tilda eyed her, no doubt formulating an argument. Regina stared back. She'd learned early that nine-tenths of mothering was being able to out-stare her daughter. Tilda rolled her eyes and handed the sketch pad over.

Regina smiled at the somewhat hideous portrait of baby Anthony, although Tilda had captured the shape of his newborn head accurately. "It's lovely, poppet. Anthony will be pleased to have you for a sister."

Tilda beamed at her.

As Regina started to return the book, a loose page fluttered to the floor. She bent to pick it up, and her heart stopped.

Missing Countess. Her heart stuttered back into motion. It climbed into her throat, choking her. Tilda looked at her oddly, waiting for the sketch book. Regina smiled weakly then handed it to her. She kept the bill for herself.

Questions fired through her mind one right after the other. Alex knew who she was? When? How?

Why hadn't he said anything? And more importantly: There was a reward for information on her whereabouts?

She thought of his trips to the market, his new trousers, the supplies for the roof. Where had he gotten the funds? Oh no. Hot dread filled her, weighing her down. Foxwald was probably on his way. She stood and gathered her papers together, then paced the parlor.

"Penny," she called.

Penny came from the kitchen carrying Anthony, a question on her face.

"We need to go. Start packing."

"My lady?"

"We need to go. Now. There isn't time to explain." She turned to the stairs, stopped and retraced her steps. She went to the kissing bough in front of the kitchen, tore it from the low rafter and pulled it apart. She let the pieces rain down onto the floor, tears burning the backs of her eyes.

How could she have been so stupid? She'd suspected him of lying from the beginning, and yet she still fell for him. She'd told him about the poet. Had almost told him more.

Part of her mind whispered, *He would not deliberately hurt and deceive you*. Another, louder part shouted, *You should have known better*. She swiped a hand over her cheek, surprised to feel moisture there. No. She would not cry. Tears would serve no purpose.

"My lady?" Penny said again, clutching her hands together.

Regina turned and gave her a wobbly smile. "Yes, Penny?"

"Where, exactly, are we going?"

And that was the question, wasn't it? She released her breath in a slow exhale. There was nowhere for them to go.

She thought of the painting in the wall upstairs. She'd have to try to sell it again, and quickly. Whatever she could get for it, that's what they'd have to work with. She doubted it would be enough for ship's passage for all of them, but perhaps she could purchase seats on a stage.

They could travel east, toward Dover, away from London. Book a room at an inn. And then what? They couldn't stay at an inn indefinitely. And Robert . . . they'd have to leave the pig behind. Maybe the farmer would take him back.

"I don't know, Penny," she whispered. "But we can't stay."

She resumed her march up the stairs and went to the corner of her room. She moved Anthony's basket and knelt to remove the wood slat. With her stomach churning, she knew, even before she slid it back, what she would find. An empty black hole stared back at her, and the tears flowed in earnest. *You should have known better.*

"He's returned," Penny said, looking out the window across from the bed. Regina didn't need to ask who "he" was. She stood and went to look. He rode down the lane on a new horse. A horse!

He must be preparing to leave, then. His audacity amazed her, and her capacity for amazement confounded her. Given all the warning signs, she should not have been surprised by anything.

"Penny, please take Anthony and Tilda out."

"Out? Out where?" she asked.

"I don't care, just take them out. Go for a walk. Please. I need to speak with Mr. Marchand."

After Penny left, she looked at herself in the small looking glass on the washstand. She would not let him see that she'd cried. She pinched color into her cheeks, smoothed her hair and straightened her skirts before marching to the top of the stairs.

———

THE FIRST THING ALEX SAW when he entered the cottage was crumpled bits of kissing bough. Dried leaves and twigs sprinkled the floor beneath the torn linen ribbon.

Next, he saw the "Missing Countess" bill from the tailor's shop, crumpled on the dining table. And finally, the missing countess herself. She stood at the top of the stairs, and the heat of her gaze seared him.

"Reggie?" He took a step toward her.

"Don't call me that," she whispered. She descended the stairs, elegant countess evident in every rigid line. Her eyes were red, but dry. He swallowed. He'd never meant to make her cry, but he supposed it had been inevitable. He should have seen it.

"How long?" she asked. When he didn't reply right away, she asked again in a stronger voice. "How long have you known who I am?"

He looked at the crumpled bill on the table and told her. "Since my first trip to Brighton."

"Who have you told? Are you working with Foxwald?"

"What? No! I haven't told anyone, and I'm not working with anyone. I just—" How did he explain that he'd not wanted to entangle himself? And then, that he'd longed to hear the story from her? That he'd waited for her to trust him enough to share her troubles? Given her state right now, she wouldn't believe him. She pressed her lips together and gripped her hands harder. "You need to leave," she said, her eyes snapping.

He opened his mouth, then closed it again, unsure what to say to fix this. There was a feverish light in her eyes, a hint of desperation that made him uneasy. "What do you mean to do next?" he asked.

"What I do is no concern of yours."

He looked out the window at the cold winter's day. "Don't run," he told her. "Don't do anything rash. If you leave, be sure you think things through, for Tilda and Anthony." *Don't do anything rash.* He'd uttered those words before, to Gaston, and look where that had gotten him.

Her eyes hardened even more when he mentioned her children.

"I know I'm not an honorable man. But whatever you think of me, know that I never meant for you or the children to be hurt. Bloody hell, I lov—"

She held up a hand. "Don't. Don't say it."

He pressed his lips together, stemming the flow of words that threatened.

"I'm going out," she said. "Make sure you're gone when I return." He opened his mouth again, but she stopped him. "Just go." Her words were all the more painful for being uttered on a near-silent whisper.

He watched her leave, the door closing softly behind her. His heart pounded in his chest, uncomfortable and suffocating. He'd anticipated he might lose her, but the reality of it was more than he'd imagined. He recalled their kiss in her room from—was it just last night? She'd been tender toward him then, a stark contrast to her manner today. He'd lost her regard, and that pained him more than he would have thought possible.

He went to his room, numb, and gazed at his few belongings. They went into his bag haphazardly; he gave no heed to wrinkles. Tilda's painting lay on the table beside the bed. The one she'd painted of them as a family. He wasn't sure why he wanted to torture himself, but he slipped it into his bag with everything else.

He left the woolen cap he'd found upstairs and took his own battered hat from the peg on the wall. Finally, he cast one last glance at the little window with its lace curtain and the newly painted spot on the ceiling where the roof had leaked.

He would leave as Regina asked, but first, there were a few things he needed to do.

CHAPTER NINETEEN

REGINA RETURNED TO THE COTTAGE with Penny and the children, spent. She couldn't feel anything anymore. She was numb from both the cold and her own thoughts.

She'd been wrong about so many things, but she'd gotten one thing right. Alex was infinitely more dangerous to her peace of mind than the poet had ever been. The poet had bruised her pride, maybe hardened her heart a little. But Alex had ripped her heart from her chest and stomped on it. And not just *her* heart.

She watched their little party as they walked across the cold ground to the cottage's entrance. Penny was silent, her eyes cast down. Even Tilda, who was unaware of what was happening, was subdued. How would she explain Alex's absence to her? His leaving without saying goodbye? She inhaled deeply, shuddering as she held back a sob.

They stepped into the cottage and removed their wraps and cloaks. The air about them seemed stale, less alive somehow, with him gone.

"My lady," Penny whispered.

Regina followed her voice to the parlor, then her gaze to the fireplace. Next to the fireplace, between the hearth and her knitting chair, was a wooden cradle. Much more substantial than Anthony's basket, the cradle rested on two curved rockers. She walked over to it and looked at it more closely.

It was simple, and one side appeared taller than the other. That must have been what he was doing in the stable. She pressed a fist to her mouth and closed her eyes.

Alex had moved Anthony's blankets from his basket to the cradle and nestled them in. On top of the blankets sat a leather pouch and what appeared to be two letters.

No, she thought. No. She didn't want anything from him, certainly not more false words.

Tilda bent to examine the cradle. She ran her small hand along the top and pushed it with one finger. It rocked a little unevenly, but Tilda smiled and looked up at Regina.

"Alex made a bed for baby Anthony," she exclaimed unnecessarily. Her little teeth gleamed in her smile as she gazed at Regina, awaiting her reaction.

When Regina said nothing, Tilda took her hand and asked, "Why are you sad, Mama? Did Alex—did he lead you astray?"

Regina nearly choked at her daughter's astute words. She smiled and rubbed a hand over Tilda's brown curls. She almost said, *Yes. Yes, he did.* But she stopped herself.

As much as she wanted to protect her daughter from future pain, Tilda was too young to feel today's hurt. So she said instead, "No, poppet. He didn't, but he had to leave to . . . to take care of some matters."

Tilda's eyebrows angled down. "When is he coming back?"

"He's not coming back, poppet."

Penny sniffed behind her, and Tilda's eyes narrowed. "But he's s'posed to paint with me," she insisted.

"I know, but—" She didn't get to finish her sentence. Tilda stomped from the parlor and raced up the stairs. Regina looked at Penny helplessly. The other woman gazed back at her, eyes damp. Regina turned to leave, but Penny stopped her.

"Wot about his letters?" she asked, waving a hand toward the cradle.

Regina looked again, then shook her head. She needed to figure out what they were going to do next. "Keep packing, Penny."

ALEX RENTED A ROOM ABOVE The White Stag. He couldn't bear to go far from Regina. From his family. He needed to know that they were all right.

The White Stag wasn't the east side of the Steine—far from it, in fact—but for convenience, it suited. He entered the taproom and moved to the corner table, intent on a pint or three. He placed his back to the wall and watched the clientele absently.

His last conversation with Regina repeated in his mind. Like touching his tongue to a sore tooth, he felt the pain over and over.

Had she found his offering? Had it softened her toward him? Given the flinty stare she'd leveled on him that afternoon, he doubted she was in a softening frame of mind.

What were they doing now? he wondered. How could he assure himself they were well, that she hadn't decided to run to Lord-knew-where? More importantly, what would they eat for supper? It was Christmas Eve, and he'd planned a fine meal that none of them would enjoy.

An idea occurred to him, and he motioned Betsy, the buxom barmaid, to his table. She sauntered over with flattering speed and did her leaning-with-the-cleavage thing.

"I need to send food to a friend," he said.

"Send food?" she asked. "I'm sorry, sir, we're not

the post. But I can get you another pint." She smiled at him broadly.

"No. How can I get food to a cottage on the cliff road?"

Her smile slipped, and she looked at him in confusion. "Sir, we're not running a delivery service."

He looked up and spotted Cosgrove heading to the bar. "Cosgrove!" He motioned the man over.

"Aye, guv?"

"Betsy, here"—he looked at her questioningly to confirm he had her name correct—"Betsy is going to arrange for a leg of mutton and some boiled potatoes. Can you deliver it to the cottage on the cliff road?"

"You want me to deliver a leg of mutton? And potatoes?" Cosgrove asked.

"Yes," Alex nodded decisively. "And a note for the lady that lives there. I'll pay you, of course."

Cosgrove nodded knowingly and winked. "Oh, aye, guv. I'm yer man."

As Cosgrove rattled off with his cart, a basket of mutton and potatoes at his feet, Alex wondered if he was mad. Most men wooed with flowers and poetry, not mutton. Not that he was wooing, he reminded himself. He was just making sure Regina and Tilda and Penny had a proper supper.

And, he thought, it was a good way to stay

informed if she decided to run. He couldn't protect her if he didn't know where she was. He hoped, if she did run, that she'd make use of his letter of introduction to Lady Ashford. She'd be safe—relatively so—in Kent, and he knew Lady Ashford would welcome her without too many questions.

——

THAT EVENING, REGINA STARED AT Alex's cradle in the parlor. She'd removed the blankets and placed them back in Anthony's basket. The cradle sat empty next to the fireplace, save for the letters and the leather pouch.

She'd left them all untouched.

She knew she was being petty. She felt guilty for depriving her son of a night in a real cradle instead of a basket, but she couldn't bring herself to accept Alex's gift. To do so would be to accept his lies, and she wouldn't do that.

But she was growing ever more curious about the leather pouch and the letters. What could he possibly have to say to her?

She rocked the cradle with her foot, watching it wobble a little on uneven runners before settling. Even with his imperfect gift, the man was charming. She pressed her lips together and tucked Anthony into his basket.

Penny and Tilda joined her at the dining table for a lackluster bowl of porridge. Alex had shown her how to get the consistency right, and it was the only thing she could make passably well. But it was still . . . porridge. She wasn't the only one disappointed in the evening's meal.

"We're having porridge, Mama?" Tilda asked, poking her spoon into her bowl. "For Christmas Eve supper?"

"Yes, poppet. I thought we'd try something different. It will be fun."

"Castle Soup would be better." Tilda sighed.

"I know, poppet. Put your spoon down until we say grace, please."

They'd just bowed their heads when a clatter in the lane alerted them to a visitor. Regina's immediate thought was Foxwald. He'd found them. A hot rush of panic flashed through her until Penny said, "It's a cart. The impertinent delivery fella from Brighton."

"Delivery? We haven't ordered anything. Don't answer it, Penny."

"Oh lud, he's seen me," she said. "Wot should I do, my lady?"

Regina sighed. "Very well. See what he wants, then send him on his way."

Penny returned to the table carrying a heavy basket, confusion wrinkling her brow.

"What is it?" Regina asked.

Tilda rose on her knees as Penny lowered the

basket to the dining table.

"I'm not sure my lady, but it smells like . . . yes, it's mutton. And potatoes! And a note." She handed the folded page to Regina.

"No," Regina said. "Send it back."

"Wot? Send it back? But . . ." Penny eyed her bowl of porridge, then the basket of food, her meaning clear.

"Is the letter from Alex, Mama? What did he say?"

Regina eyed them both, and they watched her expectantly. The rattle of the cart sounded in the foreyard, signaling the delivery man's departure. It seemed they were stuck with Alex's mutton, but that didn't mean they had to eat it, she thought peevishly.

She unfolded the note. It contained a rough sketch of Tilda picking a flower and a single line. *Before you say no, remember that Tilda needs to eat.* Drat the man. He'd said the one thing she couldn't argue.

And then she thought he'd probably paid for their meal with the proceeds from *her* painting, and her ire rose all over again. But they ate his offering. Tilda grinned around a mouthful of potatoes, pleased at her good fortune to avoid porridge for Christmas Eve supper.

———

THE NEXT NIGHT'S OFFERING INCLUDED a sketch of Regina stroking Anthony's downy head. His note was brief: *In my experience, the fish pie could use some seasoning, but I'm certain it's better than porridge.*

Was he *spying* on them? How did he know she'd prepared porridge again? Then she acknowledged, to be fair, the assumption wasn't a far stretch. She sighed and forked a bite of fish pie.

The night after that: Tilda in her magic cape. *My apologies. They don't know how to make Castle Soup here.*

This went on for nearly a sennight. Each evening they sat down to bowls of gray porridge, and each evening the delivery man's cart arrived with a basket of pub fare. The man refused to accept a coin from them for his troubles. He assured them that "the guv" had covered his fee.

Alex must be staying in Brighton, she thought. While that should have frustrated her, it gave her comfort. As angry as she was with him, knowing he was close made her feel . . . safe. She was able to breathe, to think rationally about their next step.

He'd assured her he wasn't working with Foxwald, and she had to admit the logic of it made sense. If he had been, they would have seen Foxwald long before now.

Still, they'd been in Brighton too long, and it was only a matter of time until Foxwald did locate them. He had to assume she'd had her baby by now, and he would want to assure his claim on the earldom was sound.

As much as she wanted to remain angry with Alex, she felt herself softening toward him. He was a river to her sandstone resolution. He flowed and she eroded.

On the sixth night, she finally decided to look at what he'd left in Anthony's cradle. She knew she would regret it, but she couldn't help herself. And that about summed it up, she thought. She knew he was bad for her, but she couldn't help herself.

Penny watched as she opened the leather pouch. They both gasped when Regina pulled out a thick stack of banknotes. She dropped them back into the cradle as if they were on fire and narrowed her eyes at the pile.

He'd held up a stagecoach. That was the only explanation for such an obscene amount of money. Then she recalled the letters. She opened the first one and read to herself.

She felt Penny's eyes boring into her, but she ruthlessly ignored her.

Regina,

You'll notice I didn't address this to "My Dearest Regina." For while you are very dear to me, I didn't think you would appreciate the sentiment.

I apologize if, in not telling you about the bill, you

feel I've deceived you. I suppose I did. It was a lie of omission. My only excuse is that I hoped you would trust me enough to tell me your troubles yourself. I was wrong to keep it from you, and I'm sorry. Please know that I never meant to hurt you, or Tilda or Anthony. My only wish is for your happiness. I don't know what drove you from your home or why you feel you must continue running, but I want to be sure you're safe. I've included two things to help you on your journey, should you decide to leave.

First, a letter of introduction to Lady Ashford of Redstone Hall, Kent. She is a fine lady and will be only too happy to welcome you and your family for an extended stay, should you wish to meet her.

Second, the proceeds from the sale of your painting. A man is looking for it—and me, by extension. He's dangerous. Please believe me and know I wouldn't have you hurt by my past deeds, so I sold your painting to put an end to his search. I know you meant to use it to fund your investment plans. I hope the proceeds are adequate.

I'm staying at The White Stag, should you need my assistance. I don't expect you will but know that I'm nearby.

You're not alone,
Alex

Penny continued watching her expectantly. Regina shook her head and wiped her cheek.

He could have signed the letter any number of ways. When he'd left, he'd started to tell her he loved her. She was certain of it. She'd stopped him, not wanting to hear the words; they would only have added to her confusion. But in his letter, he'd written three different words. *You're not alone.* They swirled inside her head, solid and deep and resonant in a way that *I love you* could never be.

Her hand shook as she picked up the second letter. The letter of introduction. It was unsealed, brief.

Dear Lady Ashford,

I trust this finds you well and enjoying autumn at Redstone Hall. Please convey my regards to Lord Ashford and Lady Celeste.

The lady who bears this letter, the Countess of Foxwald, is a dear friend. I've apprised her of your generous and agreeable nature and appealed to her to seek your company when next she travels to Kent. You'll find her and her little family a delight, I'm certain.

Your servant,
Alexandre Marchand

Regina sat back in her chair, the letters dangling from her fingers. Her forehead wrinkled in confusion as Alex's words tumbled in her mind. His letter to her didn't make sense.

He mentioned a man looking for her painting. That could only be Foxwald, so he must be close. But Alex wrote as if he didn't realize Foxwald and the man seeking the painting were one and the same. He spoke as if Foxwald was looking for Alex, not Regina. She rubbed her forehead and stared at the stack of banknotes.

She'd wasted a week. They'd remained at the cottage when they could have been fleeing to Kent and beyond.

Nothing made sense—not Alex's letter, not her feelings for him—but one thing was certain. He'd given her exactly what she needed to secure her freedom. Funds and a safe place to hide until she could leave the country. And the sooner, the better, since it sounded like Foxwald must be nearby.

She recalled Alex's notes and pictures over the last week. His gifts of food. With each one, he'd reminded her that he was there, waiting should she need him.

She thought of his letter and closed her eyes. *You're not alone.* He'd offered himself, and she repaid him by running. It was as much a rejection as any words could be. She pressed the guilt down to a place where she wouldn't be tempted. She couldn't afford sentiment if she was to protect her family.

"Penny," she whispered. "We're going to Kent."

CHAPTER TWENTY

IT HAD BEEN ALMOST A week and doubts peppered Alex. He questioned the wisdom of remaining in Brighton.

If he left, surely Roger would follow, but he couldn't bring himself to leave Regina until he knew she was safe. What if he was mistaken, and his leaving didn't draw Roger away? He couldn't leave Regina here, alone, unprotected. He had hoped she trusted him enough to go to Lady Ashford, but still she remained. He scrubbed a hand over his face. He'd do anything to help her if he only knew how.

He also questioned whether there was an end to this madness. How and when would he know Regina was safe? He'd watched Lafontaine's shop, but no one matching the description of his buyer had approached. How long would this uncertainty hang over them?

And, the most painful doubt of all, he questioned whether there was any hope of a future for them. *If*

Regina was safe, and *if* she could forgive Alex, then what? With no funds, and few prospects, he had no future to offer her.

Unsure how to proceed, he continued sending food and notes and drawings, if only to learn whether she remained. He was running out of options from the pub's limited menu. He'd have to go back to mutton soon, and that seemed anticlimactic, somehow. He was debating whether the proprietor of The White Stag would let him into the kitchen tomorrow to prepare Castle Soup—*cassoulet*, he reminded himself—when Cosgrove slid into the chair opposite his.

"Oi, Nicky," Cosgrove said. Alex narrowed his eyes at the name and Cosgrove winced. "Sorry, guv."

"How are things at the cottage?" Alex asked.

"Yer fancy piece seems well," Cosgrove said, glancing from side to side.

"Cosgrove," Alex said, firming his jaw at the man's disrespect.

"Aye, guv?"

"Don't make me bloody my fist on your nose. This is my last good shirt."

"Right. Well, yer fancy—that is, yer lady bird"— Alex glared at him—"Sorry. It appears she's about to fly."

Alex sat up straight at that. "What makes you say that?"

"The other lady. Miss Penny." Cosgrove ducked his head and smiled.

"And?" Alex motioned with his hand for Cosgrove to continue.

"I think she's sweet on me. She tol' me I've got 'soulful' eyes. Can you imagine? Or mebbe she said 'soulless' now I think on it. I can't rightly recall."

"Cosgrove," Alex growled, closing his eyes and pinching the bridge of his nose.

"Right. Miss Penny said they're packing the rest o' their things and lightin' out for Kent on the morrow."

"Kent? You're certain?" *Finally.*

Cosgrove nodded. "They're 'iring a post-chaise at The Dandy Rooster. Said a farmer's comin' to give 'em a ride in 'is cart. You want me 'n Perkins to follow 'em?"

Alex sipped his ale, thinking. "Yes. Follow them, and make sure they get there safely, but tell Perkins to stay put. He's still watching Lafontaine's?"

"Aye, guv," Cosgrove replied.

Alex stroked his bottom lip. Something still wasn't right. Something about Chesterton was off, but he couldn't put his finger on it. The feeling made him itchy.

He looked up from the table, over Cosgrove's shoulder, and surveyed the taproom. The customers were the same crowd that had filed in each day he'd been staying there. No new faces. If Regina left tomorrow and made it safely to Redstone Hall, perhaps he could relax. He doubted it, but it was a nice thought.

——

THE NEXT DAY, ALEX SECURED a table at The Bull and Fox in line of sight of The Dandy Rooster. He wanted to see them, assure himself they were well and truly on their way to Kent. He'd arrived early and confirmed with the post-chaise driver that he was indeed awaiting passengers for Kent. Now the man idled next to the chaise, picking his teeth with a thin reed.

Cosgrove slid into the seat across from Alex and ordered an ale while they waited. Alex studied the man. He was as crooked as his nose and would steal a grandmother's cane from beneath her hand, but, from what Alex recalled, he had a thief's honor.

There was truth to the saying about honor among thieves—Cosgrove could be trusted among his own. Unlike swindlers... swindlers were different. Cunning and solitary. Thieves traveled in packs and watched out for one another, but swindlers were lone connivers, watching out only for themselves. You could trust a thief, but never a swindler.

"Why are you here, Cosgrove? Why did you leave London?"

Cosgrove wiped his mouth with the back of his

sleeve and belched. "You know 'ow it is, guv." At Alex's raised brow, he continued. "People in London are too suspicious, always watchin' their pockets. 'Ere people are just 'appy to be on 'oliday. The pickin's are much better."

Alex supposed the man had a strange sense of logic. People in the sparkling seaside resort did seem relaxed, more carefree. Less attentive to their pockets.

"Did you ever think to leave the life?" Alex asked, studying his own ale.

"And do wot?" Cosgrove said incredulously. "I ain't got your fancy manners, Nicky."

"But you could do honest work, and not worry about a noose around your neck. Your delivery cart, for example. Surely there's enough work to keep you busy with deliveries."

"Where's the thrill in that?" Cosgrove chuckled and shook his head.

"There are plenty of other thrills to be had, my friend," Alex said. He wouldn't have thought it six months before, but the anticipation of seeing Regina as she boarded the post-chaise was exciting enough for him. His stomach flipped and rolled when he thought of her, then he sobered.

He knew it would likely be his last glimpse of her, and Tilda and Anthony. They'd journey to Redstone Hall, but eventually they'd leave Kent for somewhere else. Would he never see them again?

The backs of his eyes burned, and he stared into his mug. How would he know they were safe? Happy? Would they think of him?

"I'll make sure they get there all right, guv," Cosgrove said.

Alex nodded.

"Oi," Cosgrove said, sitting up. "'Ere they come."

Alex looked to where Cosgrove pointed. A broad farmer's cart pulled in at The Dandy Rooster. Other vehicles passed, blocking his view, and he watched through the gaps in traffic.

Tilda climbed down with Robert on his lead. Her curls bounced beneath a woolen hat, and even from this distance, her nose was red. Mittens covered her hands and a red wool muffler wrapped her neck. He recognized it from Regina's knitting basket and smiled.

Penny followed at a more sedate pace, a bag over her shoulder and a bundle in her arms. Anthony. He couldn't see any of his pink skin from here, he was bundled so tightly. Good, he thought. It was too cold for any of them to be outside for long.

He squinted, waiting, looking for Regina, but he couldn't see her. Then the farmer pulled away, and his cart disappeared down the lane. Where was she?

Alex looked at Cosgrove, who shrugged. Tilda and Penny crossed to the post-chaise, and Robert snuffled the ground at the end of his lead. The driver eyed the pig skeptically before tossing Penny's bag into the chaise.

Alex panicked. He'd never see Tilda or Anthony again once they got inside. He pushed away from the table and raced out of The Bull and Fox.

"Wait!"

Penny and Tilda looked up at his shout, but a tall peddler's cart rattled by, blocking his view again. When it passed, Tilda recognized him, and she beamed. Even around her hat and scarf he recognized her big smile with her little teeth. She bounced on her toes. "Alex!"

He raced across the lane and went to her. He knelt, intent on telling her goodbye, but she threw herself into his arms. Stunned, he rocked back then regained his balance. He knelt on the cobbles with her arms wrapped about his neck. Her curls tickled his nose and he inhaled.

He rose with her in his arms and turned to Penny, who stood with her mouth agape, staring at him. He bent and kissed the top of Anthony's bundled head.

"Where is she?" he demanded on a whisper.

"She sent us ahead to The Dandy Rooster," Penny replied. "Said she had some things to take care of first and she'd follow."

Things? What things? Before he could voice the

question, Penny continued.

"She's at The White Stag."

Alex's eyes widened. She'd gone to The White Stag. A smile started to curve his lips, but he tempered it. Better to know why she was there first. For all he knew, she'd gone to berate him before leaving town. He needed to go. Find her.

"Cosgrove is going to stay with you," he said, motioning to the big man behind him. Penny ducked her head shyly and Cosgrove blushed. Interesting, he thought, but he didn't have time for Cosgrove's budding romance. "We'll get you a warm parlor," he told Penny. "Cosgrove will see you're taken care of."

"Are you coming, too, Alex?" Tilda asked, sniffing. Her nose was runny, and there were tears in her eyes.

"No," he said. "Not yet." But soon, he decided. They were his family. He wasn't letting them go without him. If Regina thought otherwise . . . "I'll bring your Mama," he told Tilda. She hugged him again, hiccupped and dropped a wet kiss on his neck.

He handed Robert's lead to the driver, who looked at him like he'd gone daft. "Sorry, guv," he said, handing the lead back. "I'm no' a pig keeper."

Alex flipped the man a coin. "He's a good pig." *Mostly.* He flipped him an extra coin.

CHAPTER TWENTY-ONE

REGINA WATCHED THE FARMER'S CART roll away with Penny and her children. She'd checked and double checked their wrappings, ensuring they were snug and warm before sending them on to The Dandy Rooster.

Alex's words had been echoing in her mind all morning, a rich refrain that played over and over. *You're not alone.*

As the farmer's cart had trundled toward The Dandy Rooster, she'd seen the sign for The White Stag. She'd asked the farmer to stop before she knew what she was about.

You're not alone.

Had he merely said he loved her, she would have taken his money and the letter and left for Kent without stopping. Another artist had once said he loved her and look how that had turned out. *I love you* was too easy to say.

But *you're not alone* ... Those three words

resonated within her. She'd been alone for so long. Too long.

But more important than that, *he* was alone.

He'd arrived at the cottage alone. He'd lost his brother alone. Even as he sat at supper with them, he'd been alone, separate from Regina and her little family. He was a man without family, without a home.

Until, as weeks went by, he wasn't. Despite her barriers and defenses, he'd become part of their small family. She didn't know when or how it had happened, but their home was his home. And now, she'd cast him out, away from them, when deep down she knew he belonged with them.

She didn't know what forces had brought them together. What mysterious fates had prompted her to pick up *that* painting at Briarly while conspiring to send him to her. Something else beyond their comprehension was at work. Something wonderful, because she knew one thing: She'd once lost her head to a scoundrel masquerading as a poet, but she'd lost her heart to an artist masquerading as a scoundrel. When she thought about it—truly thought about it—he'd never lied to her.

He was an artist.

He was from Paris.

His name was Alexandre Marchand.

She'd seen lies where there were none.

He'd taken her painting and left choices in its place. Whether she agreed with his reasoning or not, he'd done it to protect them. Despite weeks of confusion and resistance, she trusted him. She loved him. And if Foxwald was also looking for him, then Alex was in danger. She needed to warn him. Or better, ask him to accompany them to Kent.

And so, she'd sent Penny ahead with her children, because this was not a conversation that needed an audience.

The inn's sign swung above, faded green lettering surrounding a white deer. The White Stag Inn. She straightened her spine and gripped the edges of her cloak before entering.

The interior was dark, and warm smells of ale and grease from the inn's adjacent taproom greeted her. She waited a moment, allowing her eyes to adjust. How would she find Alex?

Before she could answer that thought, a hand gripped her elbow hard.

"I've found you at last, my dear." Warm breath whispered into her ear. She turned and found Roger Chesterton staring at her with his hard blue eyes. She tugged on her elbow, but he tightened his hold.

"If you're looking for a room, I'm afraid we're full up for the night," a pretty barmaid said as she passed them with a tray.

"My wife and I would like a private parlor if you

please. She's unwell," Chesterton added.

Regina started to speak up, to dispute his words, but he squeezed and whispered in her ear. "I know you don't want to do anything to endanger your brat."

Cold, queasy dread snaked through her and she nodded.

The barmaid, Betsy, showed them to a small parlor. Chesterton—she refused to think of him as Foxwald any longer—urged her inside with a firm hand on her back. Regina stepped away from him as soon as possible and placed the table between them.

Betsy offered to bring ale and luncheon. "Today's special is mutton and potatoes," she told them with a smile. Regina looked up at that.

"I don't suppose you have a cassoulet?" she asked.

Betsy looked at her in surprise. "No, my lady, but I've heard it's very good."

Regina smiled at her and nodded.

"Leave us," Chesterton ordered. "We don't wish to be disturbed." Betsy curtsied and left, throwing a last look at Regina as she closed the door.

"Sit," Chesterton said. Regina remained standing opposite him. "Sit," he barked again. She slowly pulled a chair from the table and sat on the edge of it. He smirked, pleased with her obedience. She fought the urge to stand again.

"I see you're no longer in the family way," he said without preamble.

She nodded, her mind racing, her heart pounding. She wasn't sure what to say, how to respond to what she knew would be his next question. He'd want to know if she'd borne a live child, and if she'd borne a son or daughter. Lies tumbled through her mind: the child didn't live, the child was a girl.

She thought of her son, bundled in his wool blankets in Penny's arms. If she denied his existence now, she could hardly claim the earldom for him later. But if she admitted his existence, they only had a life of running ahead of them. Chesterton would claim guardianship of Anthony and chase them to ground, if only to gain control of the earldom.

"And?" he asked. "Where's the brat?"

The small parlor was overheated; sweat pasted her dress to her back despite the cold outside. She took her time unfastening her cloak and remained silent.

Chesterton slammed his fist on the table, causing her to jump. His eyes shone as they bored into her. "I can tell by your silence that you had a son. I demand to know where he is."

"I'll not return to Briarly," she said. "You can't force me."

"Can't I?" He rubbed his hands together and leaned toward her. "This whole town"—he waved his arms expansively—"is plastered with bills advertising the *Missing Countess*. Everyone is eager to learn your fate. Imagine how sad they'll be to learn you've gone out of your mind with grief over the death of your child. They'll gleefully mourn with you. No one will fault me for sending you off to receive the care you desperately need. So you see, I *can* force you to return. It's Briarly or Bedlam."

"Why are you doing this?" she whispered.

"Why? You ask why? I've waited *years* to be the Earl of Foxwald. Do you think I'll give that up now?" He rubbed his eyes. "I spent a decade in an orphanage in the lowest part of London. Then, when my benevolent cousin, the Earl of Foxwald, found me, he brought me to live alongside his son. His sickly son, who shouldn't have lived past the age of twenty. All I had to do was wait."

"All I had to do was wait," he muttered again, massaging a thick vein on his forehead. "But Anthony wouldn't die. And then *you* came along. And now your brat is here to take what's mine." Spittle sprinkled his cravat. "I'm tired of waiting."

"Let us go," she whispered. "Just let us go. I'll take him to the Continent. To America even. You'll never see us again."

He laughed. "What? So I claim the earldom only

to have your brat turn up when he reaches his majority? No," he bit off.

———

ALEX RACED THROUGH THE BUSY streets and narrow alleys of Brighton to return to the west side and The White Stag. Vendors' carts clogged the thoroughfares and idle aristocrats dawdled on their walks about the promenade, increasing his impatience. He urged his horse around a slow-moving hackney and cut off a fruit seller. Irate shouts chased him, but he was mindful of only one goal. The White Stag and Regina.

When he reached the inn's stable yard, he leapt from the horse and tossed his reins to the hostler. He removed his hat and smoothed a hand over his hair then tugged on his waistcoat. He was about to enter the inn when a familiar voice hailed him from behind.

"Oi, guv," Perkins shouted. The shorter man approached, his scarred brow hidden beneath a greasy hank of hair. An older fellow followed at a more sedate pace. With graying hair, spectacles and a thick white mustache, he was well dressed—not expensively, but he clearly wasn't an acquaintance of Perkins's either.

Perkins reached Alex and paused to catch his breath. "This gent"—he motioned with a thumb to the man behind him—"was askin' 'bout the missing countess." He raised his unscarred brow meaningfully. Alex's eyes shot to the older man, then back to Perkins. "Aye, found 'im at the bookseller's wif one of 'em leaflets," Perkins added.

Alex narrowed his eyes on the newcomer and noticed the paper in his hand. The man held it up, then backed away at the look on Alex's face.

"Who the devil are you?" Alex bit out. "What do you want with the countess?"

The man held up both hands, the paper flapping. "I'm a concerned friend, is all. Do you know where she is?"

"No," Alex lied, slapping his hat back on his head. He crossed his arms.

"Look," the man said. "Your ... associate"—he looked at Perkins skeptically—"seemed concerned for the lady. *I'm* concerned for her. I'm afraid she's in danger from Chesterton. That is, the Earl of Foxwald. I've been searching for her for some months now, to warn her. If you can get a message to her—"

Chesterton. Foxwald.

Alex recalled now why the Foxwald title was familiar to him. It was the title Roger had repeatedly boasted he would have one day. Roger was Foxwald.

What relation was he to Regina? Surely not her husband. Alex had met Roger's wife in Paris. A high-flying piece who was Regina's opposite in every way, but that had been two years ago.

His stomach alternated between hot churning nausea and icy dread at the thought that Roger could be the father of her child. That his family was lost to him before he'd even claimed them. No. He refused to believe it.

She'd named the baby Anthony, after his father. That meant Roger was not the father, merely the new earl. He released a shaky breath.

But one thing became painfully clear. He was an idiot. Roger wasn't tracking Alex through the painting. He was tracking Regina. The pieces hadn't fit until he realized Chesterton and Foxwald were one and the same.

"You'd better tell me what you know," Alex said. "Starting with your name."

The man nodded, and said, "Perhaps we should go inside."

"Here's fine," Alex said. It was awkward, conversing in the inn yard, but Alex was reluctant to take the man any closer to Regina until he knew more.

The man blinked at him but proceeded. "Very well. My name's Underwood. Until recently, I was solicitor to the Earls of Foxwald. When the last earl died, the heir presumptive terminated my services and brought his own solicitor to handle the probate.

A man by the name of Arnold." His lips twisted with disgust.

"I've had dealings with Arnold before," he continued, "and have found him to be an unsavory fellow. I have reason to believe they've defrauded the court with forged papers. The last earl provided handsomely for his widow, but I've learned through my own sources that she's penniless. Regardless of the earl's express provision, she's entitled to a dower share."

Perkins shifted from foot to foot, watching Alex and waiting. Alex stared at Underwood, gauging his expression. He seemed genuinely concerned. And, if what he said was true, Regina's circumstances were about to change.

"Is it true?" Underwood asked. "Did she have Foxwald's child? The previous Foxwald, that is."

Alex pulled on his bottom lip, thinking. "If she did, what control would Chesterton retain?"

"If the current will is invalidated, if the original will were reinstated, none. The previous earl named me as guardian for any posthumous children until the countess remarries. I don't think he trusted his cousin."

Alex wanted to laugh and cry. He wanted to kiss Perkins for bringing Underwood to him. His thoughts must have shown on his face, because Perkins swallowed and took a step back.

"And now, sir," Underwood said. "I think you'd best tell me your name."

Alex smiled broadly. "Alexandre Marchand," he replied, clapping a hand on the man's shoulder. "I think we should go inside."

"Alexandre Marchand? The painter?" Underwood's expression was gratifyingly impressed.

"One and the same," Alex replied. "Come along Perkins."

CHAPTER TWENTY-TWO

ALEX REACHED THE ENTRANCE TO The White Stag in short order while Perkins and Underwood followed at a more sedate pace. He held the door impatiently, waiting for them to catch up. Once inside, he removed his hat and ran a hand over his hair again, ruffling the flat parts.

Betsy approached from the taproom.

"Betsy, have you—" he began.

"Sir!" she exclaimed. "She's here, and I think she's in trouble."

Alex's brow creased. "What are you talking about?"

"Your lady friend. From the cottage on the cliff road. I told her today's special was mutton and potatoes, then she ordered cassoulet."

"Where is she?" Alex asked, not following Betsy's tale.

"She's in the private parlor with her husband, Earl something-or-t'other. I don't think he's a very nice man."

Chesterton. He was here. As long as Anthony was safe at The Dandy Rooster, Roger couldn't do anything, could he?

"Perkins." He motioned the man forward.

"Oi, guv." Perkins stepped up, preening before Betsy.

"I need you to go for the constable."

Perkins' face blanched. "Guv!" he whispered. "I ain't gettin' within fifty yards of that queer cuffin." Betsy smirked behind her hand, and Alex turned to the solicitor.

"Underwood?"

"I'll go," the man said. Alex nodded, and when he turned around, Perkins was gone.

Betsy showed Alex to the private parlor and left. He stood outside the door, listening for sounds from inside. It was quiet. He had the element of surprise, he reminded himself. He straightened, threw open the door and sauntered in.

His eyes shot to Regina. She sat on the opposite side of the room's table, her hands folded primly before her and lines of tension bracketing her mouth. She gave a shaky half smile on seeing him, and her hands relaxed their grip on each other.

Roger spun from where he stood opposite her. "I said no—" he began, then stopped on seeing Alex. "You."

"Yes. Me." Out of the corner of his eye, he saw Regina's expression stiffen.

"I wondered when you'd turn up," Roger said with a twist to his lip. "You're devilish hard to track down, but now that I have you both here, I must admit this is more convenient than I expected."

"Let Lady Foxwald go," Alex bit out.

"You always did have too much conscience, Nicky. What concern is she to you?"

Alex remained silent.

"Ah, I see the way of it," Roger sneered. "Is the brat yours, then?"

Alex placed his hands on his hips and looked at Regina. "Not by blood," he said, ignoring Roger. "But in every way that matters, he's mine." Regina's smile returned, and he knew a brief moment of panic at the trust he saw there.

"You're here now, so you might as well have a seat with the lady." Roger motioned him into the room.

Alex hesitated. He needed to get Regina away to safety, but he didn't think Roger would allow her to leave without a fight. How long would it take Underwood to return with the constable? It seemed time was his only weapon at this point, so he crossed to Regina and took her hands.

"Does she know what you are, Nicky?"

Alex turned back to face Roger, dismayed but

unsurprised to find a flintlock pistol pointed at him. Again. He stepped away from Regina, dropping her hands, anything to draw Roger's attention and the gun from her.

"Does she know what a cheat you are? How you swindled your way through London, and then Paris?"

"I know exactly what kind of man he is," Regina said from behind him.

Roger ignored her and waved the gun at Alex. "I thought you were dead. There was no way you could have survived that cliff. But then your paintings of Le Havre started turning up, and I knew you'd survived somehow. What was your plan?" he asked. "Did you mean to draw me out?"

"Would it surprise you to know I didn't have a plan?" Alex asked. "I didn't remember much from that night. The paintings just . . . happened." He moved further from Regina, positioning himself so Roger's back was to the door.

"Stop moving," Roger commanded.

Alex held his hands up, palms out. "I'm not moving," he said. Their positions were eerily similar to that night in Le Havre: Alex standing before Roger, Roger holding a gun on him, sneering.

"Gaston was a fool," Roger spat.

Alex recalled Gaston's last words. *Can you get my ten thousand back?* He looked at Roger's cold blue eyes, and realization clicked into place. Blood rushed in his ears and all noise ceased.

The trickster had been tricked. Never trust a swindler. Every swindler worth his salt knew the adage. And yet, he'd let his conscience and empathy for Gaston guide him, rather than good sense and self-preservation.

"Was Gaston ever the mark?" he asked Roger. "Or was I always the target?"

Roger smiled, pleased with himself. "Oh, he was the mark initially, but he caught on quickly. He had the brilliant idea to turn a five thousand job into ten. It would have worked, too, until the fool tripped over his own feet. Then I was obliged to get rid of you, before your conscience destroyed us all." He gazed at Alex with speculation. "And I think you would have paid, too, wouldn't you?"

"Why would you assume that? Five or ten thousand, it didn't matter. I've never had that kind of money."

Roger stared at him, and the barrel of the gun dipped and wavered before he straightened it. Then he snarled. "Don't take me for a fool, Nicky. I know about the money."

"What money?" Alex asked. Where was Underwood? This dance with Roger was becoming tiresome.

"Of all the people I could have worked with, you

don't think I chose you out of friendship, do you? Out of some sense of kinship from our time in the orphanage? I make it a point to learn everything about my associates. A few well-placed questions, and I learned what I needed to know, so don't play the impoverished artist for me. I know your parents were wealthy. You were a ripe fruit just waiting to be picked."

Alex's attention snapped to Roger. "What are you talking about? My parents died during the Terror, and their estate was stripped bare. All that was left was a defunct barony."

Roger's face reddened at Alex's words, and he waved the gun at the room at large. "We're done talking."

"What's next, Roger? You can't think you'll get out of this. There are too many witnesses in the inn for you to shoot us here. And we're not going anywhere with you, so your hand is played."

"Stop talking," Roger commanded, rubbing his head with his free hand.

Alex nodded at Regina, urging her toward the door. She didn't move, so he slowly edged away from her.

"If it's money you want, let Lady Foxwald go and we'll talk," Alex said slowly. He cringed at the words. They sounded eerily similar to the false promises he'd made to Gaston, but he knew he had to get Regina out of the room.

"I said be quiet," Roger shouted at full volume. "Let me think."

Alex kept his hands up. If he could get close enough to Roger, he might be able to wrest the gun from him, but Regina could be hurt. A bead of sweat slid down his temple. This was a position he'd never thought to be in again. Even though the actors were the same, this was nothing like the first time.

In Le Havre, he'd gambled with his life because he'd not had much to lose. Now, he had everything to lose, and he found he didn't have the temperament for gambling.

Roger's blue eyes flashed as he darted his gaze from Alex to Regina and back again. His finger trembled on the trigger. If they were to get out of this unscathed, it would have to be soon.

Alex waited until Roger's eyes were on Regina then he took a step closer. Stopped when Roger turned back to him. Inch by inch he moved closer as Roger's attention flitted anxiously between the two of them.

When he was close enough, he looked to Regina and caught her eye. He wanted her to be prepared for what he was about to do. He nodded slightly, encouraging her to ready herself, and her eyes widened. She gave a small shake of her head as Roger's finger tightened on the trigger.

"Go!" Alex shouted, lunging for Roger and the gun. Several things happened at once.

A gunshot cracked the air.

Regina screamed.

And Roger crumpled to his knees on the carpet, the gun falling from his limp fingers.

Alex stood still, waiting for pain that didn't come. His ears rang and his hands shook. He looked down, but everything seemed to be intact.

A man—the constable, he presumed—stood in the open doorway. He looked in surprise from his own hand to where one of The White Stag's dinner knives lodged in the back of Roger's shoulder.

Alex looked up and found Regina. Her hands covered her mouth, and her eyes were wide. She looked as pale as he felt.

CHAPTER TWENTY-THREE

REGINA STARED AT ALEX, NUMB. She thought he'd been shot—she'd heard the deafening crack of a gun—but he stood there, whole, looking back at her. Her mind refused to cooperate.

Things happened in quick succession after that. There was no time to think. No time to make sense of what had occurred.

The constable arranged for a surgeon to attend Chesterton before he was taken to the local gaol. Next, the man took statements from Alex, Regina and Underwood in The White Stag's parlor. He'd heard enough of Roger's gun-wielding confession to support their accounts of the day's events.

Alex sent a message to collect her family from The Dandy Rooster.

Betsy brought plates of mutton and potatoes. Sadly, she reported, the kitchen didn't have any cassoulet.

Regina was pleased to see Mr. Underwood again

and listened in amazement as he explained the terms of Anthony's original will. "He truly did intend to provide for us?" she asked.

Mr. Underwood patted her hand and assured her, "He truly did."

She couldn't quite reconcile herself to her new circumstances. She'd been fearful of the future for so many months. It was hard to accept that Chesterton's threats couldn't hurt them anymore. They didn't need to flee to America or the Continent. She didn't need to hide her family any longer. "Are . . . are you quite sure?" she asked.

"Quite."

"What of Mr. Arnold?" she asked. "And Lady Foxwald? The other Lady Foxwald, that is."

"They'll both be questioned regarding their role in Foxwald's deception. If they can be found, that is. No one's seen Arnold for several weeks, I'm afraid. But regardless, I think it's safe to say that Chesterton will have legal issues for some time."

Mr. Cosgrove arrived then with Penny and the children. Regina ran to them and scooped Anthony into her arms then she pressed Tilda to her in a smothering hug.

"Mama, are we not going to Kent?" Tilda asked when Regina released her.

"No, poppet. We're going home." It struck her then. Briarly might be their official home once baby

Anthony's title and inheritance were sorted. But their drab little cottage was the home she'd thought of when she'd spoken to Tilda. It still leaked, and it was tiny, but it was where she'd felt part of a family. She looked up to where Alex stood on the other side of the parlor. Alone and separate.

"Mr. Cosgrove," she said. "Can you see Penny and the children home?"

He grinned broadly and twisted his cap in his hands. "Yes, mum. My lady, that is."

She made sure Anthony's wrappings were secure and tucked in the ends of Tilda's muffler. When they'd gone, when she and Alex were alone in the parlor, she turned to him. She smiled and opened her mouth to say something but surprised them both with a sob. She put a hand to her mouth to press it back, and he rushed to her side.

"Reggie?"

"I'm sorry!" She waved a hand at him and tried to rein in her emotions. *No tears*, she told herself, but they'd started, and she couldn't make them stop.

"Reggie, love," he whispered, then gathered her into his arms. She went willingly and cried. Hacking sobs that shook them both. When she pulled back, his eyes were red as he rubbed tears from her cheeks with his thumbs.

"I thought he shot you," she whispered on a hiccup. She patted his chest with both hands, assuring herself he was still there, solid and warm.

He tightened his arms, hugging her tight, then he kissed her firmly. When he raised his head, she opened her eyes and waited for the room to right itself.

"I've been so scared," she confessed on a whisper. "For months, I didn't know who to trust. I wish I'd told you about Foxwald, but I couldn't take the chance."

"Hush," he said. "It's over now."

"I'm not finished," she said, and he stopped, waiting for her to continue. "When you arrived at the cottage, we made you fall off your horse, and we dragged you through the mud. Penny dropped you on your head, and we put you in a filthy room and fed you horrible food and—"

"Reggie. It's all right."

She looked at him, her smile wobbly. "You came to us, and you were everything we needed. You fixed our roof and our pig pen, you cooked for us, but most importantly, you were there for us. I don't know how you and Foxwald know each other, but it doesn't matter. I'm so sorry I didn't trust you enough."

"It's a long story," he said. "One I hope you'll let me tell you some time. But I meant what I told him."

She raised her eyebrows. Wondering at his meaning, hoping.

"Anthony, Tilda, you . . . you're my family. I mean to make you my wife, if you'll let me convince you, if you'll let me try."

She smiled at his words. They reminded her of when he'd asked to stay and cook for them. *Let me try.*

"You may try," she said, smiling.

———

WOOING WAS EXPENSIVE WORK. WHO knew hothouse flowers were so precious in January? But Alex couldn't complain, so he didn't.

Regina and the children had settled back into the snug cottage on the cliff road to await Mr. Underwood's handling of the legalities. When all was complete, Regina would return to Briarly and claim Anthony's birthright. Alex knew it was best, but he suspected Regina—and he—would both miss the little cottage with its leaky roof and persistent vines.

Alex remained at The White Stag. He was determined to woo her properly, so he took flowers and walked with her and the children when the sun shone. The remaining kissing bough had dried and crumbled, and Regina removed it. That didn't stop him from trying to steal a kiss, though, whenever he thought he could get away with it. He continued to send them food, because truly, he couldn't allow them to starve. And the fact that Regina often invited him to dine with them didn't hurt either.

But yes, wooing was expensive.

He stood across from Lafontaine's shop with two rolled canvases. His muse had returned at last. He allowed a moment of relief to relax his shoulders before pushing it aside. It wouldn't do to become too complacent. He knew all too well that an artist's muse was capricious and could withdraw her favors at any time.

He hesitated before entering the shop, unsure how he would be received. He didn't know if Roger had carried through on his extravagant offer, or if Lafontaine would feel he'd been cheated. Swindled. The thought put a bitter taste in Alex's mouth. Best to get it over with. He squared his shoulders and pushed the door open.

The little bell rang. The spaniel with her pink ribbon wasn't there to greet him. Her wool blanket was gone, leaving an empty spot of wood between the door and the first oak cabinet. His stomach turned. Where had she gone? Had Roger cheated the man, and then his dog died? Fate could be cruel indeed.

"Where's your dog?" he asked when Lafontaine finished with his customer.

"Monsieur!" The man smiled broadly and waved a lace cuff for Alex to follow him. Alex did, his boots thumping softly on the thick carpets. Lafontaine pulled a curtain aside at the back of the shop. The little spaniel lay on her blanket, nursing a litter of three . . . four . . . six pups. Alex grinned his relief as the proud mother gazed up at him.

"Congratulations," he said, clapping Lafontaine on the shoulder.

"Do you need a good hunting dog?" Lafontaine asked. "They'll be ready to train in a couple of months."

Alex shook his head. "I don't suppose they're good for herding pigs, are they?"

Lafontaine scratched his head. "Pigs?"

"Never mind," Alex said. They returned to Lafontaine's table, and he asked the question that was clouding his thoughts. "Did your buyer return?"

"Oh, my, yes," Lafontaine said. "Although he tried to change the price, but I held firm. I'm not sure what he sees in that particular painting. It's clearly not in the artist's typical style."

Alex exhaled slowly. He'd been prepared to return the money to Lafontaine. He wasn't sure how he would have accomplished that, though, since he'd given the funds to Regina. It was a relief to know he wouldn't need to.

Lafontaine motioned to the rolled canvases Alex carried and rubbed his hands together. "You've brought more Marchands?"

Alex nodded and unrolled the first one. He stepped back, crossed his arms and stroked his bottom lip while Lafontaine leaned over the canvas with his loupe.

"Yes, yes," Lafontaine murmured, head bent. "This is much more like it. The artist has a unique style that's evident here in the light and shadow. This is a fine piece. What else have you?"

Alex showed him the remaining canvas. Lafontaine made a reasonable offer for both, and Alex readily agreed. While he was pleased to have wooing funds, he was even more pleased to think his painting might be able to support a small family. They couldn't live on Anthony's inheritance after all. He glanced at his boots, still worn and scuffed, and his hat, still sadly crushed. He'd gladly forgo boots and hats if it meant having Regina.

Today was the day. He would ride to the cottage and ask her to marry him. He'd already spied a wedding band that he wished to purchase, although he wouldn't curse his chances by anticipating her response. The ring wasn't much, but perhaps in time he could buy her something fancier. Something suited for a queen.

In a few short hours, he hoped to be a happy man indeed. That is, if she agreed. If she said no, which he acknowledged was a possibility, he'd simply have to keep trying. There was no other option.

He placed the sad hat on his head and prepared to leave. As he reached the door, Lafontaine stopped him. "Sir, might I have your name and direction?"

Alex pushed the door open and paused beneath the tinkling bell. "I'm staying at The White Stag," he said. "And the name's Marchand." He grinned at Lafontaine's gaping mouth, then exited into the sunshine.

———

ALEX RETURNED TO THE WHITE Stag and was surprised to meet Mr. Underwood exiting the inn. Another gentleman walked alongside him, and both men carried leather cases.

Dressed in a brown coat and dark brown pants, the newcomer resembled a wren. A beak-like nose and small dark eyes completed the image.

"Mr. Marchand," Underwood greeted him. "You're just the gentleman I was seeking." He introduced the man with him as Mr. Jasper Smythe and begged a moment of Alex's time.

"What's this about?" Alex asked once they were seated before the small fireplace in the inn's private parlor. "Do you have news for Lady Foxwald?"

"Yes, in fact, I do. The court has agreed that the papers Arnold filed were forgeries. They're allowing the earl's previous will to stand. I've just come from sharing the happy news with the lady herself, but that's not why I'm here," he said.

Alex's eyebrows lifted, and he waited for the solicitor to continue.

Underwood looked at Smythe then pulled a stack of papers from his leather case. He adjusted his spectacles, then peered over the tops of the lenses at Alex. Alex resisted the urge to shift in his seat.

"Chesterton made some interesting comments when he . . . well, during The Event."

Alex snorted. The Event. That was an understatement. Alex remained silent, waiting for Underwood to get to the point. He had wooing to do. A proposal to make. A troth to plight.

"One thing in particular caught my attention, and I made a few inquiries." Alex uncrossed his legs and sat up straighter at that. Was Underwood about to charge him with a crime? Who did he say the Smythe fellow was again?

"Your parents," Underwood began.

Alex narrowed his eyes. "What of them?" he asked.

Underwood gave a half smile and consulted the papers before him. "I understand they perished during the terrible events of '93."

Alex nodded, waiting.

"And you left France with your grandfather, correct?"

Alex shifted and crossed his arms. "Yes, my mother's father, Mr. William Warner. And my brother, Gabriel," he said.

"Just so," Underwood nodded then smiled at Mr. Smythe.

Smythe spoke for the first time. "Mr. Marchand, I'm pleased to inform you that you're a wealthy man."

Alex uncrossed his arms and leaned forward. "I think you'd better explain."

Smythe pulled papers from his own case. "When your parents entrusted your grandfather with your safety, they also entrusted him with funds, which he invested. When he passed, my firm was named the trustee until you and your brother came of age. Through an unfortunate series of events"—he inhaled deeply—"my predecessors ... Well, I'm ashamed to say, they forgot about the funds."

"Forgot?" Alex asked, his brows lifting. His mind couldn't quite comprehend what he was hearing, so he asked the only question that made sense. "How does that happen?" How, indeed, did one *forget* money?

Smythe smiled apologetically. "My firm is a very large one, with very large accounts. I'm afraid your grandfather's account was simply lost in the paperwork until Mr. Underwood here came to me with his questions. A clerk in my firm recalled a man making inquiries a few years back—we assume that was either Chesterton or his man. But the clerk—he didn't realize the funds had been overlooked."

Alex leaned back and rubbed his bottom lip. "Wealthy, you say?"

Smythe nodded.

"How wealthy?"

Smythe dipped his beak and gazed at Alex. "Your grandfather was very astute. Either that, or he was a fortune teller." He chuckled at his own joke, his small dark eyes nearly disappearing in his face. When Alex remained silent, staring at him, he cleared his throat and continued. "He invested heavily in firms that were well positioned when the war began. The corpus has grown substantially." He handed a page from his stack to Alex. "Here's your current balance."

Alex took the page and looked at the number. It was long. Stunningly, embarrassingly long.

He knew he should be elated. He could buy a thousand queenly gems for Regina. New boots for every day of the week. But he frowned, thinking of the coins in his pocket from Lafontaine. They were warm and heavy. Satisfying. The page before him was cool and crisp. And unearned. Undeserved, given his life and past sins.

"There's one more thing," Smythe said, feeling in his pocket. He pulled out a small velvet pouch and untied the drawstring. "This has been in our vault as well." He emptied the pouch and handed the contents to Alex.

Alex stared at the small ring. He recalled it on his mother's hand as she stroked his hair, or soothed Gabriel's bruised knee. It was simple, a single pearl surrounded by small diamonds. It glowed and sparkled in his palm, and he smiled as he closed his fingers around it.

"Thank you," he whispered. He stood and placed the ring back in its velvet pouch, placed the pouch in his pocket. "If you gentlemen will excuse me, I have somewhere to be."

They looked at him in surprise. "What about the funds? How would you like me to proceed?" Smythe asked.

Burn them. Give them away. Forget about them. He wanted to say all of those things, but his new wealth was the result of his parents' final actions. He couldn't dismiss it. And although he didn't want it, hadn't earned it, could it be used to advantage for someone else? He'd have to think on it.

He couldn't make a decision now as he had more pressing matters to attend to. He looked at the clock on the mantle. It was growing late, and he had a basket of food to deliver.

"Leave your direction with the innkeeper. I'll be in touch," he said.

CHAPTER TWENTY-FOUR

THE SUN WAS LOW IN the sky by the time Alex reached the copse at the end of the lane. He shifted the basket in front of him and turned his horse's head toward the cottage.

Regina and Tilda came out to greet him, and Regina took the basket from him as he dismounted.

"This smells wonderful," she exclaimed. "Although you truly don't need to continue to bring us food."

He looked at her and raised his brows meaningfully before exchanging the bundle of roses he carried for the basket.

"Thank you," she said, inhaling the flowers' warm fragrance. He suspected she appreciated the food more than the flowers, but she deserved both, and more.

"What is it?" Tilda asked, lifting the lid of the basket and sniffing.

"Coq au vin," he said. "Or an approximation

thereof." They stepped into the cottage, and the tension he'd been feeling since learning of his new wealth left his shoulders.

"Coq au vin?" Regina asked. "Since when does The White Stag offer that on their menu?"

"They don't," he said simply.

Penny joined them with Anthony, and he leaned down to kiss his downy head. It was no longer misshapen, which he admitted was a relief. He'd been worried for a bit, but Anthony was growing into quite a handsome lad.

Tilda set five places around the small table, her chubby fingers carefully arranging forks next to each plate. He was pleased the ladies no longer asked him to join them. It was assumed that he would. But five?

"Who else is joining us?" he asked.

"Mr. Cosgrove," Regina whispered, motioning to Penny as she settled Anthony in his cradle.

Cosgrove? He frowned. The man had no business interrupting his proposal supper. He sighed as a cart clattered down the lane to stop in the foreyard. A knock sounded on the door, and Penny rushed to answer, smoothing her hair. Alex shook his head. Cosgrove. There was no accounting for taste.

"I saw Mr. Underwood," he told Regina.

"Yes," she said with a smile. "Did he tell you? Anthony's previous will, the real one, will stand. I can't tell you what a relief that is."

"He did mention it," Alex said. He didn't tell her Underwood's other news. There was time enough to explain that, once he figured out how he felt about it.

He looked up at Cosgrove's entrance.

"Oi, guv," Cosgrove said, doffing his cap. "Didn't know ye'd be 'ere." He spied the basket on the table. "I'd 'ave been 'appy to bring yer basket."

Alex narrowed his eyes on the man as they moved to take their seats at the table. Tilda folded her little hands and bowed her head, waiting.

Cosgrove looked at her in alarm, then at Alex, who smirked. Once Cosgrove bowed his own head—eyes still open—Alex began.

"Dear Lord, thank you for the gifts you've provided in this food, and in the company we share. Forgive our sins and grant us the strength that we may seek and accept redemption. And please keep Robert out of the cabbages. Amen."

Regina raised her head and smiled at him with approval. He lifted the lid from the pot and steam curled from it in savory tendrils.

"Oi, I don't recall anythin' so fancy from The White Stag," Cosgrove said to the room at large.

Alex scowled at him, then began spooning chicken, mushrooms and little onions onto their plates. The innkeeper at The White Stag had been happy to allow him in the kitchen for an extra fee.

The man was an extortionist.

He passed servings to the ladies, then placed a scanty bit onto Cosgrove's plate. He looked up and caught Regina's frown then added a tiny bit more. She continued staring at him, frowning, until he added another onion. He grudgingly passed the plate to the other man and looked in the pot. One tiny drumstick and one mushroom. He placed them on his own plate side by side. Pitiful.

Regina pressed her lips together, hiding a smile. She avoided his gaze as she leaned over to cut Tilda's portion.

"Oi, this is delicious," Cosgrove said around a mouthful of tender chicken.

Alex scowled, then relaxed as he surveyed their crowded table. Regina sat straight and poised. Polished and countess-like. Unconcerned that she shared her meal with a nursemaid and a petty thief. With a swindler—former swindler, he reminded himself. Granted, he was a wealthy former swindler, but still . . .

How had her poet missed seeing her beautiful heart? He didn't care. What the poet had lost was his gain. He hoped. He hoped she returned his regard and was willing to take a chance on him. His stomach fluttered with nerves. Who was he kidding? He couldn't have eaten even if Cosgrove hadn't taken all the food.

When they'd finished supper, when all stomachs were full—save one—Alex pushed back from the table.

"Cosgrove, why don't you assist Miss Penny in the scullery," he suggested. "You can return the pot to The White Stag when you leave," he added meaningfully.

Apparently, *Miss Penny* was all the encouragement Cosgrove needed. He nodded eagerly and said, "O' course," before trailing after her with the pot.

Tilda followed them to wash up, and Alex turned to Regina. He thought of the words he'd rehearsed, but he couldn't ask her now. Not with Cosgrove thumping about in the kitchen.

"Thank you for the meal," she said. "It was lovely, although I'm sorry you didn't get to enjoy much of it. It was nice of you to share with Mr. Cosgrove." She smiled, and the last of his irritation evaporated.

"I'm glad you liked it. Will you walk with me?" he asked. "When Penny returns to watch the children?"

She nodded, biting her bottom lip.

———

ALEX WAS BEHAVING ODDLY. HIS irritation with Cosgrove was normal, in character for him. She knew how much he enjoyed his food, and to give it all to Cosgrove . . . She pinched her lips to keep from laughing at the look that had crossed his face when he'd stared down at his own sparse plate.

But he seemed nervous tonight. Distracted. Regina placed a hand on his arm and watched him as they left the cottage. The moon reflected on the chalk stones in the lane and the hint of golden whiskers on his cheeks. He rolled his shoulders, settled a hand over hers, and curved his lips in a close-mouthed smile.

They walked to the end of the lane, then across the cliff road to the precipice above the sea. The water shimmered below, a silver ribbon splitting it where the moon cast her glow. She shivered in the cold and pulled her cloak more tightly around her.

"You're cold," he said. He set to removing his own coat. She tried to stop him, but he ignored her pleas. He settled the heavy wool about her shoulders and his clean citrusy warmth flowed into her.

"Now you'll be cold," she protested.

"It's a small price for your company," he said. She stiffened at his words, then forced herself to relax. Her natural inclination was to reject his charming words, his flattery, but she knew enough of Alex now to know he meant the words sincerely. She wasn't surprised when he told her so.

"Reggie, you must believe me when I tell you

how much I value your company. It's worth a little chill to have you by my side. I'm not trying to charm or deceive you."

She nodded, silent. How had he come to be so dear to her in such a short time? He ran a hand over his jaw and stared at her. His eyes dropped to her lips, then returned to her eyes, and she felt fluttery inside. Finally, he spoke.

"I had words prepared, but they seem inadequate. Reggie, love, I'm not a good man, but I'm trying. I've done things of which I'm not proud. I want to change that. You make me want to change that."

She looked into his eyes and saw truth there, but she needed to make one thing clear. "I can't be your redemption," she whispered.

"No," he agreed. "None of us on this earth are ever truly redeemed. But you make me feel *redeemable*. And that makes all the difference."

She sucked in a breath, and he took her hands in his. "When I arrived at your little cottage, I was broken, but you allowed me to stay. You took a chance on me and gave me time to put myself back together."

"Silly man," she said with a chuckle. "We were hungry, and you fed us."

He smiled. "I'm asking you to take another, bigger chance."

She knew what he was asking, and tears pooled in her eyes.

"Reggie, love, will you take a chance and become my wife? Let me love you, and Tilda and Anthony? Let us be a family?"

He waited, brows raised, for her reply.

"You weren't the only one broken, Alex," she said. "I haven't cried since the poet left. And you make me cry."

He looked at her in confusion. "And that's good?"

"Yes, that's very good. You make me feel again. You helped me see that there are people worth trusting. People worth loving, enough to risk crying."

"So, are you saying . . . yes? Will you marry me?"

"Yes." She placed a hand on his cheek. "It would be my honor."

He stepped closer and pressed his perfect lips to hers. She settled into the kiss, relishing the warm softness of his mouth on hers and the light stubble beneath her hand. His arms came up to circle her, holding her tight as he deepened the kiss.

When he pulled back, he pressed his lips together and gazed at her with a hesitant look.

"I should probably tell you, I'm absurdly wealthy. I could use your investment advice, although I'm not sure that I'll keep the funds."

EPILOGUE

TWO MONTHS LATER

REGINA ENTERED ALEX'S STUDIO AND stopped. He lay on the velvet sofa, eyes closed, Tilda sprawled atop him. Sunlight filtered through the floor-to-ceiling windows to highlight his face. It sparked off his hair, and although it was only mid-morning, hinted at evening whiskers to come. He was no saint, she thought, blushing. But lying there in repose, she could almost believe it.

She paused to give silent thanks to the poet. She finally had the home and family he'd promised. Although it had taken longer than expected, every bit of it was worth her reputation. She'd cursed Albert Durand for years, but he'd set in motion a series of events that brought her first Tilda, then baby Anthony, and now Alex.

Before Alex married her, he'd insisted on sharing

his tale of Le Havre. She knew he continued to blame himself for his role in Gaston's death—he was convinced if he hadn't agreed to Roger's scheme in the first place, Gaston would still be alive. She'd argued that Gaston's own greed had led to his presence atop the cliffs that night, but only Alex could decide to forgive himself.

He was well on his way to making amends, she thought. He'd begun meeting with a physician acquaintance from Kent—Dr. Julian Grey—and together they were making plans for an orphanage. One that would be well staffed by a physician and compassionate administrators.

Alex had purchased an old manor house in London, and they'd soon travel there to set it to rights. They wouldn't be able to save every child, but if they could help one, she thought that would go a long way to easing Alex's guilt over Gabriel. It was also a wondrous use of his parents' legacy.

Anthony stirred in her arms, and she shifted, adjusting the soft linen of his christening gown. Or *dress*, as Alex called it. She smiled. Alex's lip usually had a little curl to it when he referred to the long, lacy gown that Anthony would wear for his baptism.

The ring on her hand caught the sunlight and sent tiny sparkles across the room. The band was simple but precious, a small pearl edged with diamonds. When their wedding vows had been exchanged, he'd lifted her hand and slid the ring onto her finger. It had been a perfect fit.

"This was my mother's," he'd whispered, and tears had filled her eyes for the woman who would never see the man her son had become.

They still had time before they needed to leave for the stone parish church.

Alex's paints were carefully arranged on a table, his brushes clean and straightened on a linen cloth. Tilda's painting of them as a family hung in a place of honor above the table, but it was Alex's easel she sought. He'd turned it toward the corner, out of view. Uncovered for once. He'd been so secretive about it. Perhaps . . . perhaps she could take a quick peek. Just a tiny one.

She looked at the sofa where they still slept, Tilda's small hand flexing and curling on Alex's chest. Regina took a step on her toes, then another, and winced when the floorboard creaked. Neither Alex nor Tilda stirred, so she crept closer.

When she rounded the easel, she wasn't sure what to expect, but . . . Robert? He'd spent hours closeted in his studio to paint a portrait of . . . the pig?

———

ALEX OPENED ONE EYE AND watched Reggie creep across his studio. Her dark hair caught the sunlight and held it, warm and shimmering. Anthony stirred in her arms, his dress trailing below his little feet. *Gown*, he reminded himself with a grimace.

The lad would need a steady male influence, that much was certain. He'd caught Tilda trying to dress him like one of her dolls yesterday.

He angled his head to look at her sprawled atop him. She was made of knees and elbows. Lots of pointy bits. He gently shifted her to the sofa and rose on quiet feet to join Regina at his easel.

"It's a good likeness, don't you think?" he asked.

She jumped and he chuckled. "I suppose so," she said and leaned into him. He wrapped his arms around her and Anthony, relishing the faint lavender scent of her hair. "This—*this* is what you've been working on so secretively?" she asked.

He thought to tease her, but he couldn't wait any longer. He smiled into her hair. "No. This is what Tilda and I painted this morning. *This* is what I've been working on *so secretively*, as you put it." He pulled the portrait of Robert down to reveal the canvas behind it and waited.

He felt her inhale sharply then go still. The only sound was Tilda's rustling as she turned on the sofa. Alex looked at the canvas, trying to see the portrait through Regina's eyes.

The three of them—Regina, Tilda and Anthony—stood in a sunlit room. Tilda smiled at Anthony in his lacy dress—*gown*—and Reggie gazed at them both. His madonna.

She covered her mouth with her hand. "It's stunning," she whispered behind her fingers. "But . . ."

"But?"

"But you're not in it," she said.

"Oh, but I am," he assured her. He squeezed her and Anthony closer to him. "I'm in every brush stroke. I'm in Tilda's curl there, and every blessed ruffle on Anthony's . . . gown." He bent and nuzzled her neck. "I'm in the curve of your cheek and the sunlight on your face."

She sniffed, and he nuzzled harder. "Is there time?" he asked.

"Time for what?"

"Time to lead you astray," he whispered.

She laughed softly and stopped sniffing, as he'd intended. She turned in his arms and laid a palm on his cheek. "No," she said with apology in her voice. "Penny said Mr. Cosgrove is ready with the carriage. But the christening is what I came to talk to you about. I'd like to make a change."

"A change?" She'd decided they'd both stand with Anthony at the front of the church. As Anthony's stepfather and guardian, it made sense for Alex to join Regina. Had she changed her mind?

She pressed her thumb on his brow and smoothed the wrinkle there.

"Anthony's name," she whispered.

He pulled back in surprise. "We've been calling him Anthony for months. You want to change it?"

"Not the Anthony part." She paused and chewed her lip. "You know I planned to name him Anthony Edward after his father." Alex nodded and she continued. "I'd like to name him Anthony . . . Gabriel instead. With your permission." She waited.

He closed his eyes. He had a lot to make up for. Atonement. Crimes for which he owed penance. It would take a lifetime. But she saw the best in him. Wanted the best *for* him. He didn't deserve her, or them, but he nodded and pressed his forehead to hers. "Yes."

THE END

THANK YOU!

If you enjoyed Alex and Regina's story, be sure to subscribe at klynsmithauthor.com/tar and receive an **exclusive extended epilogue** as a thank you!

Return to the cottage where Alex and Regina fell in love and witness little Anthony's first steps. This couple has a special place in my heart, and I simply couldn't let them go without one more visit. I fell in love with their story—and their new family—and I hope this additional glimpse warms your heart as much as it did mine.

Alexandre Marchand first appeared as a potential love interest for Lady Celeste St. James in *The Astronomer's Obsession,* and he reappears with Julian Grey in *The Physician's Dilemma.* Read on for an excerpt.

BOOKS BY K. LYN SMITH

Something Wonderful
The Astronomer's Obsession
The Artist's Redemption
The Physician's Dilemma

Hearts of Cornwall
Discovering Wynne
Jilting Jory
Matching Miss Moon
Driving Miss Darling
Kissing Kate
Saving Miss Swan
Charming the Captain
Engaging Miss Enderby*
Regarding Rebecca

Love's Journey
Star of Wonder
Light of a Nile Moon
Stars of Twilight Fair
Beneath a Brighton Sun

* Part of the Hearts in Bloom Regency Anthology.
Visit klynsmithauthor.com for the most
up-to-date list of titles.

THE *Physician's* DILEMMA

"Prescription for a Wonderful Book Hangover... Such a beautifully written book that I really can't see myself reading anything else for a while..."

- 5-star reader review

A physician seeking love

Julian Grey has led a charmed life. His every endeavor has been easily achieved, and he doesn't want for much. Freedom from the females in his family. A man-sized scone. A bride so he might join his friends in wedded bliss. He's even found the perfect lady to court. But first, he needs to hire a surgeon for Heloise Manor, London's newest foundling home. If only it weren't for the annoying Miss Grace, whose brash manner and freakishly accurate memory irritate him like a pebble in his boot.

A surgeon seeking employment

Charlotte Grace has watched her sisters abandon their

own desires and step off the matrimonial cliff. That life is not for her, thank you very much. She wants nothing more than to be a surgeon, but she'll be content making rounds with her father and helping him treat his patients. That is, until he retires.

Set adrift, Charlie goes to London to further her studies and seek like-minded doctors for intelligent discourse. Instead, she encounters small minds and Dr. Julian Grey, a physician who studied with her father years ago. Life is too easy for Dr. Grey—even London's stubborn traffic parts for him. With little effort he's gained the entrée into the medical world that she desperately longs for. But she's willing to overlook his failings if he'll hire her on as surgeon at Heloise Manor.

Will he realize that the best things in life don't come easy? Will she learn that shared dreams are the best dreams before it's too late?

EXCERPT FROM
THE PHYSICIAN'S DILEMMA

CHARLIE SUFFERED THROUGH THREE HOURS—three hours!—with Emily's modiste. Despite her assurances that new dresses were unnecessary, Emily had insisted.

"Let me do this for you, sister," she'd pleaded. "It gives me great joy."

As it seemed there was little enough of that in Emily's life, Charlie had relented.

Emily's taste ran toward stylish gowns of little substance, unlike Charlie's own serviceable attire. Indeed, few of the evening dresses Emily selected for her had a sufficient amount of coverage in the bodice, so Charlie had insisted on a fichu if Emily expected her to wear them in public.

"Oh, stuff, Charlie! This is the style," she'd told her. "I assure you, you'll be no less covered than any other young lady."

"That may be, sister, but I'd like a fichu, please." Why a lady would purchase a gown that necessitated the expense of yet another garment to fill in the gaps made little sense to her, but she'd never been one for fashion like her sisters.

Emily had grumbled but eventually agreed, and the modiste added three fichus to their order.

So it was that they returned to Russell Square with no less than twelve boxes containing ready-made dresses, stockings, gloves, bonnets, shawls, spencers, and fichus. There were more custom pieces on the way, and Charlie's head spun at the extravagance. Colonel Watson must be quite flush indeed, and a very indulgent husband to allow his wife such latitude with his purse.

"What time do we ride in the park?" she asked Emily, checking the clock on the mantle.

"I should think five o'clock will be perfect. Everyone will be there then."

"Then I should like to go to . . . the lending library," Charlie said. By way of Barts, although she didn't mention that she intended to visit the hospital. If she left now, she'd arrive in plenty of time for today's lecture.

"Fine, if you must. Would you like company?"

"Oh, no, there's no need. I know the lending library is not to your taste, and I'm sure you must have other things you'd like to do."

"Very well, but be sure to take one of the maids. Agnes, perhaps. And you might as well look lovely while you're there. Wear the blue dress, Charlie. It looks so nice on you."

Charlie hadn't thought to change her gown—she was only going to the hospital, after all—but she gave in to please her sister.

The dress *was* quite pretty, she admitted. In a printed blue muslin a shade darker than her eyes, it provided a soft, tempering effect to her red hair. She pulled on an ivory spencer and grabbed a chipped straw bonnet before hurrying down the stairs.

Agnes trailed her on the short walk to Barts, never more than five steps behind, never less. For one unaccustomed to having a servant shadowing her movements, the maid's presence felt awkward.

After a few wrong turns, she finally reached the hospital and surveyed the expansive square complex. She'd long made a habit of arriving early to every appointment, so she had ample time to fully appreciate the sight before her.

She faced a broad wing on the north side of the square, with an arched entry above which Henry VIII gazed down on all who entered the hospital. Additional wings on the east, west and south contained the wards and completed the square around a spacious central green.

She'd read the history of St. Bartholomew's Hospital in her father's library and was curious to see the painted murals on the north wing's grand staircase, but she was even more eager to find the lecture hall.

"Favored Techniques in Wound Dressing" the advert in the morning's *Times* had said. She crossed the green and advanced toward the north wing, Agnes trailing a precise five steps behind her.

——

As it turned out, no one was inclined to provide her with direction to the lecture hall. Each person she stopped shrugged and hurried on their way, giving her and her maid skeptical glances.

She blew a stray curl from her forehead and began methodically checking each corridor of each wing. At this rate, the lecture would be long over before she found the hall, no matter that she'd arrived well in advance of the advertised time.

Finally, as she passed the pathology department, she spied a group of young men gathered before a set of double doors. They looked as though they were waiting . . . for a lecture to begin.

She hurried forward and peered through the throng into the room beyond. It was arranged as a small auditorium, with raised semicircular seating around a central lecture stage. She'd found it!

"Pardon me," she said to the gentleman nearest her. "May I pass, please?"

Two men turned and looked at her. "Are you lost, miss?" the first one asked.

"This is the lecture on wound dressing, is it not?"

They looked at each other hesitantly, then the others around them, before nodding.

"Then no, I'm not lost. If you'll let me through, please."

An older silver-haired gentleman stepped forward, blocking her way. "I'm sorry, miss. You can't go in there. Allow me to see you back to the entrance."

"I'm here for the lecture," she protested, ignoring the titters of the young men—boys, really—that surrounded them. Truly, you'd think they'd never seen a lady before. "The *Times* said it's open to the public."

"It is," Mr. Silver Hair said. "To the *male* public. I'm afraid it's not appropriate for"—he eyed her skeptically—"ladies." As Charlie's heart rate increased, so too did the blasted warm flush creeping up her throat. She willed it down but suspected she wasn't successful.

Charlie felt, rather than saw, Agnes shrinking into the wall covering behind her. She drew a breath, then tucked a curl behind her ear. "With all due respect, sir, I'm fair certain all of you"—she looked at the gaggle of men—"had mothers who dressed your wounds when you were children. And I'm fair certain every one of them was female, so there's nothing inappropriate about it." They chuckled, then sobered when Mr. Silver Hair narrowed his eyes at them. As one, they turned and entered the lecture hall, closing the door behind them and leaving her firmly outside.

———

JULIAN WAS SURPRISED TO SEE men still milling about the entrance to the lecture hall. He was running late, as usual, and expected everyone would have been seated by now. But as the crowd near the doors shifted, he realized the source of the delay: a lady.

She was tall for a woman, with curly red hair—hard to miss, really. As he drew closer, familiarity struck him. He was certain he knew her from somewhere.

He listened to Dr. Fletcher inform her the lecture was not open to ladies, then he heard her crisp tones as she told him what she thought of that. Recognition furrowed his brow on hearing her voice. She turned to the side, and he caught more of her profile, which only confirmed what her voice had told him. Mr. Grace's bluestocking daughter.

He'd spent the summer of his twenty-first year with the kindly surgeon in Little Tarrington . . . Torrington? Tarlington. Little Tarlington. That was it.

Miss Grace had been attractive in an earthy, wholesome sort of way, and he'd not been immune to a pretty face. She'd accompanied them on all her father's rounds, asking questions and answering her father's queries like any medical student.

At first, Julian had discounted her, enjoying the novelty of her presence as he suspected any healthy male would have. But once he realized she answered more of her father's questions than he did, he'd started paying more attention.

His collar grew tight as he recalled how often he'd shown to poor advantage before Mr. Grace, coming up short against Miss Grace's freakishly accurate memory. She was brilliant, he recalled, a fact of which she was well aware.

But, as irritating as she was, she was Mr. Grace's daughter, and he'd learned much at the man's side. He sighed, knowing he couldn't turn away now no matter how tempting the thought.

"Dr. Fletcher," he said, catching the older man's attention. "Miss Grace is with me." He assumed she was still Miss Grace, as no husband in his right mind would allow a wife to attend a lecture at Barts.

She was staring at him, and Julian resisted the urge to loosen his collar. Did she recall him? How lowering if she did not. She opened her mouth, no doubt to dispute his words, then snapped it shut and narrowed her eyes. She did remember him then, it would seem.

"Dr. Grey." Fletcher nodded at him in greeting,

then pressed his lips together. "But . . . she's a female."

"She's my assistant." He gave a slight shrug. "Highly irregular, I know, but she keeps my notes organized," Julian said. And although he would probably regret it, he added, "I can vouch for her."

Dr. Fletcher sucked on his teeth and looked from Miss Grace to Julian and back again. It was quite comical, truth be told. Finally, the older man gave a short, terse nod and opened the door for them to precede him.

Miss Grace motioned to her maid to await her at the end of the hall, then she swept in. All the seats were taken save two in the center of the top row.

The polite thing for the gentlemen to do—the only proper thing—would have been to move to the center and allow them the seats on the end. But they remained stubbornly seated, obliging Julian and Miss Grace to navigate knees and feet to the center of the row.

It was abominably rude for the gentlemen to remain seated in the presence of a lady, and Julian glared at them as he passed. If Miss Grace noticed the slight, she gave no indication, thankfully. Finally, she took her seat next to a pale blond man with broad sideburns, and Julian settled next to her.

"Your assistant?" she asked in a sharp whisper once they were seated. Her affront was obvious.

"You're welcome," he said.

She pressed her lips together and shifted her bonnet in her lap. "Thank you," she whispered, though it was clear the words pained her. Then, after some moments had passed, she added graciously, "It's a pleasure to see you again, Dr. Grey."

He nodded, and they sat in silence as the lecture began. Julian surveyed the attendees, searching for new faces he could approach about the position at Heloise Manor.

There. He recognized a gentleman on the front row: Mr. Thomas Williston, if he wasn't mistaken. A young surgeon who'd recently arrived from Edinburgh. He was green but had achieved high marks from what Julian had heard. He'd read some of his papers and found them to be well-founded and of sound argument. He'd approach him after the lecture. With his plan decided, he settled back to listen to Dr. Fletcher.

———

CHARLIE WATCHED DR. GREY FROM the corner of her eye. Why he'd jumped to her defense she didn't know, but she wouldn't question her good fortune. She was here, in the lecture hall of Barts, and she reveled in the experience. How many women could say such a thing? How many *men* had such an experience? She couldn't recall ever having a better day.

That was, until Dr. Fletcher misspoke about the proper application of pressure when caring for a wound. She frowned, waiting for someone to correct him. When no one did, she shifted in her seat and moved to stand, but Dr. Grey placed a warm hand over hers and shook his head slightly.

"But he's incorrect," she whispered to him loudly.

"Yes," he agreed. "But he's only too eager to toss you out, and me along with you. So be quiet if you wish to stay," he urged.

She shook his hand off. The heat where he'd held her lingered, and she tried unsuccessfully to wipe it away on her skirt.

One of the students asked a question about the best type of material to wrap a wound, and Fletcher answered. Incorrectly, yet again. Charlie opened her mouth, and Dr. Grey shook his head again. She clamped her mouth shut and glared at him. "He's giving them the wrong instruction," she protested on a whisper. "Evidence has shown that the wound needs to breathe."

"Shh," the blond student next to her hissed. She glared at him, then turned back to Dr. Grey.

"Shh," he said.

She settled back in her seat and faced forward, but the words on her tongue wouldn't be silenced. She couldn't allow the man's inaccuracies to stand.

She stood up. "Dr. Fletcher."

Dr. Fletcher's head came up at her words, but he continued droning on about infection. From the corner of her eye, she saw Dr. Grey wipe a hand over his face. "Dr. Fletcher," she said again, more loudly.

Finally, Fletcher stopped and looked at her. He sucked on his teeth for a moment before saying, "Yes, Miss Grace?"

"Your instruction to wrap the wound tightly . . . Evidence has shown greater results with a looser dressing."

"Miss Grace," Dr. Fletcher began with a twist of his lips. "A tighter dressing is beneficial to prevent bad humors from infecting the wound." The room murmured their agreement.

"Yes, but—"

"Dr. Grey. Please ask your assistant to refrain from comment."

Dr. Grey reached a hand to hers and tugged her back to her seat.

When the lecture ended, Dr. Grey whispered to her, "Please wait here, Miss Grace. I need to speak with Mr. Williston for a moment, and then I shall escort you out."

What? She turned to him, but he was gone. She watched him navigate the crowded room and approach a young man of about twenty years. She turned away and gathered her bonnet to leave. His business was really none of hers.

As excited as she'd been to attend today's lecture, it had been a tremendous disappointment. She thought she'd best head back to Russell Square as she knew Emily had *Plans* for them to go driving in the park. But as she passed Dr. Grey and Mr. Williston, she couldn't help overhearing bits of their conversation.

"—seeking a surgeon for twenty residents at Heloise Manor. The wage is good, and the work is rewarding."

"I thank ye for considerin' me, Dr. Grey. I'll give it some thought. Can I let ye know in a few days?"

"Yes, although our need is rather immediate. Please do let me know soon."

Mr. Williston nodded and placed his hat on his head before turning toward the exit.

"You're looking for a surgeon?" Charlie asked at Dr. Grey's shoulder. He startled, then turned toward her.

"I thought you were going to remain where you were."

"Pish," she said. "I heard you talking to Mr. Williston. You're looking for a surgeon," she said again.

"Yes. Do you know any?" He steered her toward the exit and held the door for her. She sailed through, and Agnes jumped up from where she'd been sitting on a bench at the end of the corridor.

"Let me do it," Charlie said. The more she thought about it, the more the idea appealed. Meaningful occupation would make London more bearable. She could remain in London indefinitely if she had worthwhile work to perform.

Dr. Grey looked at her and laughed, then sobered when he realized she was serious. "No."

"No? Why not? You know the quality of my work. Or I could serve in the position on a trial basis so you can decide."

"No," he said again, this time more firmly. "For one thing, you're not licensed. I'm looking for a licensed surgeon."

She chewed her nail. "Yes, I can see your dilemma, but I'm as good as licensed. All but degreed, even. I've studied all the same texts. I even wrote a thesis for the Medical College at Edinburgh."

He stopped walking and turned to her. "You wrote a thesis for a curriculum you didn't attend? For a degree for which you're not eligible?"

She nodded. "Yes. You can read it if you like. *The Merits of Uniting the Complementary Disciplines of Medicine and Surgery*."

He stared at her for a moment, then nodded once. "A controversial subject, to be sure, but one on which we would find accord. I've long thought the divide between the two disciplines is detrimental for patients, which is why I studied both."

She looked at him with surprise, both at his admission and his agreement. A physician who was also a surgeon was . . . unusual. Not unheard of, but not the normal way of things, either.

He resumed walking, and they exited the building into the April afternoon. Mindful of her freckles and her mother's frequent admonitions about the sun, Charlie hurried to don her bonnet, tying the ribbons haphazardly.

"You said *for one thing*. What's the other thing?"

He slanted her a look from the corner of his eye. "You have to ask?"

"What other objection do you have? Speak plainly, Dr. Grey."

"You—you're a woman," he said. Rather unnecessarily, she thought.

"And?"

"What do you mean, *And?* Isn't that enough?"

"I fail to see how the fact is relevant, so long as I'm qualified. And you know from the summer you worked with my father that I'm more qualified than many of the men in that lecture hall. Most of them," she muttered.

They'd reached the front of the central green and stood next to the street. A boy approached leading a horse, and Dr. Grey pulled a coin from his waistcoat pocket. He tipped his hat to her and gave a short bow. "Miss Grace, it's been a pleasure seeing you again, but this is where we part. Please give my warmest regards to your father."

She nodded, her brow wrinkled as she watched him ride away.

ABOUT THE AUTHOR

K. Lyn Smith writes sweet historical romance about ordinary people finding extraordinary love. Her debut novel, The Astronomer's Obsession, was a finalist for the National Excellence in Romantic Fiction Award, and many of her other titles have been shortlisted for honors such as the American Writing Award, the Carolyn Reader's Choice Award, the HOLT Medallion and the Maggie Award.

When she's not lost in the pages of a book, you can find her with family, traveling to far-off places and binging period dramas. And space documentaries. Weird, right?

Visit www.klynsmithauthor.com, where you can subscribe for new release updates and access to exclusive bonus content.